Central panel from Paula Rego's *The Fisherman Triptych*, 2005
Pastel on paper, 187 x 135 cm
Printed with the permission of the artist

A DESIGNATED MAN

Moris Farhi

A Designated Man

TELEGRAM

ISBN: 978-1-84659-068-9

This first edition published in 2009 by Telegram

A full CIP record for this book is available from the British Library.

Manufactured in Lebanon

TELEGRAM

26 Westbourne Grove, London W2 5RH
Tabet Building, Mneimneh Street, Hamra, Beirut
www.telegrambooks.com

To Nina, my eternal inspiration.

To Mai Ghoussoub, soul-sister and mentor, who believed in this work. I carry your beautiful soul everywhere and all the time.

And to Womanhood – the only blessing that can save the world from its armoured people.

ACKNOWLEDGMENTS

With gratitude to my family for their love and support: Ceki, Viviane, Deborah & Yael Farhi; Rachel Sievers & Hamish & Zara MacGillivray; Eric, Danièle & Nathaniel Gould; Phil, Rachel, Samuel, Joshua, Kezia & Joseph Gould; Jessica Gould; Emmanuel, Yael, Noam, Amit & Adi Gould; Guy, Rebecca, Ela & Uri Granot; Sara, Christopher and Sean Coil; Nicole Farhi & David Hare; Dennis & Elizabeth Hull.

With gratitude to the late Asher Fred Mayer whose beautiful soul sustains me.

With gratitude to Barry Proner, purveyor of insights into the mysteries.

With gratitude to my brilliant and devoted editor: Rebecca O'Connor.

With gratitude to my friends and mentors for their guidance: Peter Day; Ahmad Ebrahimi; André, Lynn & Salwa Gaspard; Jana Gough; Agop Hacikyan; Dmetri Kakmi; Robin Lloyd-Jones; Christopher New; Sharon Olinka; Maureen Rissik; Anthony Rudolf; Nicholas Sawyer; Ros Schwartz; Evelyn Toynton; Rod Wooden.

With gratitude to my agents: Jessica Woollard, Paul Marsh, Camilla Ferrier & Caroline Hardman.

With gratitude to my kindred spirits for their unflinching support: Tricia Barnett; Selim & Nadia Baruh; Ian & Anthea Davidson; Marius Kociejowski; Julian & Karen Lewis; Sallie Lloyd-Jones; Robina Masters; Elizabeth Rosen-Mayer; Faith Miles; Richard & Ceinwen Morgan; Christa New; Ayşe & Mehmet Önal; Şafak Pavey; David Picker; Lucy

Popescu; Nicholas, Maggie & Rosa Rankin; Paula Rego; Hazel Robinson; Elon Salmon; Enis Üser; Juliet Wedderburn; Ateş Wise.

With gratitude to my alter egos near and far for their solidarity: Ergun & Rengin Avunduk; Attila & Ayşem Çelikiz; Rajko Djuric; Semra Eren-Nijhar, Indirjit & Ilayda Nijhar; Bensiyon Eskenazi; Sylvie Finkelstein; Andrew Graham-Yooll; Brigitte Hacikyan; Bracha Hadar; Nina Kossman; Julita Mirkowicz; Hazem Saghieh; Saliha Paker; Donné Raffat; Mariantonella Saracino; Isabella Zani.

With gratitude to the other members of my dedicated 'family' at Saqi & Telegram Books: Ashley Biles, Rob Fakes; Rabi Fatihi; Lara Frankena; Amin Jawad; Lina Kayali; Safa Mubgar; Shikha Sethi; Anna Wilson; Rukhsana Yasmin.

1

KOKONA

Hungers are legion. Some, like the hunger in empty bellies, can kill; those that are weathered leave woeful scars. But there is one hunger – only one – that is gracious, that exhorts us to live, that gives meaning to our lives: the hunger of the flesh. It is Creation's gift to us.

Many of you will be angered by this chronicle. You will want to ignore my words, ridicule them as an ancient woman's prattle. But somewhere in your innards you'll listen. Because you know that I, Kokona, am truthful as the sea. You know my memory is like the Earth's and errs not. You know I bear this island's history. You know I have never blinkered my eyes, never shielded my heart. Everything that's happened in Skender is written on my body. And written in salt on open wounds.

No need to dwell on the other hungers. We've all suffered them, especially the fatal ones. They are the Earth's ferrymen. They follow a timetable scrolled somewhere in the ether. If we survive, we survive only because Providence throws us a reprieve at the last moment. We've all buried kin who haven't been so lucky.

But the hunger of the flesh, the craving to touch another's body, to find a soul with whom to become one, is a hunger that must be celebrated with open hearts and minds. No one can live without love. Yet you've spurned it like martyrs spurn the bodies they inhabit. That's why you're so dead.

I sense scorn rising in you. I hear the adherents of the Law furiously rattling their bones in mimicry of cobwebbed Toma whom you still revere as your prophet. You're primed to drown the music of the flesh with the carpentry of coffins.

But, deep down, you know I'm right. You're dead because you've chosen to renounce the ways of Creation. You've elected to bed not with love, but with hatred. You draw breath only to kill and be killed. And you're doubly proud when your victims are lovers who want nothing more than to live with their faces upon each other. You've drained your cocks of sap, filled your *amatas* with stones. Only the sight of blood engorges your loins.

But I, Kokona, old as I am, still keep myself ploughed, like good earth. My body can still receive sky, water and fire. And before I end my days, I want to bring you to life again.

I want a future for Skender.

That's why I've put this story together.

Our island is the furthest from the mainland, more than half a day's journey from Turnu, the nearest headland. Though there are almost eight thousand of us, we don't have an airstrip. Our only link with the rest of our country is the ferry. And that, much as we're entirely dependent on it for medicine, fuel and other necessities, is always at the mercy of the Maritime Lines. According to them, the restricted service – once a week, if we're lucky – is due to the vagaries of the elements. We Skenderis know better. We know, in this part of the world, that governments abandon certain regions like parents who desert their children.

So we're isolated.

Our nation thinks we're a colony of hydras.

Our government officials visit us once every forty moons – always escorted by a squad of gendarmes – only to fling scraps at us as if we were animals in a zoo.

Europe looks upon us as primitives who have never learned how to be a people – hence, lawless. And, except for a superpower or two who deem that, at some future date, we might have strategic value and so glance at us occasionally from their war-rooms – or so our government speculates – the rest of the world doesn't even know we exist.

The lawlessness is both fact and fiction.

The fiction is that we have a legal system; it is called the Law and is based on the *Kanun*, that ancient charter of the Balkans, which raptorial warlords imposed upon us some two hundred years ago. And it is the Law, with its injunctions about honour and the imperative to redeem it with blood feuds, that makes us lawless.

Evil, we know, is a Trojan horse; it arrives at people's gates wrapped up as a gift.

The warlords came, as warlords do, when this remote island was prosperous and harmonious. They came to protect us, they said, because the Ottomans had abandoned us. We trusted them. We were innocents. Infants. We swallowed their lies. They wanted privileges. So they blindfolded us. Poured poison into our ears. Abased our women to chattels. Preferring to save our skins rather than our souls, we scurried before them.

Those who had the audacity to challenge them ended up in limepits or over the cliffs. Strangers, immediately branded as threats, had their hides ruddled and were sent to slaughter. Bards had their tongues torn out because they dared voice the truth.

Then they forced open our gullets and goose-fed us with honour. With what we now call the Law.

Yet we knew, even as we slopped it up, that this deadly lotus could be garnished in countless ways to justify every wrongdoing. Mindlessly, we evangelized its brutal sacraments. Like memorizers of sacred books, we chanted that nothing had greater importance in life than honour – least of all, the miracle of life itself!

They stuffed us with this toxin so easily, our warlords. But then, over the centuries, we had laid ourselves bare for such conditioning. We had given credence to religions that glorified death. We had accorded loyalty to those who believed they could forge armour that could soar to the sun without ever melting. We had accepted doctrines that dispossessed women of their rights and of their femininity. And we had venerated the dust devils that fomented ancient grievances into tempests.

Thus, if our neighbour's pig devoured our crop and we chased it away, we were reviled as a Muslim or a Jew! If we got tired of eating fish, we insulted the Christians! If our eyes fell on the rump of a shepherdess helping a sheep to lamb, we accused all womankind of prurience.

Quite simply, our superstitions made us easy prey to the warlords. Any idiocy became a good enough excuse to kill for honour. And when our turn came to die, we choked on our own blood, sad and bitter, not because we were giving up our life before its time, but because we felt we had not done enough to protect our honour.

So it went on.

And so it still goes on today.

Which explains why we have become outcasts. Why those Skenderis who left the island in search of better conditions came back, destitute and hungry. No one would give them work. Fortunately, even in its devastated state, Skender can still feed them. Money is scarce, but there is no unemployment and old-fashioned bartering, particularly with Turnu, meets our meagre needs.

Occasionally some mainlanders – youngsters mostly – take an interest in us. Thinking Skender is a lost Eden, they overlook our lawlessness. What do spoonfed youths from cities know about violence and the way it turns rabid? They think carnage is fanciful, akin to what they see in partisan films: flag-waving, drumbeating racists massacring their fellow men without once shitting in their pants. We've seen those youths, rucksacks on their backs, getting off the ferry. And we've seen them leave, not always alive, on the next ferry.

Other mainlanders – businessmen – thought they could bring in tourists. But since Skender has a cliff-gouged coastline with few beaches, they soon abandoned the idea. Some of them, too, left in coffins ... killed either for fear that they were allies of an enemy family or that their aims might threaten our way of life.

But, of course, there have been – and they're still around – the invisible men. We call them Gospodins after the absentee landlords of the Balkans. Nobody knows their identity or where they came from or where they're burrowed. Not even our very own Viktor Mikhail, who acts as their agent, as his father did before him. But we have come to think that these Gospodins are a cabal within the government. They bought – and still buy whenever they can, and very cheaply – the abandoned properties in Skender. There have been many suppositions – from drug smuggling to money-laundering – about their interest in this forgotten island. Those of us, like me, who are aware of what's going on in the world, think that Skender's so-called 'strategic value' is the cause of their speculation. I think they believe this island could be another Diego Garcia, in the Indian Ocean, and hope that one day a superpower, wanting a military base in the Mediterranean, will buy those lands from them at a hefty price. That's not too far-fetched a deduction. Skender was indeed used as a base by the Germans during the Second World War.

Then, one day, to this aberrant island, he came.

Xenos.

One ordinary day, he washed ashore.

And, soon afterwards, he exposed our lifelessness.

You always called him 'Xenos', 'Stranger', even though he was born here. Son of a wealthy family that perished in the feuds. Some of you went to school with him when we still had a school. When I was the teacher.

Xenos. A man in search of a haven. Returning to an island that was itself in need of havens.

Dev and I were the first to meet him. We were on our way back from Turnu, where I had delivered a batch of my tapestries to the National Handwork Cooperative. Dev, as you all know, is my name for my man, Mordo. You refused to call him that. Instead you taunted him for being a dwarf. 'Shrimp', you mocked him to his face. But then you've never had eyes to see what's in front of you. Compared to anyone in Skender, he was, true to the name I gave him, a giant.

Anyway, there we were on the ferry. For once it was a pleasant crossing. The gales they had forecast had run out of breath and the passengers had settled on the deck. Since Skenderis, unwelcome anywhere in our country, seldom leave their island, the only passengers, apart from us, were tourists cruising in the archipelago.

Dev and I noticed him immediately. Though of average height, he stood out like Triton's rock. One arm resting on his duffle bag, he was sitting cross-legged on a bench, staring at the sea and smoking. A chain-smoker, his fingers had the colour of autumn leaves. And his moustache, no doubt originally as silvery as his hair, looked as if it had been basted in turmeric.

We had left Turnu late in the afternoon. The tourists were busy consuming their packed suppers. We brought out our meal – bread, cheese, olives, figs, wine. Then we saw he didn't have any food.

Dev, who would feed the whole world if he could, fretted. 'Shall I ask him to join us?'

I nodded.

He went over to him.

Xenos, surprised, hesitated a moment, then came and sat by us. 'Thank you.'

He had a deep voice, but spoke almost in a whisper. He had the accent of the mainlanders, but clipped his words as we do.

I pointed at our meal. 'Help yourself.'

He shook his head. 'That's your fare.' Then he took a fig. 'But refusing a fig would be against nature.'

I was intrigued by the fact that he knew Skenderis held figs sacred and mistrusted those who did not.

He toasted me with the fig. 'May you live a century, Teacher.'

That took me aback. 'How did you know who I am – was?'

'You taught me.'

'I did?'

'I still remember your first lesson.'

I laughed. 'I can't believe that ...'

'I know it by heart.'

Dev, always disposed to be joyous, clapped his hands. 'Let's hear!'

Xenos shook his head. 'You don't really want to ...'

Dev clasped Xenos' arm. 'Yes! I had no schooling!'

Xenos stared at him, charmed by his childlike excitement.

Dev insisted. 'Go on!'

Xenos shut his eyes as if reciting a ballad. 'Skender, an appellation that means "defender of mankind", is an island as legendary as Odysseus' Ithaca. It was named after Alexander the Great, who was sent here by his mentor, Aristotle, to study what was then the most peaceful domain in the Sea of Seas. And as he watched the way Skender's yeomen – tillers of the soil – and her mariners – tillers of the waves – lived in harmony, the idea of marrying the East to the West arose within him. Though he failed in that, the gods were impressed with Skender for so inspiring Alexander. As a reward, they endowed the island with Olympian fruitfulness. That's why our figs, olives and wine, our sheep, game and fish have no equal anywhere in the world.'

Dev swayed about in enchantment. 'That's the truth!'

I was astounded. That was indeed the first lesson I used to teach, almost word for word. 'What made you memorize it?'

He smiled. 'It was one of the few constants I took with me. It has been a staunch friend ever since.' Then he held up the fig he was eating. 'This is not a Skenderi fig.'

'Sadly, no. From Turnu.' I pointed at the wine. 'But the grape is.'

This time he did not refuse. He picked up the bottle and drank a good mouthful. He nodded in recognition. 'Definitely.'

'Have your fill. We've got plenty.'

He bowed his head in thanks.

'You know me, Xenos. But I can't place you. Remind me.'

'Osip Gora.'

'Osip Gora ...?'

He nodded shyly.

Osip Gora! I should have recognized him. I had known him very well. And had thought about him for years. A restless boy. But with a mind as breathtaking as a peacock's tail. Family dying fast in endless feuds. Father, an intellectual. And, unusually, a redoubtable gunman. Killed several feudists. But inevitably, eventually, he was killed too – trapped by four families in alliance. The boy, Osip – fourteen or so at the time – was next in line to take up the feud. He'd have been killed immediately. The family still had some money so I convinced his mother – a fearsome woman known as 'Eleanora the Falcon' – to send him away and so spare him.

'Gone all these years …? Fifty? Sixty?'

'Fifty. Exactly.'

'Seems longer since I put you on the ferry.'

He stared at me, surprised. '*You* put me on the ferry?'

'Yes.'

'No … It was my mother …'

'It wasn't.'

'Are you sure? It must have been my mother …'

'No. It was me.'

I had found him a place at a training school in the capital. He'd not wanted to go. He'd wanted to stay and avenge his father. He had wept frantically when I'd handed him over to the ferry's captain – even though boys from feuding families are instructed never to cry.

'It's all hazy in my mind – that day.'

'You were a boy – and fearful …'

He smiled bitterly. 'I remember crying …'

'And many times after that, I imagine.'

'No. Only once after that. Decades later.'

'What about at the training school? Homesickness? Discipline?'

He drank more wine. 'Easy. I took it like medicine.'

'Doesn't sound easy to me.'

'It is. If you grow a shell.'

'After the training school – where did you go? Somewhere vocational? University?'

'Here and there.'

'Doing what?'

'Whatever came my way.'

'Always on the mainland?'

'All over.'

I could see my questioning was troubling him. That was typical of most of the mainlanders, particularly after the Peoples' Wars. Minds trying to erase the horrors the eyes had seen. 'Were you involved in the Wars?'

'That, too. But they called it ethnic cleansing.'

I sighed bitterly. 'The antiseptic names we give to slaughtering our own.'

To my relief, he nodded. His expression hardened.

Dev took some wine, then passed the bottle to him.

He hesitated. 'I'll get drunk.' But he took the bottle and drank a good amount. Then he offered us his cigarettes.

We both took one. He lit them for us.

I inhaled deeply. Nobody's better at smoking a cigarette than the aged; not knowing how many breaths we have left, we like indulging our lungs. 'What brings you back to Skender? Revenge?'

'Revenge?'

'To take up your family's feuds?'

'That was a long time ago.'

'Time means nothing when it comes to feuds. You must know that. They're our way of life.'

'I thought – expected – all that had changed.'

'Change is not a concept in the Skenderi mind.'

He shook his head, dismissing my words. 'Even so – there

can't be any enemies of my family left. And if there are, they'll be disappointed. I won't get involved in feuding.'

'What brings you back then?'

'Time to return, I thought. To end my days where I began them.'

I raised my eyes sceptically.

Then he added: 'Also, in a way, to start living. I love water. I want the sea around me. And rivers running wherever I look. Water teaches us how to live. It's time I learned.'

'Life has a poor harvest in Skender. It has become a place for dying. Even our crops and animals – the best in the world wither or die prematurely.'

'When you taught us mythology, Teacher – remember telling us about sacred grottoes? Which the ancients consecrated as sanctuaries to water spirits?'

'Yes ...'

'A metaphor for withdrawing from an existence that man constantly despoils, is how you put it. That's what I'm looking for. A place where I can start a new life. Where I harm no one and no one harms me. I thought my island – my wellspring – might be that place.'

The way he spoke so spontaneously impressed me. Skenderis, apart from Dev and me, seldom express their emotions.

'You're very frank.'

'You're my teacher. I wouldn't hide things from you.'

'What makes you think you might find this refuge in Skender?'

'Well, I've got a water-mill to start with ...'

Dev, who knew every blade on the island, interrupted. 'Only one water-mill. On the south coast.'

'That's the one.'

'Wasn't it sold?'

'No. It's Gora property. All that's left. Years ago a lawyer contacted me. I'm the only heir. He said there was a buyer, but I refused to sell.'

I chuckled. Skender, which suffers at least a couple of killings a week without regard for the country's legislation, is as scrupulous on such statutes as inheritance and proprietorship as a weaver-bird building a nest. Of course, the real reason for this diligence is our infamous Law. Feuds must be handed down in perpetuity until the enemy family is exterminated. Thus anyone with blood links to a family, particularly an inheritor, is required, in the perverse logic of feuds, to uphold the honour of that family and take on the historic fight – whether he wants to or is capable of it is immaterial. That, of course, automatically makes him a legitimate prey for his family's enemies.

I offered Xenos more wine. 'Your family had feuds with several families. For all you know, there may be some descendants. They'd expect you to uphold the Gora honour.'

'Honour has no meaning for me.'

'That's a grand statement.'

'I mean it.'

'How come?'

'That's something else you taught me, Teacher. It took me a long time to accept it.'

'But your family's enemies – they won't accept it. That would be against the Law.'

'I won't get involved.'

'Wouldn't make any difference. You'd still be targeted. And before you knew it, you'd be sucked in. Until now only a handful have managed to avoid feuding. That, despite the fact that there are some who'd like the Law abolished. But, alas, honour has many crusaders.'

Dev muttered in disgust. 'And a prophet – Toma!'

'Toma? I remember him – vaguely. He and my father often clashed. He must be quite old now.'

I took some more wine. 'He is. Older than me, in fact. Now known as "the Righteous". Honour is his sacred hymn. And you're right: he and your father were bitter foes. But your mother revered Toma, worshipped him as her mentor.'

'I'll steer clear of him.'

'You won't be able to – if you stay ...'

'Are you trying to dishearten me, Teacher?'

'I'm reminding you – warning you – how it is in Skender.'

'I'll keep myself to myself. That's all I can do.'

'You could sell the water-mill. The people who wanted to buy it – our absentee landlords, very likely – would still be interested.'

'And then what?'

'You could go back – with money in your pocket.'

'I am back. Skender is where *back* is. There's nowhere else.'

'Then watch your step. And set your eyes behind you.'

Dev interrupted again. 'The water-mill – it's derelict.'

'I imagine so.'

'But you can restore it. Get it working again.'

Osip nodded. 'That's my intention.'

Dev, being Dev, became animated. 'I can help. I'm good with my hands.'

'I'll remember that.' Osip stood up. 'Thanks for the fig, the wine – and the advice.'

He went back to his seat and sat down again cross-legged. Except for the repeated movement of lighting cigarette after cigarette, he looked like an ancient statue on a remote, abandoned site.

The next time he moved was at daybreak, when we were approaching

Skender. I had slept on a bench all night and was stiff all over – one of the joys of being old.

But Dev, who, though almost seventy, glides like quicksilver, went up to him. 'Home. Recognize it?'

Osip leaned against the railings and gazed at the bay. 'There was an old song: "Skender, the heaven of heavens, where dolphins teach gods how to swim and skylarks compose melodies for mermaids."'

Dev offered him some wine. 'We still sing it.'

Osip drank fretfully. 'Looks more like Scylla's perch.'

By then I had gathered up my bones and joined them. I could see what he meant. The sea-sated air that normally makes each dawn promise a better day was mottled as if stricken with blight.

Dev tried to be encouraging. 'Wait for the sun.'

'Ah, yes – the sun ...' Osip looked like a sailor who knows he's heading for yet another shipwreck. Or maybe like one who always expects to be marooned. Or even like one who, preferring the hazards of wreckage to the perils of sailing, feels grateful for any lesser misfortune. 'But the sun always goes down. Then the demons come out.'

I looked at him. 'Demons?'

'In a manner of speaking.'

'You believe in demons?'

He smiled. 'Don't we all?'

'I think you're carrying too many troubles, Osip Gora ...'

He shrugged. 'No more than most people.'

Dev tried to lighten the conversation. 'Make things grow. Best medicine against demons. Skender has fine soil!'

Osip looked doubtfully at Dev's stunted frame. 'Make things grow?'

Dev grinned amiably. 'I know. You're thinking: make yourself grow first. I can't. But everything else, yes.' He pointed at our carpet-bag. 'Asparagus – know it?'

'Yes.'

'Very popular now on the mainland. Not known in Skender. So I bought seeds. Next year, we'll have a whole field.'

Osip smiled uncertainly. 'You must be a very happy man ...'

Dev chuckled. 'Yes.'

I nodded. 'A fulfilled man, Dev is. If you want to know what life's all about, he's the teacher.'

Osip turned to me as if to say something. Instead he stared at me. His gaze lingered. I sensed a gust of warmth from a time long past. A boy-man gaping at a woman in adoration. For a moment I felt he was looking at me the way Dev looked at me when we first got together – the way he always did. I thought if I hadn't loved Dev, I could be captivated by this man.

2

OSIP

The day, at least, was sunny and welcoming.

Save for an old boy whose frayed sailor's jacket identified him as the harbour master and who supervised the ferry crew unloading barrels of fuel and bales of consignments, the pier was empty.

Kokona, Dev and I were the only passengers to disembark. The rest, the tourists, were returning to the mainland. Skender, I'd been told, was always excluded from sightseeing excursions.

Kokona indicated a solitary van parked on the main road. 'We've got a motor. We can take you to the water-mill.'

'Thank you but I'd like to walk.'

'It's some distance.'

'I want to get a feel of the place. It's been a long time.'

Kokona shook my hand. 'I understand.'

A strong grip, in defiance of bent, arthritic fingers.

She smiled. 'Our farm is just east of the Citadel. Visit us whenever you like. We're old hands at chasing away demons.'

Her smile glowed and rose from her soul. Her eyes, now that I could see them clearly in daylight, had not been dimmed by the attritions of a long life: still inquiring, vivifying and self-assuredly female in the way a woman boldly assesses a man. Despite her years, despite being dressed in the shapeless shift common to Skenderi women – though in her case it was yellow instead of the usual black or grey – she was entirely feminine. Tall but earthy, as Aphrodite would be if she ever succumbed to time.

Why had she assumed the ancient name for grandmothers, Kokona?

When I was a boy, I was in love with her. Maro, her name was. Effervescent as sea spray, she imparted colour wherever she went as if she were a rainbow. 'Almond Blossom' was my secret name for her. Widowed three times before she was thirty. Husbands killed in feuds. But she never wilted. Battled like a Fury against the killings. That's how she came to urge my mother to send me to the mainland. Don't sacrifice him to what men call honour; there's no honour in feuding, she told her. Boldly. And unmindful that I was in the room, begging not to be sent away. Surprisingly, my mother took her advice. Wept as she put me on the ferry as if tears could requite honour. Little did she know that if there really is such a thing as honour, it's somewhere beyond the reach of mortals.

Ah – fickle memory!

It was Maro – Kokona – who put me on the ferry, not my mother. It's time I stopped clinging to that lie.

I remember it clearly now. Mother had stayed at home, cleaning her gun. Father had just been killed and Mother, the formidable Eleanora the Falcon, could hardly wait to engage his killers. Feuds had priority over children's welfare. Besides, appropriating my right to serve as the next feudist, she had already declared herself the family's designated man.

Was it Kokona, then, who had wept for me? Yes, it was.

I'd sit at the front of the class and imbibe every word she spoke, worship every gesture she made. And at nights, in bed, I would fantasize about being her hero. I'd be the boy – braver than any man in Skender – who kept saving her. Not just from feuds and those islanders who tried to vilify her, but also from all kinds of perils like rapists, ferocious animals, sinking boats, fires, earthquakes and the rest ...

'Good fortune.'

Dev had taken my hand with both his. Farmer's hands, strong and calloused. Hands too big for a dwarf. Hands, I imagined, that protected lame deer from jackals. I felt glad he was Kokona's man – even envious of their natural intimacy.

My hands clasped his. 'Thank you.'

I watched them walk to their van – Dev adjusting his pace to Kokona's. They looked like a mother and her child, an image embellished by Dev's opulent ebony hair, which I secretly admired because it still gleamed like a young man's.

I surveyed the harbour as they drove away.

Both my father and Kokona had taught me that Skender had been an important commercial outpost in antiquity, a free port for Hellenes, Illyrians, Phoenicians, Egyptians, Hebrews, Romans and Etruscans. Its prosperity had reached its apogee under the Ottomans' liberal rule. Thus Turks and Greeks, Armenians and Jews, Serbs and Croats, Dalmatians and Albanians, Macedonians and Bulgars, Saracens and Arabs, Berbers and Egyptians, French and Italians, even Germans and Russians had traded with their word as their bond. Then, late in the eighteenth century, after one of the countless wars Europe had waged against the Ottomans, its sovereignty had passed from one warlord to another. Thereafter it had plunged into the Dark Ages.

When I left fifty years ago the harbour had an array of historic monuments: columns of Greek and Roman temples on the cliffs;

Ottoman mosques with arrow-thin minarets on the hillocks; picturesque churches on the slopes; small homes for artisans along the bay; and, by the waterfront, hugging the Divan – once cherished by the islanders as a depository of historic artefacts – residences and warehouses in vivid colours, like a Gypsy tapestry, for notable merchants. And all of them imbued with a pastoral tranquillity as cattle, sheep, goats, pigs, chickens and geese moved freely through the human throng.

Could I trust my memory here? Might I be idealizing the time of my boyhood?

Now, wherever I looked, I saw discolouration and rubble. Temples, mosques, churches, houses and the Divan pockmarked by history's debris and dust. The famous stone and wood pier that had introduced European engineering to the Balkans, and had then been reinforced with iron around the time I was born, stood encrusted with algae and rust. A reef formed of refuse, sewage and bloated animal carcasses barricaded Homer's wine-dark sea. Even the sand on the nearby beach sprawled lustreless as if long untouched by children's games. And those buildings that had remained erect stared eyeless at the world with scorched windows.

This was a landscape I had come to know well. After the Peoples' Wars, we had reduced the mainland to a similar state. This was desolation that only man could wreak. After which, inevitably, nature had taken over.

Yet Skender, by virtue of being remote and isolated, had not been touched by the Peoples' Wars. So what had happened? How had these stones crumbled so rapidly?

Should I have returned?

The harbour master came running up to me. 'Looking for a bus?'

'No.'

He chuckled. 'That was a joke. No such thing. Hardly any vehicles here. A few belonging to tradesfolk. And a handful to the well-to-do – like the couple who arrived with you.'

'I see.'

'Maybe you want a hotel?'

'No.'

'That was a joke, too. No hotels either.'

'Why?'

'No one lives here any more. Want a telephone?'

'No.'

'Third and last joke. What lines we had are long dead. You'll need a radio if you want to reach the mainland. A few people in the Citadel have one. So do I – thanks to the Maritime Lines.'

'You said no one's living here ...'

'No one. Except me.' He pointed at a derelict shack near the pier. 'That's my palace.'

I indicated some of the houses that were still standing. 'They look habitable.'

'Yes. But they're ghoulish.'

'Ghoulish?'

'The killings ... Everybody moved inland. Easier to hide there. Hills, woods ...'

'I thought the Peoples' Wars hadn't reached Skender ...'

'We have feuds. Just as bad ...'

His words roused the ancient bitterness in me. 'Haven't people had a bellyful of that? Aren't they worn down? Don't they shout: enough?'

'They haven't so far.'

I pointed at the barrels and bales that had just been unloaded. 'What about these goods? They must be dependent on them ...'

'The consignees pick them up on truce days. Usually the second morning after the ferry's arrival. That's how long it takes to organize them.'

'It's hard to take in.'

'Yes.' The old sailor offered me a cigarette. 'Where are you heading?'

I offered him mine. 'Try these. Stronger.'

He took one. 'Ah, the expensive kind!'

I lit his and mine. 'The water-mill – on the south coast.'

He shook his head. 'Don't know it. Barely moved from here since I got this job – ten years or more now.' He waved the cigarette. 'Good stuff.'

'Keeps one going.'

He gestured towards his shack. 'If you want to rest your balls, you're welcome. Haven't had company since Noah sailed past. I've got a hammock you can use. And flagons of *rakiya*.'

I heaved my kit onto my shoulder. 'Thank you. I must be on my way.'

He smiled to cover his disappointment. 'Course. Mind how you go. Here they kill you for a fart.'

I walked in a trance.

When eventually I surfaced I found myself on the eastern cliffs.

There were no sheep grazing. And the few goats were emaciated; judging by their hides, which bore no brands of ownership, they seemed to have been living wild.

All through my childhood, this part of Skender had been my favourite haunt. Gazing at the horizon from here, with only sheep and goats for company, I could see the Earth's curvature. This had been my captain's bridge where I had strutted about and imagined that I was a great explorer defying storm-tossed seas in order to discover lands where no man had yet set foot.

Equally important to me, these were the cliffs where, in late spring, colonies of Eleanora's Falcons came in to nest and breed. My father and I would spend much of the summer watching them. One year, we even tried to tame an injured fledgling; but he recovered and flew off. That pleased us even though we missed him.

I realized why, seemingly inadvertently, I had come up to these cliffs.

Memories.

But not the memories of the countless villainies that haunt me. Nor memories of Sofi that assail me day and night. Specifically the survivor's memory, the one I'd assured myself I'd cauterized years ago, but which is still sitting, immovable, on my shoulders.

It was here that my father, Anibal, had been killed. Right there, by that rock cluster, I watched as they gunned him down. He'd pushed me behind a boulder to protect me from stray bullets. That had given his killers the few seconds they'd needed to open fire. They had continued firing into his body long after he was dead. Then they had left, courteously nodding at me, as decreed by the Law. And intimating that we'd meet again, no doubt soon, when, as expected, I'd be appointed my family's new feudist.

My father died because of me. I've never been able to accept that. But surely it's time I did.

Is that why I've come back – to make amends?

I advanced to the edge of the cliffs and scanned the sea. And there, where water and sky blended their different hues, was the Earth's curvature: a gentle blue arc, perfectly defined. I was transfixed by it – as when I was a boy. Also, boyishly, I felt that at the point where the arc disappeared there was an abyss, the edge of the world from which, as the ancients thought, we would tumble into infinity, some to spin into hell, others to land airily in heaven. This feeling was powerfully enhanced by another stirring view: the refracting silhouettes of five countries in the far distance, like the last formations of land before nothingness.

Then my ears recognized the harsh *kee-kee-kee* sounds. I spotted them immediately: dark brown; the chin, throat and face buff; the underside chestnut with streaks of black; the tail with dark grey feathers barred rufous here and there; the cere and feet pale yellow – Eleanora's Falcons. In my father's judgement, the most beautiful bird in the world. The bird that Icarus had sought to emulate.

Some were settling on cliff ledges; others, on the open slopes, under rocks. True to their Spartan habits, using no nesting material. This being early May, the beginning of the breeding season, they would still be coming in. Those that had already arrived were either solitary or in small groups. By July, when they'd start laying eggs, they'd flock into larger groups. Then they'd hatch, fledge their young and by October they'd be on their way back to the other end of the Earth, to Madagascar.

Much as my father and I loved all birds, we had a special affinity with Eleanora's Falcons. After all, they migrate all the way from another hemisphere, and, although the Mediterranean is dotted with islands where they could breed just as easily, they choose to come to Skender. That's a tribute to us, Father had asserted, because seeing how our cliffs reflect our rugged selves, the falcons consider our island as their rightful place; that, in turn, gives us an idea why they were named after Eleonora d'Arborea, Sardinia's fourteenth-century legislator and greatest heroine: these eminences of the air possess the same passion for independence as their namesake who fought off the invading Aragons.

Nor is it surprising, Father would wryly add, that my mother, the staunchest defender of the family honour, should have borne the sobriquet of a bird of prey. True, it had been my father who had jokingly dubbed her so because of the shape of her nose, but the fact that all Skenderis had found the designation apt proved what a daunting person she was.

I had come to realize, over the years, that my father would have preferred a less potent woman for a wife – one less fanatical about honour. For, though he had been the best feudist in Skender, he only killed when he had no other choice. Given that he was swift enough to take his prey on the wing, it should have been my father who carried the falcon's name. Maybe if he had had a gentler wife – say, a woman like Kokona – his life might have been different. Certainly my life would have been.

I spotted a newcomer alighting on the rocks. A large one, therefore a female. She strutted around, cursorily marking out a patch for her nest. No sooner done than off she flew, no doubt in search of a mate.

Dawn or dusk was the best time to watch them, my father had instructed me. That's when they preferred hunting. Ready to start roosting and breeding, they needed all the food they could get. In the fading light, they surprised other migrant birds exhausted after their long journey from wintering lands by swooping upon them over the open sea.

Unfolding reminiscences of my father compounded my own exhaustion. Wasn't I a migrant bird, too – a migrant all my life? And the question remained: much as I maintained I had to come home after my relentless journey, would fate be clement enough to allow this migrant to roost?

I perched on a boulder. And this time dared face the memory of my father's death.

The excitement of watching the falcons' return – such a natural, innocent thrill for a child. Yet it had killed my father. Knowing what a precise timetable the falcons kept, he had worked out the day they would be arriving. On that day, at dusk, we would go to the cliffs and welcome them. Keep it a secret, he had cautioned, it's best that people don't hear about our excursion; otherwise God knows who might come and spoil our day. But I'd become so excited that I had blurted out our secret to some classmates. They must have mentioned it to others. Eventually word had got round to Father's enemies.

And so, on the set day, as we reached the cliffs, they had appeared. Four men. Each from a different family. Four men I should eventually have had to kill by becoming the Gora feudist, but who, I learned in due course, had been killed by my mother, the self-appointed designated man. Not long after that she'd been killed, too, by one of the sons of the four men.

Why did I come back?

To atone for running away?

I wouldn't know how to atone ...

That fantasy I told Kokona about a new life in a grotto? Do I believe that?

I do, in a way. But I also know, in my bones, that if Fate allows a person a new life, she never lets him enjoy it.

As for finding a grotto, that's just a dream – harmless. But at least I can still dream.

Why did I come back, then?

To die?

That would make sense.

And yet ...

I left the cliffs and took the main road again.

Inland, Skender's desolation was even more evident. Every stretch from the cliff-top to the Citadel's walls, visible in the distance, had been abandoned and was withering. No cattle or sheep grazing; vineyards dried into dead wood; terracing crumbled from disuse; orchards and olive groves forlorn, their ungathered fruits rotting on the branch; and many irrigation canals, which had been the islanders' pride in Ottoman times, clogged and stagnant.

Striding through this landscape, I felt as if I were the last man alive: that Proteus whom even Charon wouldn't take into his boat and row to the underworld.

Yet I had spent most of my life stomping through lands more desolate than this. And had often contributed to the devastation myself. Lands that, during the Peoples' Wars, we had denuded of populations whom unprincipled politicians had decreed to be not of our kin, hence vermin. Lands where every person screamed for a final solution. Where, overnight, friends and neighbours became barbarous foes. Where the ghosts of the unburied hung around like low clouds. Where bellies of pregnant women were thrown to the dogs. Where men and boys were tied up like bunches of flowers and either scythed with machine-guns or drowned in rivers. Where children's clear blood ran in confusion like streams barred from a river.

Why did the destruction of Skender affect me more than the horrors of the Peoples' Wars?

Was it because this was my crucible, and the Skenderis, though I'd forsaken them all these years, were still of my own ethnicity?

Or because I knew there was no reprieve for me and, therefore, to perish under the same sky as my people, indeed, as my father, Anibal, would be my most honest achievement?

Sofi always disagreed when I told her we'd all been allotted a decaying star at birth.

But Sofi, I am right, I am right.

So I trudged on. An Odysseus praying for the sleep of the earth.

I banished the thought. I didn't want oblivion. Not yet. I wanted wakefulness, awareness. I wanted to embrace life. And to live it decently, truthfully. If I could turn myself round a few degrees and raise enough pith, I might become what I would have wanted to be; or, at the very least, discover whether, as Sofi once told me, I could have chosen a finer path out of the forty allocated to every person.

I started to feel uneasy. One of those churnings of the stomach I'd acquired during the Peoples' Wars warning me of impending danger. I surveyed the area. My neck, an equally dependable antenna, sizzled.

I'm not afraid of dying. I know that large parts of me have already died. So I can think of death as the polarity of my unlived life. I am even inclined to imagine it as the woman of my fantasies who would make love to me for all eternity, living and dying with me time after time after time. What makes that illusion ridiculous is the fact that Death is never merciful; it never shrouds a person without humiliating him.

But I have accepted that paradox.

There is beauty in the world. And where there is beauty, there is goodness. And though that world of goodness has never opened its doors to me, I believe it exists because Sofi assured me it did. I've had intimations of it – even the odd glimpse.

I walked more quickly. Despite my years, I'm pretty fit – thanks to the Peoples' Wars. Not long ago, a woman I slept with said I looked ageless, like driftwood.

I love women. If I could, I'd give all I have to a woman.

But what would I be offering her? How can I say: take me;

have all of me? What is there in me of any worth? What I'd really be saying is: please, make me live; I don't want me for myself; I don't know how to live. What woman would want such a burden? When I was still a doctor, when I treated wounded soldiers, and some of them looked upon me as God – waited, with unwavering faith, for me to heal them even when Death was closing their eyes – I persistently buried my feelings. All that interested me, I admonished myself, were their broken bodies and the possibility, if any, of repairing them.

What woman would want a man so lost to life?

Sofi. Sofi would have.

She'd have said: what sense is there in a life without feelings? What's more sublime than being able to give yourself to another so that you can receive all that the other can give? That's what bestows meaning onto Creation.

The presentiment of danger flared again. Instinctively, I dropped my bag, threw myself to the ground and rolled to the side of the road as a shot whistled past.

I scrambled towards the fields.

Instinct rather than good judgement propelled me to dive into a ditch. I swallowed mouthfuls of slime. I had taken cover in one of the abandoned irrigation channels.

When under fire, both the best and the worst move to escape from the enemy is to seek cover in water. A deep stretch gives some chance of swimming away from danger. Conversely, water is also the first place attackers search. And heaven help you if you're caught wading; there's no way you can dart out of the water and rush at your pursuers.

I had no choice. Keeping my head just above the slime, I moved away from the direction of the gunfire.

I trundled about fifty metres.

At a point where a cluster of bulrushes rose from the channel, I paused. There had been no other shots so I raised my head and looked about me.

There wasn't much to see. The fields had been reclaimed by coarse grass.

In the far distance, a man on a horse was galloping towards the Citadel.

I assumed he was the gunman. But why had he fired on me? Perhaps, as Kokona had suggested, an enemy of the Goras, pursuing a feud? But how could he have known I was back? Or known who I was? Even Kokona hadn't recognized me.

I turned round to climb out of the ditch when I became aware of a presence: a sheepdog, crouched, panting and alert as if it were ready to herd a flock. Next to it, I saw a man's legs in loose pantaloons – the sort Skenderis prefer – but with smart, shiny city shoes.

I looked up.

The man was pointing his rifle at my head.

Fine-looking, fair-haired despite his severely cropped hair. Unusually for the islanders, no moustache. Though there were some deep lines on his forehead, he had the smooth, effeminate skin of the bald. About mid-thirties. He was wearing a striking coat, the traditional garb for funerals, black but elaborately embroidered, which, as with his shoes, looked new. And he had a large poacher's bag slung over his shoulders like a bandolier.

I raised my hands.

3

BOSTAN

He stood upright. Condemned men beg from head to foot. Not he. No concern. That's what struck me about him. Arms slackly raised. Eyes idly gauging the way I stood.

But he wasn't really looking at me. Not at me as a person. Not even as one who was going to send him to his ancestors. More like a vet examining an animal that had lamed itself.

I growled. 'Who're you?'

He spoke calmly, quietly. Eyes still unreadable. 'You don't really mean to kill me, do you?'

I bellowed. 'Who are you?'

Suddenly his eyes changed. Like the sea, turning dangerous without warning.

I hissed menacingly. 'I won't ask again. Who are you?'

His eyes turned blank again. 'Nobody.'

'Nobodies sneak up from behind. And kill.'

'I'm not that sort. Just a stranger, a *xenos*. And who might you be?'

'I'm asking the questions. Your name?'

'Wouldn't mean a thing to you.'

I aimed my rifle at his forehead. 'My patience is running out. Your name!'

'Osip Gora.'

'Gora?'

'Yes.'

'That's an old Skenderi name. Plucked it out of the air, did you?'

'No.'

He dropped his arms, moved to climb out of the ditch.

Castor, my dog, rose from his haunches, ready to hurl himself at him.

'Don't move! Keep your hands up!'

He did so. Still ignoring my rifle. Not troubled by Castor.

He was powerfully built, but craggy and ageing. Also of a strange lightness, as if trying to squirrel away his strength, putting half his ballast aside. That, too, struck me. Not puffed-up like Skenderi men.

'You a hired hand?'

'Hired hand? No!'

'Don't lie! Hired hands are against the Law!'

'Against the law?!'

'But some families have been talking about it – secretly. Many mercenaries on the mainland – from the Peoples' Wars. Now redundant, looking for jobs.'

'That's how it goes with wars.'

'So the truth! A hired hand, are you?'

'No.'

'The truth, I said!'

'Who'd employ me?'

'The Rogosins!'

'I don't know any Rogosins. I just got off the ferry.'

'Off the ferry? You must have been the only passenger.'

'No. There were others ...'

'The Rogosins?'

'I told you I don't know the Rogosins. But I got talking to Kokona and Dev. You might know them ...'

'I do.'

'We were the only three to get off.'

'So why are you here?'

'Inheritance.'

'What?'

'The water-mill. On the south coast. Maybe you know it.'

'I know it.'

'It's Gora property. I inherited it.'

'A clown, are you? The water-mill was sold. To absentee landlords – Gospodins, we call them.'

'It wasn't. Somebody made an offer – through a lawyer – but I decided to keep it.'

'A story-teller! Maybe *you* are one of the Gospodins, making an appearance!'

'As I said, the name is Osip Gora. I have an identity card.'

He lowered one arm to put his hand in his pocket, then realized he was still up to his knees in slimy water. 'But it'll be soaked.' He pointed at his duffle bag. He'd dropped it down the road. 'I've also got documents, deeds and things. If you'd let me get out of this ditch.'

A man with a well-known Skenderi name. Claims to be a stranger. Heir to the water-mill that everybody thinks has been sold. I'm supposed to believe all that? But who'd think up such a tale? 'Stay where you are!'

He sighed. Then he ran his eyes over me – again looking at me as if I were not a person.

I scratched my groin, as we do in Skender, to show off our manliness. 'Gora. Once a famous name here. The Rogosins' new allies?'

'I don't go in for alliances.'

What did I have to do to get a proper answer? 'He escaped, thanks to you.'

'Who?'

I pointed at the horseman, barely visible now in the distance. 'Stefan Rogosin. Had him in my sights. Right between the eyes. One bullet. Then you turned up!'

'I was on my way to the water-mill.'

'Didn't come to help him?'

'No.'

'He didn't ask you to sneak up behind me?'

'No.'

'Well, you helped him all right. I had to take care of you first. It gave him the chance to escape.'

'You nearly killed me.'

'Count yourself lucky. I rarely miss.' I lowered my gun. 'You can get out now.'

Castor uncoiled from his crouch.

Xenos climbed out of the ditch, started scraping the slime off his clothes.

I took out a bottle of *rakiya* from my poacher's bag and offered it to him. 'Have a drink.'

He took several gulps. 'Thanks. That's good.'

'Keep it.' I pointed at my bag. 'I've plenty more. I'm one man who always goes around well stocked.'

Why was I reacting like this – almost offering him a welcome?

He toasted me with the bottle.

Then he approached Castor. Was he mad? Why wasn't he afraid? Of me, of my gun, of Castor?

'Handsome dog. What's his name?'

'Castor.'

He started stroking him. 'Pollux's brother?'

I was amazed. Castor isn't a dog who fraternizes with anybody. He can tell about people. Won't let many touch him. Even my son fears him.

'Who's Pollux?'

'Castor's twin. In mythology. They're a constellation now.'

I felt pained. 'Oh, that Pollux. I didn't realize ...'

'Sorry, I was talking to myself.'

'Actually, that's how he got his name. Kokona suggested it. I had another dog. He was called Pollux. Also named by Kokona. He died. So it made sense this one should be Castor.'

'It's a good name.'

'It is. Castor's amazing – so was the one who died. Twins in every way.'

'That I can understand.'

'Just like in mythology. I'm pretty good at mythology. Even though we don't have a school.'

'So Kokona said. Not since she stopped teaching.'

'Even in her time, it was rare for ...' I was about to say something I shouldn't. I stopped just in time, annoyed with myself. Why was I telling him things?

'For?'

I muttered. 'Schooling for kids like me. We had to work on the farm. But at least I can read and write. I learned that.'

He smiled. 'That's good.'

I ignored the remark. I'm not one to be patronized.

'Were you really going to kill that man?'

What a question! 'Stefan? Definitely! But don't worry. I'll get him! No one escapes Bostan.'

'Bostan – that's you?'

'Yes.'

'Greetings.'

'Send them to your guardian angel. She kept you alive.'

'Why do you want to kill Stefan?'

Why doesn't this man keep his mouth shut? Why doesn't he show any fear? 'You wouldn't understand ...'

'More relevant to me: why try and kill me – someone you've never seen before?'

Maybe he's a djinn. That's how they appear. Suddenly. 'I told you. I thought you were Stefan's ally. His family – the Rogosins – and mine – the Kristofs – are engaged in a feud. That includes allies.'

'Ah, that old Minotaur!'

'I said you wouldn't understand.'

'I understand all right. But I see no sense in it.'

I was getting hot. I opened my coat. 'A life for a life. If your family has been dishonoured, it's like being dead. Only blood purifies honour. So, as a man of honour – that's what I must do.'

Xenos stopped stroking Castor. 'Who says?'

'The Law says. *We* say.'

'Who are we?'

'All of Skender.'

'Not Kokona. Or Dev.'

I snorted. 'She and the dwarf live in another world. You should meet Righteous Toma, our elder. He'll tell you what's what.'

He shook his head. 'Righteous? Must be a formidable man.'

'He is. Knows the Law inside out. He trained me. Best feudist from his stable – I'm proud of that.'

Xenos' eyes turned murky. 'He certainly taught you how to shoot ... But his law sounds like that of every righteous charlatan ...'

That angered me. Who was he to bad-mouth a great man? 'Watch what you say! He's God-sent! And it's not his law. It's the Law! Our law!'

'The one that forbids hired hands?'

'Exactly.'

Xenos nodded. Mockingly, I thought.

Then he took out his cigarettes. He saw they had disintegrated in the water. He turned to me. 'Got a cigarette?'

I took out my packet. 'I shouldn't give you any! You blasphemed against the Law and Righteous Toma ...'

He smiled. Surprisingly, a natural smile. 'As you please.'

I threw him my packet. 'But I'm not heartless. Help yourself.'

He took two. 'One for later, if it's fine with you.'

'Keep the pack.'

He nodded thankfully. 'Want one?'

'Why not?'

He came closer and offered me the packet. I took one.

'Got a light?'

I gave him my matches. 'You can have those, too.'

He lit his cigarette and mine. His eyes stayed on my girth. 'Wise of you.'

'What?'

'To wear protective clothing – bullet-proof vest, is it?'

I buttoned up my coat again. 'Observant of you.'

'Sensible – for feudists.'

'Not that it helps those I'm after. I always aim for the head.'

'A past master ...'

'I'm the best there is ...'

'There's always one better.'

'Not in Skender. Not yet. There won't be for a long time.'

He sighed, as if he was really concerned. 'I hope so. For your sake.'

I'd had enough of this *xenos*. I whistled to Castor, started walking. 'Watch where you put yourself!'

He nodded, still looking at me.

I strode off.

Castor followed me.

I walked uneasily. I could feel his eyes watching the way I moved. I thought I should have killed him anyway. But I don't kill for the sake of it.

4

DEV

I soon hear about Bostan's attack on Xenos.

I go to the Citadel to get bread. But the baker – a Jew – has gone to a circumcision and is late lighting his ovens. I don't sit in the Plaza. Too many chickens, stray cats and dogs, donkeys hitched to carts and a few sheep waiting for slaughter. Promised land for flies. So I go for a drink.

Most afternoons the tavern is empty. Browned photos of famous feudists are the only patrons. They're put on show after they've been killed. All have big moustaches. Even women who became designated men – like Eleanora the Falcon – wearing false ones.

But this day the *Morituri* have a lesson. Eleven boys, four girls. Aged thirteen to twenty. Schooling to be feudists. Toma is their teacher. '*Morituri*' means 'those who are about to die'. That's how Roman gladiators saluted Caesar. Kokona coined the name. Toma calls them Paladins of the Law: after the Palladion, the stone house by the Citadel gate which people restored for him. Now the Academy for Instructing The Law. And his home.

Today the *Morituri* are learning to drink like men. Without puking. When they become feudists, they won't smell of their mothers' milk. All with guns. After drinking, they'll practise shooting. Another of Toma's classes. Six generations of feudists he has trained. Toma forbids the term 'feudist'. He says it's archaic. He insists on 'paladins'. People still say feudists. We Skenderis don't use grand words.

Gavril Rogosin, Stefan's nephew, is sitting with Zemun, Bostan's son. One day, they'll be fodder for the Law. Now they're just comrades marking time.

Gavril waves to me.

Zemun doesn't. He's a boy like a ferret. No one likes him much. But a very good shot. Toma's favourite student.

I see Zemun is in rapture. Lila sits at his other side. She's the island beauty. All men lust after her. I bet even Toma.

Zemun's nostrils are wide. He's smelling Lila like good Turkish coffee. Both are approaching seventeen. So naturally Nature is nudging.

Big smile from Anton Kaplan. He's playing his lute. Singing softly. Poor Anton – not a good drinker. Forces down *rakiya* like hemlock.

Where Anton goes, there goes his brother, Marius. They're very close. Two persons in one. But Marius is not a *Morituri*. He sits apart. Reads. He's always reading. Always asks for books from Kokona.

I wave at Gavril and Anton.

I buy a *rakiya* and sit facing the Plaza.

I listen to Anton. Master lutanist. Gentle boy. Clear-water voice. When he sings he makes the world beautiful. Everybody likes him. Me – and Kokona – love him. His lute teacher, Stefan Rogosin, says one day Anton will be better than Orpheus.

Strange thing. His brother, Marius, is not musical at all. But Kokona says reading is also a great gift. Marius is a year older than Anton. As the first-born he was marked as the family's future feudist.

But Marius is against the Law. So Anton took his place. He'd rather he was killed instead of Marius. Why? Anton says, because one day Marius will change the world. Maybe. At least Marius watches over Anton all the time. Always ready to save him. If he can stop Anton feuding, I'll believe he can change the world. Shows what an insult to the Creator the Law is.

I glance at Toma. Skinny and lined like terracing. Tallish with large features. But so bent you think he'd rather be a dwarf. Wearing a purple cloak, as usual. In these parts we never wear purple because it's the colour of gods and heroes. A superstition we inherited from our ancestors. Shows Toma's hubris, Kokona says.

Also he has his special goblet. Reputedly belonging to Skanderbeg, the Albanian national hero named after Alexander the Great. He took it from the Divan. In fact, impounded whatever was left there and put the objects in the Palladion. Only he is allowed to keep them, he said, because he is the only incorruptible one among us.

He is waving his mace. In rhythm to Anton's music. A mainland smith made it for him. Toma boasts it is silver. But I know it is iron. Keeps rusting. Has tassels and a wood-carving of a skull for a knob. It sums up the man.

His eyes are shut. Anton's magic is possessing him. It does everybody.

But will he spare Anton? Never! The Law is more important than the music of the gods. We must worship death – nothing else.

That's why Toma hates Marius. Always reviles him. Always afraid Marius will pull Anton away from the *Morituri*. Make him defy the Law. Bring the temple down.

Maybe Toma has shut his eyes because of me. I don't exist for him. He and I are so different. Gull shit and egg yolk. But elfin Fate – she put our stars in the same coop. Axed us from feuding. Me, because dwarfs don't count as men. Him because, long ago, in a feud, he had his testicles shot. In Skender no balls means no right to be a man.

Kokona thinks it's the castrato's grief that makes Toma the prophet of blood-letting. Happens with the unsexed, she says. More so when they get old. They embrace savage traditions. Convince the young and virile that living for death is the noblest life. The more cemeteries they fill, the more they swell their lost balls. Kokona says history is full of politicians, generals and religionists who have nothing dangling between their legs.

I finish my drink, get up to leave.

I see Stefan Rogosin gallop into the Plaza on his horse.

He ties his horse to a post. Stumbles in.

Anton stops playing. Goes to Stefan. Very happy. Kisses his hands. 'Master ... Welcome ...'

Stefan strokes Anton's cheek. He's shaking. 'Good man, Anton ... Carry on ... Play ...'

Anton goes back to Toma's table. Starts playing again.

Stefan sinks into a chair. Shouts at the taverner. 'Large *rakiya*, Jiri ...'

He looks paler than the moon on a luckless night. And he's shivering.

Jiri serves him.

Toma and the *Morituri* stare at Stefan. Watch in puzzlement.

Marius stops reading. Watches also.

I go to Stefan. 'All right?'

He snarls. 'Get lost, Shrimp!'

'What's up?'

He drinks his *rakiya* in one gulp. 'Disappear, I said!'

Toma puts on his fatherly voice. 'Something the matter, Stefan, my boy?'

Stefan tries smiling. Prophets – especially false ones – get more respect than dwarfs. 'Nothing, Righteous Toma. All's well.'

Toma loves the 'Righteous' title. All the *Morituri* call him that.

Stefan was a *Morituri*, too – two generations ago.

Toma raises his goblet to him. 'As it should be, my boy. As it should be.'

But Anton is unsure. Again he stops playing. Once more he comes to Stefan. 'Master, you're very pale. Are you unwell?'

Marius watches Anton.

Stefan waves Anton away. 'I'm fine. Just need a drink.'

Anton goes back to his table. Unhappy. Looks at Marius.

Marius shrugs. When Anton sits down, Marius continues reading.

Stefan's still shaking. I sit with him. 'Something's up, Stefan ...'

He manages to light a cigarette. 'Get me another drink!'

I get him a *rakiya*. 'Tell me.'

Stefan hisses. 'Shrimp, you mean well, but you always go too far. Fuck off!'

I don't move. I sit quietly. Stefan's not a man who keeps things to himself. He will spew. Soon.

He finishes his drink. Pushes his glass for more.

I bring it. I wait.

'Just had a close shave, Shrimp, didn't I?'

Toma's still watching. 'What's that, Stefan?'

'Nothing, Righteous Toma. I'll tell you later.'

Toma nods. But keeps watching.

Anton, too. He can see Stefan's in trouble.

I nudge Stefan. 'What close shave?'

'Bostan. Ambushed me. I only had my pistol. Useless against his rifle.'

'You got away? How? He's a crack shot!'

'Miracle! Suddenly this man appeared ...'

'What man?'

'Never saw him before. A *xenos* ...'

Toma shouts. 'Stop whispering, Stefan! Let's all hear what you've got to say!'

I press Stefan. 'This *xenos*. Just off the boat?'

'Dropped from heaven, for all I know. Bostan spotted him and started firing. I grabbed my chance and ran!'

Toma struggles to get up. 'What's that about Bostan? He's one of my paladins. One of the best ...'

I stand up. 'Did Bostan kill Xenos?'

Stefan shrugs. 'I wasn't going to wait and find out. But Bostan never misses.'

Toma rises, staggers over. 'What *xenos*?'

Anton follows. Anxious.

Marius stops reading. Watches Anton.

I rush out.

Stefan bawls. 'What the hell, Shrimp ...?'

'Can't leave a man lying dead!'

I jump into the van. Drive as fast as I can.

Half an hour later, I spot Xenos!

Alive. Walking. Agile as pollen in the air. Bag on shoulder. Smoking.

I stop. Jump out. 'Thank God! You're safe!'

He smiles. Cautious. 'Yes.'

'Not even wounded?'

'No.'

'Wonder of wonders! But wet ...'

'I dived into a ditch.'

'That's how he missed – Bostan?'

'News travels fast! How did you hear?'

'I saw Stefan – the man Bostan's after ... You're lucky Bostan didn't pursue you ...'

'He did. He cornered me.'

'He let you go?'

'Yes. After we talked a bit.'

'Maybe it makes sense. Bostan kills only feudists.'

Xenos thinks for a moment. 'Something about him, though. Troubled. Like the Sphinx. Stuck with a riddle ...'

'What do you mean?'

'The riddle of life and death. But then we're all stuck with that, aren't we?'

'Talking above my head, Xenos ...'

'Sorry. Just muttering ...'

'You're safe. That's what matters.'

'When you and Kokona spoke about the feuding ... Then when the harbour master went on about it – I didn't realize I'd come across it so soon. It's really this rife, is it?'

'Yes. Everybody's involved.'

'You, too?'

'No. Many are unhappy, but do nothing. Kokona and I are the only ones outside. Also a young man, Marius.'

'How come?'

'Kokona – when, after her third husband died, his family asked her to feud, she refused.'

'How did she manage that?'

'Kokona is Kokona.'

'That's the craziest part – women getting involved as much as men.'

'It's the Law. When a family is without men – when every boy after puberty is dead – a woman becomes the designated man.'

'Yes, I know that. Even men consider them men. Yet ...'

'No yets. They live like men. Behave like men. Drink, play cards and backgammon with them. Even piss standing up. And once designated, there's no going back. They have to stay men. Nobody thinks – or talks – about what they were. Their pasts are erased. They become a secret everybody knows but no one ever betrays.'

'I'd forgotten much of that. That's how it was, too, when I was a boy. My mother was a designated man. What I've never understood is why they agree – willingly – to give up their womanhood.'

'Importance. For most. As designated men they have men's rights. All the rights. So they have status in the community. As women they have no say. Good only for work, for bedding and for making babies.'

Xenos stares into the distance. 'My mother was certainly very willing ... Often I felt she couldn't wait for my father to die. Maybe even prayed for him to get killed. She wanted to be head of the family. That's why she agreed to send me away. She didn't want me around.'

'You were lucky!'

Xenos' eyes turn dead. 'Terrible woman, my mother. No feelings. Not so my father. He was all heart. You expect women to be gentle – so gentle that we men might learn from them. But that's not always true, is it?'

'No.'

'And the children suffer like orphans.'

'Yes.'

'Well, she didn't last long, my mother. Some months after I was sent away, Kokona wrote saying she'd been killed. She urged me not to come back ...'

'Now you *are* back. And safe.'

'The women who refused to be designated men were treated as outcasts. Are they still?'

'Yes.'

'Is Kokona?'

'No. Not for years. They gave up. Kokona can beat the Devil.'

'How do they look upon her now?'

'Village fool. Or wise. Sometimes a freak – like me.'

Xenos nods. There's a sadness on him like grey skies. He brings out his cigarettes. 'Smoke?'

I take one. 'To please you.'

He looks at me. As on the ferry when I said I make things grow. 'You really like pleasing people, don't you?'

I smile. 'Oh, yes.'

'You must be the last good man in the world.'

I laugh. 'Funny!'

'How come you're not involved in feuds?'

'They don't think dwarfs are men. Same as castrati.'

'Castrati? I thought they left these shores with the Ottomans ...'

'We have new ones. Shot in the goolies. Some feudists prefer that to killing. Primitive stuff, Kokona says. Like drinking blood. You strengthen your balls with the enemy's balls. It's also insurance for some feudists. Castrati lose the right to feud. They're no longer a threat.'

'Castrati can't feud because they've lost their nuts. But women who've never had any nuts can feud as designated men. That's some logic!'

'The Law. Feudists are like sacrificial animals, Kokona says. They must not be blemished. Men with no balls have a blemish. Women don't have balls so they're without blemish. Acceptable for sacrifice.'

Xenos' eyes go blank. He talks softly. Almost to himself. 'Who can say what a man is? Or what makes him one?'

'I can. You are.'

'You, too, Dev. Better than most.'

'But still a dwarf.'

'Look at it as a blessing. You're closer to the earth. Touching good soil. Chest high, the air is evil.'

He makes me laugh again. 'You have sunstroke.'

'This other person you mentioned – Marius? How come he avoids feuding?'

'Anton, his brother, took his place.'

'I see. I think that's what my father did – decided to feud to spare others.'

I open the van door. 'Hop in. You need a drink.'

He nods. 'Best way to celebrate the day.'

'That's Kokona's saying. When she thinks man has befouled life.'

He smiles. 'I must have pinched it from her – all those years back.'

He watches me clamber up the steps I've added to reach the cabin. Then he settles in his seat. He examines the manual controls I've put on the dashboard. 'Amazing, Dev ...'

'What?'

'Brake, clutch, accelerator – everything at your fingertips.'

'Otherwise I can't reach the pedals.'

'Did you adapt them yourself?'

'Yes.'

'You can make even a van grow, eh?'

'I try.'

'Kokona's right. You are a giant. She's lucky to have you.'

I don't know him. But I feel his despair. A thirsty soul. A plant desperate for water. '*I* am lucky. Kokona saved me.'

'How so?'

'One day everybody kicks me. A freak. Next day, I have life. Happy man.'

'How did she do that?'

'By loving me. And letting me love her.'

'Ah. Love.'

He shuts his eyes, falls asleep.

Back at the Citadel, Stefan's still in the tavern. Toma and the *Morituri* have gone to the Palladion's *meydan*. For shooting practice. Which we can hear. Marius has gone too – to watch over Anton.

Stefan calls us. 'Drinks on me.'

We join him.

He orders *rakiya*.

Jiri brings the drinks.

Stefan plays with his prayer beads. Stares at Xenos. Maybe he thinks Xenos is a ghost. 'You survived? How?'

Xenos shrugs. 'He let me go.'

'Bostan? That's never happened before.'

'I'm not you.'

'Even so. He takes no chances.'

'He'll still be going after you – he said so.'

'Naturally. We'll hunt one another – until one of us is killed.'

'Why don't you just stop?'

'We can't. It's the Law.'

'Damn the Law! Break it.'

'You don't understand.'

Xenos sighs. Offers cigarettes. 'Bostan thought I was your ally. Will you now think I'm his ally and consider me your enemy?'

Stefan takes a cigarette. 'That would be ungrateful of me. And against the Law. You saved my life. Besides, you're outside all this.'

Xenos lights cigarettes, mutters. 'I intend to be.'

Stefan finishes his drink, stands up. 'See you again. Then you can tell me what misfortune brought you here.'

He goes.

We drink on.

We watch Stefan mount his horse. His head, in the setting sun, shines like a halo.

I chuckle. 'Sunset makes things glow. Look at Stefan.'

Xenos glances casually. 'But eventually it gets dark. What can glow in the dark?'

I draw an oval on the table. 'This.'

'What's that?'

'Hope.'

'Looks like a vagina.'

'Yes. We call it *amata*.'

Xenos looks into the distance. 'Is it that simple?'

'*Amata*, Kokona says, comes from the word "love". A complete woman's *amata* – that's where love is always ready. Where life begins.'

'But you need to find that complete woman, recognize the hope she offers. You need to know how to begin life. How to make things grow. Bleak otherwise.' He stubs his cigarette. 'Time I was on my way ...'

I hold his arm. 'The sun's going. Gets dark quick. Stay with us. I'll take you to the water-mill tomorrow. Have some more *rakiya*.'

A shot rings out. This one's very near. It hasn't come from the Palladion's *meydan* where the *Morituri* are practising.

We jump to our feet.

Stefan on the saddle, catapults backwards, falls from his horse.

His horse gallops in panic.

A sheepdog races in. Stops by Stefan. Sniffs him. Zips away.

We run out of the tavern and hurry to Stefan.

People come out. From shops and houses.

Stefan is hit in the head.

Xenos feels his throat.

I ask. 'No pulse?'

Xenos shakes his head, then squints towards the Citadel gate. 'The dog – it was Castor. Bostan's dog.'

Toma and the *Morituri* – and behind them, Marius – come running from the Palladion.

Anton spots Stefan's body. Rushes to it.

Cradles Stefan's head. Weeps bitterly.

Toma shouts at Anton. 'No crying! Get up! Men don't cry!'

Anton wails. 'He was my Master. I loved him!'

Toma raises his mace to strike him.

Marius steps between Toma and Anton. 'Don't, Toma! No one touches my brother!'

Toma glares at Marius. He twirls his mace, ready to lash out at him instead.

Anton lets go of Stefan's head. Hauls himself up. Clasps Toma's sleeve. 'It's all right, Righteous Toma! It's all right!' He turns to Marius. 'I'm sorry, brother. I lost my senses!'

Toma smiles. Like a judge who's never wrong. Puts on the face of a forgiving father. 'That's right, Anton, my boy. You lost your senses. Let this be an exemplar. You're a Paladin of the Law! A true man! One of my disciples! You do not cry!'

Anton nods.

Marius holds Anton to his chest. To console him.

Toma turns to me. He speaks to the air above me. That way he doesn't have to face me. 'Bostan, was it?'

Something else catches my eye.

Bostan's son, Zemun, has daubed his face with Stefan's blood. Turns to Lila. In rapture.

Lila is shocked. But smiles approval.

Toma shouts at me. 'I asked you a question, Shrimp!'

I turn to him. 'Dev is my name. Ask again.'

'Was it Bostan?'

'Who else?'

He sighs. Very satisfied. 'Admirable. Admirable.'

I look at Xenos. He's watching Toma. As if Toma is a man who burns harvests.

Toma turns to the *Morituri*. Puts on his prophet's voice. 'See, my young ones! This is what our life is about! This is honour! For both men! As I've taught you: we're all born with weak blood, bad blood, blood contaminated by torpor, blood that slithers through life at Evil's pace. But you, the Paladins of the Law, you are men destined to be gods. You are here to cleanse the contamination. You are here to save our blood. To strengthen it. To immerse it in the only purifier there is: honour! And behold! That's what we are witnessing here! The ultimate purification! Bostan honoured his blood and killed like a god. Stefan, too, honoured his blood and died like a god. Nothing can be more sacred!'

Xenos' face is blank. 'Sacred, did you say?'

Toma nods. Pious. 'Sacred. As in holy. Sublime. Hallowed. Sanctified. Sacrosanct.' He extends his hand to Xenos. 'I am Toma. You must be the *xenos*.'

Xenos does not take his hand. 'Osip Gora is the name.'

Toma is very surprised. 'Gora? Did you say, Gora? Eleanora the Falcon's boy?'

This time Xenos is surprised. 'You remember her?'

A great light appears in Toma's eyes. 'Of course! Glory

personified. Most zealous designated man in Skender's history. Come to avenge her, have you?'

'No.'

'No? Did you say "no"?!'

'I did.'

'But she was killed to safeguard your family's honour! Four houses against her, my memory reminds me. Some of their descendants might still be around! I can find out for you – easily! You must avenge her!'

'I'm not interested.'

'Not interested? You must uphold her honour – and yours! That's the Law!'

'Not my law.'

'Have you turned soft, like your father?'

Xenos hisses. 'Soft?!'

Toma enjoys needling. 'Anibal – an illustrious name! But what does he do? Turns bird-watcher. Do you know what I ended up calling him? Skender's dove!'

Xenos gives a grim smile. 'He must have taken that as a compliment. Doves carry olive twigs and bring peace.'

Toma doesn't like to be challenged. He needles some more. 'He used to take you along, didn't he – bird-watching?'

'Yes.'

'As I said. Soft. Father and son.'

Xenos' eyes turn fiery. 'There's something you forget: my father was the best feudist of his time!'

Toma nods. 'That's true. He was. A remarkable paladin. But his marksmanship was a gift from the Fates. Like Anton's music! The real man in your family was your mother. Out of interest – did you chance to look at the photographs of our famous paladins in the tavern?'

'No.'

'Well, go and look! Your mother is there. Placed conspicuously. But not your father – though he was, as I've readily admitted, the best paladin we've ever had. Why do you think his picture is not there?'

'I wouldn't know. And I don't care!'

'I'll tell you all the same. It *was* there. One of his admirers had put it up – but I made them remove it. Because Anibal's notion of honour was heretical. He abhorred killing. He constantly tried to oppose the Law. Whereas your mother knew what honour meant. She knew that only blood purifies it. She killed without hesitation. Feudists must be hard as stone – like my Palladion. Or they might as well be women! Come to think of it, that's what your father should have been.'

'You've abused my father's name too many times, old one! Be careful what you say next.'

'I'll say what I like! Where did he think he was, your father – in the Garden of Eden? Heroes don't go bird-watching.'

'What would you know about heroes?!'

'Plenty! I am one. Look at my purple cloak – heroes' colour since time immemorial.'

Xenos is wordless as if before a madman.

Toma keeps badgering. 'Let me tell you something else! You should have been *my* son! Your mother should have married me! Not Anibal. She would have, but I was too august for her! I would have been the right father for you! Made a proper man out of you!'

Suddenly Xenos seizes Toma by his collar.

The *Morituri* try to pull him off.

Xenos doesn't even look at them. He shakes his shoulders as if he's a titan and throws off the *Morituri*.

The *Morituri* are cowed by his strength.

Only Zemun, still with Stefan's blood on his face, stands his ground.

Xenos ignores Zemun, shakes his head regretfully and lets go of Toma. As if he is pestilent.

This makes Toma mock him all the more. He spits words. 'What were you thinking of doing, Anibal's son? Smash me against the wall? You haven't the spleen! Like father, like son. He was an insult to your mother, Anibal was. A no-man of vapid blood. Whereas your mother, the best blood, blood bathed in immaculacy! Good thing Anibal didn't live too long! He would have defiled her! Like he has defiled you!'

Xenos turns to me. 'Get me out of here, Dev, before I lose my mind!'

I take his arm. Lead him to the van.

Toma shouts to the *Morituri.* He is in oration mode. 'Mind instead of guts! There you see putrid blood!'

I can't help myself. I shout back. 'What about your blood, Toma? How good is that? When did your cock last raise its head?!'

Toma ignores me. He has the *Morituri* around Stefan. And is declaiming. 'Pure, invincible blood, boys – that's the imperative! Transform bad blood into pure blood! That's the alchemy we must perform! That's what religions instruct us. Look at Stefan's blood! Sanctified! Honourable! Look at Zemun smeared with Stefan's blood. See how it glows on him like the gods' ichor? Remember, we're all born with bad blood! But people like Anibal's son are happy to let it run poisonously in their veins! Not us! Our blood is purified by extolling honour! By spilling our own blood! That's what history tells us! History knows about blood! History *is* blood! That's why, as paladins, you must never waver! You must obey and submit to our traditions! You must spurn distractions like love – be it for wives or children or parents! You must affirm that there's nothing more important in life than honour! Nothing else that keeps humiliation at bay! That's the source of our strength! And strength, first and foremost, means the consecration of Death! The will to embrace Death at any time! The readiness – always – to sacrifice our own lives! Never forget that, boys! That's how we became men! That's how we will make the earth fruitful! That's how we will ensure survival! That's how we will cleanse our souls!'

His words capture the *Morituri*.

Even Anton stops weeping.

They raise their arms. Salute Toma. Shout.

'Honour! Strength! Honour! Death!'

Zemun shouts loudest. Urges Lila.

But she looks uncertain. Maybe thinking she'd be better off married. Like all beautiful girls.

Last thing I see before I climb into the van is Marius, gently pulling Anton away.

5

TOMA

Anibal's son will be my enemy. I, Toma, know it in my bones.

I called him soft. But he isn't. Soft men are not provoked. His father, for instance, was so meek, so given to reason, that he never showed anger. Whereas this son of his seemed ready to fight all my paladins.

I don't want him in Skender.

Skender is my island. My smithy.

Word is that Anibal's son has inherited the water-mill.

How come we all thought the water-mill had been sold to the Gospodins long ago? That agent of theirs, Viktor, is useless. Never keeps records. Just happy to pocket his commission and live like a lord. He even has a new car!

So now Anibal's son will live at the water-mill. Harmlessly, he claims. Won't get involved with life on the island.

But that's not how things evolve in this world.

For a start, he's a stranger.

I don't welcome strangers. I tolerate only the Gospodins. And that's because they live in far-away warrens and are faceless.

More- over, they know I'm the power who has created stability in Skender, the leader who will enable them to make their billions when their time comes. What they don't know is that it'll be me who will use them for my purposes. What I've established here will determine the future – a future they will never be able to control or change. All they think of is money. That makes them so self-assured, so trustful of me that it never occurs to them to try and read my mind – or even ask why I've deigned to fraternize with them. They're unaware that when they move in – in all likelihood, with a great power – I will be the mystagogue who will govern Skender. And I will govern absolutely. Tolerate no dissent. And my governance will be my stepping-stone to the mainland. After that, country by country, the Law will rule everywhere.

That's what people are hankering for: a rule for order, a code to regain their honour, the hegemony of the Law, of *My Law.* And that's what I'm forging: the new order.

To come back to strangers. I hate them. They are not like us. They are the untouchable others. Barbarians at our gate. Aliens. And like all things other, they are dangerous. They bring their own ways. And there is always something new in their ways. So they always hatch changes.

Changes are perilous. They are unstable.

Moreover, a stranger who knows our ways, who once walked our land, fed on its spirit and then returned, having acquired other ways, is disastrous. Whether he intends to or not, he will precipitate change. You can't command the winds which way to blow. They have their arcane science. So do strangers.

The Law says everything has gravity; given the right conditions, even a feather can generate enough force to shift a mass. A stranger is like that. And the shift need not be substantial. A minute shift, particularly when it affects tradition, is enough to destabilize the edifice and send it crumbling down.

That's how it was here before the Law. Strangers of every hue and creed living cheek by jowl. Chaos. Ancestral homes turned into mire by heathen footsteps. Lands putrefied by alien food. The horizon despoiled by temples of every creed and denomination. And worse: children of every colour. Even today, we have women who give birth to babies with outlandish complexions. Still tarnished by the muddy blood some discoloured stranger dropped here once upon a time.

But I've corrected all that with the Law. I gave Skender its equilibrium. I've purified our people – irrespective of their religions – with the flag of honour. Our people needed order. Longed for it. Now they have it.

Those who think like Kokona – and Marius Kaplan, that anaemic brother of Anton – and who keep challenging me, claim that the Law is the only book I've read, and that I know little else. That's not true. I've read many books. Probably more than Marius will ever read.

After Anibal's death – and with Eleanora the Falcon's consent – I asked my paladins to bring his books here, to the Palladion. Not his trunk of scribbles. I didn't even look at them. The man was a fool. They'd have been muddled and unreadable; or about birds.

When they piled the books up in the *meydan*, I sermonized that it had been the books that had made Anibal meek; that whenever he challenged me and the Law, he did so not with reason, as he'd claimed, but with some absurd notion he had read in a book; that, therefore, the books had to be burned so that they would stop defiling the islanders' minds. And I told them that, as the custodian of the Law, it was my duty to burn them personally.

That night I made a huge bonfire. But I did not burn the books. I took them in, hid them and read them.

Books on history, philosophy and supposedly great novels. From the Balkans, Europe, even America. All permeated with so-called progressive ideas about how life should be lived. And, needless to say, all full of confusion. Fetching water from forty rivers and spilling it all on the way. In summary, they maintained that the pursuit of happiness can only be attained through the pursuit of love – particularly carnal love. Variations on all that I had read when, as a youngster, my parents had sent me to school on the mainland, then brought me back, terrified, because the mainland was aping the European Enlightenment – or rather what those foreigners, strangers, called enlightenment.

Books – all of them – miss the kernel of our souls.

And this time I did burn them – one by one – in my Palladion's great hall where I teach the Law. I burned them in the fireplace which has my pulpit on one side and the bookcase which contains the Scroll of the Law and my writings on the other. And as the flames consumed the pages and their shadows danced on the walls, I sipped *rakiya* and ululated. Here was proof of strength. Of my strength. Proof that the strength of the Law, the strength to embrace Death, was more important than money, learning and love.

What mankind needs is not a state of confusion about his mind and heart and the way he should live happily, but a cause for which he would *die* happily. Only a cause worthy of death gives him dignity, keeps humiliation at bay. What better preserver of dignity than honour?

That's what makes the Law the ultimate scripture, the Codex of Truth. Even religions' sacred books, much as they are supposed to contain the knowledge of God, deny God's most vowed dictum: honour.

I know. I have read those books also. And should anyone need proof of his misreading, let him just ask: if there is only one God and He is the Truth, why are religions at each other's throats; why are they foraging the market-places in search of followers; why does each pretend that his god has the bigger cock?

Speaking of cock. That was the weakness in Anibal's blood. Once, when we were arguing about the Law – he wanting to abolish it; me determined to uphold it – he said he was a loving man and killing was brutalizing him. He had agreed to feud not only to spare the other members of his family from that obligation, but also to please his wife.

A loving man! What nonsense! He was an ordinary man – with nothing on his mind beyond fornication. Eleanora the Falcon confided in me; told me he constantly wanted to bed her. Well, she wasn't interested. The purpose of intercourse is procreation, she told him, not pleasure. So she did her duty by him, gave him a son, then barred him from her bedroom. She, like me, had come to understand that the only worthy bedfellow is honour. Everything else is frailty.

Which is why she would have been the perfect spouse for me. She would have prized my emasculation as a badge of valour, considered the void in my crotch as a laurel. And we would have slept in the same bed, like two megaliths admiring each other's splendour. The rest of the time, we would have continued to consolidate the Law and crush any opposition.

I did, of course, ask her to marry me after Anibal's death. She refused only because by then I was acclaimed Prophet. And prophets, she believed, belong to the people and must remain detached. I think, in time, I could have convinced her. But not long after she became the designated man, she was killed.

A sad confession here ... Being a castrato does not stop a man from desiring. There are times, particularly since Lila joined my paladins, that I keep imagining ... No, I can't talk about that. It's debasing ... Anyway, all this babel about sex – it is perversion, nothing else.

Instead, here is a confession that really hurts. Some nights, having seen in a nightmare the death of one of my paladins, I wake up in a sweat. I'm sure I will again tonight. I'm bound to dream about Stefan.

This strikes me as 'conscience' – a word from Anibal's books. The Law calls it the Doubter within us. He's another despoiler of honour – so must be obliterated! I must live as I have always lived, a servant of the Law and its interpreter for ever.

6

KOKONA

There was a time when every door on this island was always open. Whoever wanted to visit a family just walked in and received a warm welcome. It was a custom we had picked up from the Turks when they were our rulers. Nowadays, no one – except Dev and me – practises it any more. Reclusion is another legacy from the Law. Feudists are forbidden to attack their enemies in their own homes. So a person's house is his sole refuge on the island. The feudist leaves it only when he goes to stalk his foe or due to dire necessity or on truce days.

So when Dev brought Osip home my face lit up. Like an olive tree in moonlight, Dev told me later.

I had not stopped thinking about Osip since we had left him at the pier. Incidentally, I'm calling him Osip from now on; not Xenos. He's not a stranger to me.

I had been at my loom much of the day, trying to decide on a motif for a new arras. My tapestries were selling well at the Handwork Cooperative and I was thinking that maybe I could be more adventurous, create a design of my own, perhaps try a figurative one – gleaming with bright colours – maybe depicting a love poem from Naim Frasheri's *Summer Flowers*. Much as I enjoy copying geometrical patterns from ancient rugs, I'd been doing that for years and I wanted to discover whether I could be original. But I was having difficulty concentrating as memories of Osip came rolling down into my loom.

The memories seemed to blend into a few clusters of great clarity, like photographs untouched by the tinge of time: Osip as an infant, wizened into silence by the violence that withers the air we breathe; Osip as a minor, delicate as the down on his face, trying to alchemize himself into iron; and Osip as a withdrawn youngster desperately struggling with his fears in order to become Skender's idea of a man.

I even remembered the day he was born – a very special day for his father, Anibal, because Osip was his first child. And he knew, given his wife's indifference to him, that the boy would be his only child – hence a unique fruit for a man who had yearned for the continuance of his family line. He also knew, of course, that, though still young – in his early thirties – he himself would have a short life, like all feudists.

And, of course, I remembered Osip's mother. Beautiful and regal. But heartless as religion. Aptly nicknamed after a falcon. An ardent disciple of Toma, who had already established himself as 'the Prophet of Honour'. In fact Toma wanted very much to marry her, courted her even while Anibal was still wedded to her. And she might well have taken Toma, unmanned though he was – indeed not being a loving woman, she would have thought that a boon – but having dallied with religion while still young, she believed that a 'great prophet', like the fathers of the Church, belonged to everybody and, therefore, should never get married.

Osip had several cousins – six of them. All females. Indoctrinated by Eleanora. They took turns following in their aunt's footsteps as designated men and so died in quick succession. I wrote to Osip after each death, but never received a reply.

That sensitive boy who had clung to me at the ferry – hugged for the first and the last time by maternal arms, I'd felt by the way his heart thudded – has now, somehow, matured into a man who looks stout on his legs and seems well-seasoned. On the ferry, he opened up like a flower before a bee; he didn't even try to hide the fact that he was weighed down by dark clouds.

So all sorts of questions gnawed at me: who was living inside him now – the child he had been or the man he appeared to be? Why had he come back? Was he really looking for a peaceful retreat? If so, what devastations had compelled him to seek it? Would he be able to settle down in his water-mill? Would he manage to live in Skender without incurring a feud? And if he got into a dispute how long would he be able to survive?

Dev, distraught as he always is after witnessing a death, stuck to his belief that Osip's survival was a miracle. I don't believe in miracles. But I had to admit that since Bostan's bullets seldom miss their targets, Osip's escape was, at the very least, remarkable. Was he endowed with *baraka*, the protection of deities? Or with Hermes' wings that enable soldiers, in the heat of battle, to trickle away like quicksilver? These are wonderful gifts, but they can't give protection for ever. How many calamities had he survived? How many more had he left?

So I welcomed him, took his shoes and Dev's and washed their feet. I sat them down and served them cheese, spring onions, olives, salted fish and *rakiya*.

I decided to prepare a feast. Spinach *börek* – Osip loved that as a child. Then lamb knuckles cooked with aubergines. Rice. Bread. Wine. And, of course, figs – Skender figs, straight from our garden, which I sent Dev to gather.

It took me a while to start cooking because Osip, fascinated by my weaving, kept asking questions. That pleased me. I enjoy talking about the finer points of my craft. Weaving is like creating a world. From the moment you start spinning the wool to the final knot, you feel like a god. And when you look at the finished article and say it's good, you do so with some sorrow – as the Lover of Love must have done after creating Creation – because what you've created is unique and you will never be able to relive the joys and frustrations of that labour. Then with that sorrow you start on a new work or, if you're the Lover of Love, on a new world – and then once again you're in your element.

His mother, Osip reminded me, also used to weave – but not happily like me, he said, not with her heart. I understood what he meant. She was a Penelope. And Penelope is not one of my heroines. All that nonsense about fidelity. There is even a legend that says when Penelope thought Odysseus had been killed, she threw herself into the sea only to be saved by gulls. These are legends created by men to yoke women. The reason Penelope kept her suitors at bay was self-interest. She was determined to cling to her worldly goods. She was prepared to do all she could to fit the image men had decreed for her gender. What care could she provide for anybody, let alone her child, by stifling her womanhood in order to satisfy patriarchal vanity?

When finally we sat down to supper, Osip ate with relish, though moderately. Thinking he might have acquired city habits, I had given him a plate, knife and fork, but he put those aside and, like Dev and me, helped himself with his hand from the platters.

Since a guest should never be questioned during a meal, I talked about everyday subjects: the weather; our coop and pen; our plot of land which, thanks to Dev's prodigious hands, makes us self-sufficient in almost everything; and books.

I may not be a teacher any more, but I still read a lot. The ferry brings me newspapers. I choose some titles and the captain buys them for me on the mainland.

During the meal Dev hardly spoke. He just kept shuddering. That's how it is with him after there's been a killing. But what was endearing – and unexpected – was the way that every time he quivered, Osip took his hand. Dev didn't know how to respond to that – no one except me, certainly no man, has ever been tender with him – but I could see from the way his eyes watered that he was grateful.

We keep saying in Skender – perversely echoing Toma – that men have no compassion in them, that all they know is how to fight and kill; but we're wrong. It is we – the whole community and not least our trepanned women – who push them into being so. How many among us have seen the love and tenderness men give one another as a divine act? How many of us have opened our minds and tried to provide that gentleness to the man we love?

After dinner, Dev cleared up and went to feed the animals. Osip offered to help him, but Dev would not let a guest do any work: it would be like asking payment for hospitality.

So I refilled Osip's cup with wine and sat in my corner to roll the wool I'd spun.

He sat next to me and wound the wool around his hands. 'I'll hold it for you.'

That made me laugh. 'You know how?'

He smiled and nodded.

'I'll roll it loosely. They have to be dyed before I distaff them.'

He waved a hand, indicating he knew.

'Thank you – for comforting Dev. Normally people don't treat him as a person. Dwarfs aren't expected to have feelings.'

Osip stared into some darkness. 'Seeing someone getting killed is hard to bear. Particularly if you've never killed.'

The softness of his voice, the sadness that gave lustre to his face assured me I could trust him. My heart spoke before my mind could think and I divulged the one secret that I had kept for decades. 'Oh, Dev has killed.'

He stared at me incredulously.

'Two men, in fact.'

'Killing is intolerable. No matter how many you kill ...'

I was moved by his honesty. If I'd had a son, I thought, I'd have wanted him to be as truthful. 'You've killed, too – I gather ...'

He averted his eyes. 'Yes.'

'Many?'

He mumbled wearily. 'Yes, Teacher. Many.'

'No doubt, you were often close to death yourself?'

'Yes.'

'Peoples' Wars?'

'Yes.'

'That was horrible. Seemed it would never end.'

'Forty-odd years.'

'Where do people find the energy to fight for so long?'

'Hatred. That's people's daily bread. But if you asked ...' He stopped speaking and looked away again, his mind disappearing into a mist.

I prompted him. 'Asked who ...?'

He spoke so softly, I barely heard him. 'A woman – I knew ... Young ...'

'Doesn't she have a name?'

'Sofi.'

'And what would Sofi have said?'

'Atavistic delirium. The pursuit of power. What most men – all our rulers – suffer from. Have suffered for millennia. They hoodwink us. We let them. And history forever repeats itself ...'

'Wise young woman. Where is Sofi now?'

'She died. Instead of ...' He fell silent.

'Instead of you?'

He shrugged, unable to answer.

'I'm sorry for her. But I'm glad that you, at least, know how to avoid bullets ...'

'During the Wars the soldiers had a saying: the fire next time.'

'The Wars are over ...'

'Are they ever?'

'Develop the aptitude to forget past horrors. Then, before you know it, you blossom with expectations.'

'You sound like Dev, Teacher.'

'Naturally. We think alike.'

'At the tavern, Dev drew an oval – depicting a woman's genitals ... He called it hope. Next minute, Stefan got killed. It made a mockery of hope.'

I pointed at an oval design on one of my tapestries. 'Was Dev's drawing like that?'

'Yes.'

'One of the oldest symbols in the world. Existed long before the Christians adopted it. Sign of the fish. And a woman's lagoon – where the fish swim. Symbol of life. It means life goes on – despite death. There lies the hope. When the drive for life – which is an almighty force – overcomes the obsession with death – which is often fabricated by man – the killings will stop.'

'Hope can be killed also. Despair is very good at that.'

'Yes. But you're not one without hope – not yet. Or you wouldn't be here ...'

'That's true. I can't let go of it. Or it won't let go of me. But I'd be much better off without it.'

I had finished rolling. Now that his hands were free, he glanced at his cigarettes. I could see he was hankering after a smoke.

I smiled. 'Go ahead. I'll have one, too.'

He grabbed the packet.

We started smoking.

'You were saying, Osip ...?'

He looked at me hesitantly. I could see he wanted to talk, but he was also reticent, almost apprehensive. 'I've run out of steam, Teacher. Maybe another day ...'

I didn't press him. 'Of course. Any time.'

He sipped some of his wine. 'Can you tell me what made Dev kill?'

'He was protecting me.'

'A good reason.'

'Good? Who can tell? In a way it made him the giant he is. On the other hand, how can anything good come from killing?'

'What happened?'

I hesitated. I wanted to tell him, but felt that this was Dev's secret and I shouldn't divulge it. I drew on my cigarette a few times. Then I decided to tell. I could trust Osip. 'Dev doesn't know that I know. This must remain a secret between you and me.'

'It will.'

'It was a long time ago. Thirty-odd years. I wouldn't have anything to do with feuds. Even after Petros, my third husband, had been killed. I loved Petros dearly. He was a good man. The sort who fulfils a woman – very much like Dev. A perfect match – in body as well as spirit. So I raged against feuds. Not so his family. They glorified the Law. Eventually they ran out of males. So the women came to me and asked me to become their designated man. I chased them out. They turned spiteful. Trumpeted to all Skender that I'd agreed to take up the feud. I denied it – but no one believed me. So our enemies sent someone to kill me on my way to the Citadel. Dev had been expecting that. He laid an ambush and killed that person. That made the enemy think I really was the designated man. So they sent someone else. Dev saw to him also.'

'Didn't they suspect it was Dev? Knowing how much he loved you.'

'We weren't together then. Even if we had been, who'd think a dwarf capable of killing two feudists?'

'Didn't they send others?'

'No. Dev made sure of that. He cast a curse.'

'A curse?'

'He cut up the clothes of the men he'd killed and wove them into meshwork. Then he trussed up the bodies and left them to the buzzards. When the first body was found, it looked as if the man had lost his mind and got entangled in his demons' webs. When the second was found in the same condition, all the islanders agreed that the would-be killers had been attacked by griffins. That suggested I had supernatural forces watching over me. At the time, people believed that the Law must not challenge the supernatural, that this would antagonize the Devil and make him drown us in dishonour. Toma, of course, denounced the belief as superstition, but even he couldn't quash superstition overnight. No one dared come near me after that.'

Osip shook his head in amazement. 'How did you find out it was Dev who killed those men?'

'My first and second husbands died – both within months of marriage. Then the school closed. And suddenly I was left on my own. Banished from life. No man, no children, no students. I accepted that as my fate. But I'm not one to wallow. So I immersed myself in books, sought to quench my thirst for life in the lives of fictional characters – so very real to me – in the histories of other peoples, in the ideas old and new that sought to understand the world, sought to imagine an existence without bloodshed. My mind became my only source of pleasure.

'During this time – it lasted some years – I began noticing Dev. I'd seen him around, of course, but now he kept appearing everywhere. If I looked out of my window, there he would be. If I worked on the land, the same. But always from a distance. He never addressed me or came near me. And shied away if I tried to approach him. Just looked at me as if I carried the sun. And I realized he had appointed himself as my guardian angel. Perhaps another person might have been annoyed by this. But I was immensely moved. And in a way, it was revelatory. It made me realize that since I believed in life, I should be involved in life – like Dev – indeed make myself a life-giver, inhabit myself as a woman. So I left my cocoon, met Petros, married him.

'After that Dev disappeared from view – as he told me later, discreetly withdrew from my life. Then when Petros was killed – once more soon after our wedding – Dev reappeared. Again to watch over me from a distance. Thus when those men came after me, I knew it had been Dev who'd killed them – both men were knifed in the belly; that's just about as far as he can reach. Also, after the killings, Dev got sick. I looked after him. He was delirious for a while. He blurted out everything.'

'Why didn't you tell him you knew?'

I stubbed out my cigarette. 'Dev's a proud man. I didn't want him to think I loved him because he saved me. I wanted him to know I had grown to love him for what he was – still is: my man. The best ever.'

'Maybe he knows you know. I would have known, if I were him.'

'Maybe. Dev sees everything. Senses everything. But he's never mentioned it to me.'

Osip lit a fresh cigarette with the stub of the one he'd been smoking. He stared at the smoke as if wishing to blend with it. 'I envy you both.'

I sorted out some rolls of wool. 'I have to prepare these for dyeing.'

'Can I help?'

'No. Enjoy your cigarettes and the wine.'

I went out into the yard.

Later, when Dev and I came in, we found Osip sitting in the same position as I'd left him. He'd been smoking, but had not drunk more wine.

Dev, now back to his old self, pointed at a basket filled with eggs, fruit and vegetables. 'Provisions for tomorrow, Xenos ...'

Osip was embarrassed. 'You shouldn't ... Besides, that's too much ...'

Dev smiled. 'To get you going ... Tomorrow, I'll take some cuttings from here. Start a garden for you. Get the water-mill looking pretty in no time ...'

I started tidying up. 'That's me finished for the day. I'll put two blankets on your bed, Osip. It can get cold in the night.'

Osip protested. 'Let me just curl up in the corner. I can sleep anywhere.'

Dev burst out laughing. 'Not in our house!'

Neither Dev nor I slept well that night. We could smell Osip's cigarettes and realized that he had spent the night smoking and staring into his haunted realms.

Towards first light, Dev snuggled up to me. 'I worry about him, Kokona. Even afraid for him. He looks strong. But is he?'

I held my man close. I had the same thoughts. 'He's frayed. Threadbare here and there. We'll patch him up.'

'Yes. We must.'

Dev and I love making love. But this time we did so fretfully. We couldn't free ourselves from our concerns for Osip.

7

OSIP

Dev took me round the water-mill, holding my hand as if I were a child.

I had expected my inheritance to be in an even worse state than the derelict buildings in the harbour. But I was surprised to find it relatively habitable despite the roof where many stone shingles had fragmented and needed replacing. Equally encouraging, it was neither very damp nor, save for forests of cobwebs, too dirty – a condition Dev attributed to the micro-climate in that part of the island.

Its setting was breathtaking. It stood on the left bank of a river in a dell on the island's meridional hills. The woods, thick with scrub oaks, Syrian pine, carob, terebinth, wild almond and abandoned olive trees, encircled the mill in a horseshoe; a gap at the southern end stretched into a sizeable meadow which gently rolled down by the side of the river to the sea. I could see, even with my rusty eyes, that the area had a vigorous insect and bird life. And, according to Dev, the higher slopes offered good hunting for game. The only forlorn aspect was the meadow. There were no animals grazing. No shepherds. A great pity, Dev had remarked, because the meadow was lush; but in Skender's feuding culture it was safer to corral animals in farmsteads than to put them out to pasture.

A weir, erected some four hundred metres up-river, directed the water into the mill-stream. A sluice gate controlled the volume to the millpond. A stone traverse over the pond led to the mill's entrance. Two ducts channelled the overflow onto the grounds on both sides of the mill where, in olden times, Dev informed me, there had been fruit trees and a vegetable garden that had been the envy of many Skenderis.

A sharp drop at the millpond discharged the water down onto the chamber where the horizontal wheel – typical of the Balkans was located; it then flowed out through a sluiceway at the back of the chamber and rejoined the river. The wheel itself was fixed to a crankshaft which, in turn, was connected to the millstones in the mill-room. A transmission consisting of three pairs of toothed reels was fastened onto the wheel to regulate the speed of its rotation. The wheel, its spoon-shaped vanes – twenty of them – the gearing system and the crankshaft were all moulded from hefty timber. The chamber was heavily silted and clogged with rotted vegetation – as was the millpond – and both would need dredging and draining. The task seemed impossible. But Dev just laughed: providing I pulled him out by his mercifully thick hair should he sink into the mire, I should consider the job done.

The mill-house, built of stone on three levels, with timber flooring, was exceptionally large. It was a well-known fact, Dev informed me, that in its heyday, the water-mill contributed handsomely to my ancestors' prosperity.

The basement accommodated the mill-room and the quarters for the animals. An ancient scale for measuring produce, three pairs of millstones, a fruit press, an olive press and a fireplace where the paste of such yield as almonds could be heated up to extract their oil took up much of the space. The animal enclosure, judging by the number of troughs and mangers, Dev remarked, could pen in about thirty milking sheep.

The ground floor, connected to the basement by wooden stairs which Dev called 'the miller's ladder', consisted of three rooms. The central and largest room – with an imposing fireplace on one side – served as the living area. The rooms to left and right, empty save for household detritus and rat-mauled mattresses, had been used as sleeping quarters. Exceptionally, even for present-day Skender, the one to the right incorporated an indoor water-closet complete with an oriental latrine, a sink and a rusted iron bath-tub.

Dev told stories of how people would bring their produce on donkey-driven carts and, as they waited for it to be ground, would grill fish from the river or game from the woods on *mangals* in the garden. Sometimes, particularly when there was a moon, people would choose to stay the night; then the men would spend the evening telling stories and singing while the women would sew, knit or embroider.

The top floor, connected to the ground floor by another wooden staircase, was a vast room that ran the length of the mill and functioned as storage space. Six massive beams supported the roof. A pulley by an opening at the far end enabled heavy loads to be hoisted up and down from the mill-room. The other end served as an office and, to my astonishment, still had strewn around some old ledgers, letters, even money that had long gone out of circulation.

Then a discovery: a trunk, packed with notebooks containing my father's writings. One of them proved of immense importance: a transcription of the Law with countless annotations in the margins. The Law, as far as I'd understood, had never been collated as a text, or, if it had been, copies had long since disappeared. Only Toma, Kokona had informed me, had a tattered old scroll in his

Palladion with which he instructed the *Morituri*; the rest of the Skenderis received the canon orally, either from their parents or from Toma himself.

The prospect of spending nights going through the documents and trying to get a sense of the Goras, conducting a post-mortem on my family that had remained unknown to me was a boon. And the privilege of studying my father's writings and familiarizing myself with his preoccupations, particularly his opposition to the Law, filled me with a mixture of joy and apprehension.

When eventually I rejoined Dev by the millpond, he scrutinized me expectantly. 'What do you think?'

I took out two cigarettes, lit them both and passed him one. 'There's much to be done. The roof. Dredging the silt. Some of the timber – in the mill-room and the stairs – has rotted. All the plumbing. Even so, I think I've found my grotto.'

'Don't worry. Work is work. Needs only time. I'll help.'

'Dev, you don't have to.'

'First, you need bedding. And cooking utensils. A new bath-tub. Pipes. The Citadel store stocks everything. I'll take you tomorrow.'

'Dev, this is something I should do by myself.'

'Two hands are better than one. It will be fun. Do you have money?'

I looked at him suspiciously. 'Why?'

'If you don't, Kokona and I can help ...'

I hated myself for distrusting him. I ruffled his hair. 'I have enough.' I opened up my pouch. 'Lots of gold coins ...'

He stared at them like someone who had never seen gold before. 'Kokona says, Incas call this "sweat of the sun" ...'

'Gypsies call it "sesame". It opens doors. Gold is acceptable even if Gypsies aren't. It's best to travel like them, particularly after the Peoples' Wars.'

Dev shook his head in admiration. 'What a wise man you are, Xenos.'

That was the last thing I had expected to hear. All my concerns and doubts, all the fears and wishful thinking of years of a brutal existence, all the regrets of a wasted life, all the anguish of an eternity of sleepless nights suddenly erupted. I grabbed hold of Dev's head and pressed it close to me. And, to my astonishment, tears ran down my cheeks.

Dev stroked my hand. 'That's good, Xenos. You are home now. Cry. As much as you want ...'

I wiped my tears. 'Sorry ... And I'm Osip. Not a stranger to you.'

'Yes, Osip.' He rolled up his sleeves excitedly. 'Time to start. We'll make this place smile like a sultan in his harem. While I plant these, look around again – get to know your grotto.'

'I intend to.'

Dev stubbed out his cigarette. 'You know about horizontal water-mills?'

'A little. I looked at some books before coming here.'

He nodded. 'Only wise men look and see before the eyes can see.'

'If only that were true ...'

'It is true. Check that especially. See what needs to be done first.'

'Right.'

As he tripped away to his van to collect the cuttings he had brought, Dev shouted at the top of his voice. 'Welcome back, Osip!'

I waved at him and started walking towards the weir. As if

doubting my eyes, I kept telling myself that here at last I had found my place. Here, after an endless time in the lands of the dead, I could begin to live ...

Dev shouted, over and over, as he started digging. 'Welcome home, Osip! Welcome home! Welcome home!'

I took my time going round. I made a note of everything that needed restoring. The main decision was whether to make the mill fully habitable before getting the waterwheel operational ... or get the waterwheel operational first so that I could start earning some money. Actually, earning money wasn't a priority since I had enough funds to last me a couple of years, but the idea of at last being involved in honest labour – and getting paid for it – instead of plundering whatever I could as I had done most of my life, appealed to me. Beyond this, in all my sixty-four years, I had never had a place of my own – I'd never considered the family house as my home because my parents had always used it either as a fastness or as a command post. For a leaf tossed by the winds, the yearning for a puddle where it can rest becomes irrepressible.

Still undecided, I rejoined Dev. He had just finished planting – and although there were no flowers to greet me, I could see he had already laid the beginnings of a well-planned garden.

Dev described his ideas. 'Roses – there, there and there. Interspersed with clematis there – and there. All of them climbers. To blanket that wall. Vine on the other wall. Shrubs, azaleas, with carnations, poppies – in those beds. Honeysuckle and passion fruit – also climbers – at the back. They need plenty of sun, so south-facing. Later, I'll get seeds and plant magnolia, morning glory, sweet peas and black-eyed Susan by the front door. And some geraniums and pansies in troughs and baskets.' He pointed at the terrain on the other side of the millpond. 'That section will be the fruit garden.

I'll prepare the soil. Next week we'll plant orange, lemon, cherry, pomegranate, apricot, peach and fig trees ...'

I stared at him overawed. 'You should have been God, Dev!'

He smiled. 'One of His tools – enough for me.'

I pointed at the bag of food he'd brought along. 'You're sweating like a horse that's galloped across a continent. How about some wine to cool down?'

'I'd prefer a dip in the river.'

'Great idea!'

He started running. 'I'll race you!'

We sprinted, like children, to the river west of the mill. To make sure that Dev would win the race, I kept slowing down to shed my clothes.

At the river, Dev looked in horror at my naked body. 'My God, Osip!'

'What?'

'So many scars ...'

I'd forgotten about my scars. Except for the women I'd occasionally slept with – and the doctors who had patched me up – not many people had seen them. 'Yes, well ... Do they bother you?'

'They tell me you have suffered much.'

I shrugged, embarrassed. 'Past and forgotten.' Then I put on a stern face. 'Are we swimming or not?'

'Yes!'

'Well, come on then!'

He undressed quickly and dived into the river.

I dived after him. I had seen his cock and thought how remarkable it was that, despite his deformity, it was a good size – bigger than mine, in fact. I felt pleased for him. And covetous.

The water was cold so we swam vigorously.

Then we horse-played.

Then over our laughter we heard an animal panting; we turned round.

It was Castor, by the bank, staring at us.

We both moved towards him. 'Hello, Castor!'

The dog wagged his tail in recognition then sped away.

We watched him run into the meadow.

And there was Bostan, rifle on shoulder, alert yet at ease, walking along with a group of women – all laden with bundles – towards the sea. He waved at us.

We returned his greeting.

I looked at Dev quizzically. 'What's up?'

He smiled. 'The Kristof women. Off to do the laundry. The *lavanderi* is down-river. Bostan protects them – in case the Rogosins attack.'

I watched them. Such a bizarre spectacle. 'I thought feudists attacked only feudists. Isn't that what the Law specifies?'

'Yes. But sometimes they get frustrated, go mad. They kill somebody, then say: sorry, we made a mistake, thought the person was an enemy feudist.'

'Does that happen often?'

'It happens.'

'So no one's really safe.'

Dev sighed sadly, scampered from the river. 'I'm hungry now. Let's eat!'

I followed him.

As we walked back, I took another look at Bostan ... not without admiration. He was an excellent escort – eyes constantly alert and scanning every compass point. And he had trained Castor well. The dog darted about fast, constantly sniffing for danger.

Bostan saw me looking at him and nodded. I saluted him, then noticed that his wards were laughing at me. I realized I was still naked. I covered my genitals and hurried to the mill with as much composure as I could.

Kokona had prepared us an excellent picnic: bread, cheese, onions, olives, figs and wine. I ate with pleasure. Curiously, Dev had become subdued.

'Something bothering you, Dev?'

'It's nothing.'

'If it's some bad news about the mill, you can tell me ...'

'It's not about the mill. I'm thinking about Bostan. Where's his heart? He killed only yesterday. But feels nothing ...'

'Conditioning. It soon drowns conscience.'

'It took me ...' He stopped, unsure whether to continue.

I lit two cigarettes, handed him one.

'Tell you a secret, Osip?'

'Of course.'

'No one knows ...'

'I keep secrets come what may ...' I looked away, thinking about some of the scars ...

'I've killed too. Twice. Many years back ... But for very good reasons.'

I stroked his head.

'They were going to kill Kokona ...'

'That's a very good reason – saving the woman you love.'

'No. I mean, yes. The woman I love. And have loved all my life ... But at the time, we weren't close. I loved from a distance ... She doesn't know I killed – not even now.'

'I thought she knew everything that happened on Skender ...'

'Yes. But not about those men. I never told her. Though sometimes I think she knows. But says nothing. Please don't tell her.'

I poured us some wine. 'I won't.'

'We got together afterwards. When I was sure she was safe, when I saw nobody else was going for her, I cracked … I got very ill. There was no one to help me. Who'd help a dwarf? I'd been an orphan all my life. Father killed in a feud before I was born. Mother died while giving birth to me. Brother when I was still a boy. Maybe you can tell from the way I speak. No learning until Kokona taught me to read and write.

'Anyway, after the killings, I shut myself in my hut. Waited to die. Then Kokona came. Brought the apothecary, Basil. They broke down my door. Took care of me. Made all kinds of potions. I kept thinking she knew I killed those men and was repaying me. But she never said so. I was sick a long time. She stayed with me throughout. Read to me. Taught me to play backgammon. Then one day she came into my bed. You know how it is. Bodies don't lie. I saw she had feelings for me.'

I was deeply moved by the union they had created. I even felt jealous. 'A secret from me, too, Dev. I don't know how it is – bodies not lying, I mean. I've never known it.'

That upset Dev. 'You're making fun of me, Osip …'

'It's the truth. But now that I've got your word for it, I'll pray I can find a body that doesn't lie …'

He smiled, concerned. 'Sure you will. Look at you! A real man! With a real body!'

'An empty body, Dev. Nothing in it for women.'

'Wait and see – they will swarm!'

I laughed. The secret I'd revealed had left me disconcerted. Dev's ingenuousness had stirred all my yearnings.

We spent the afternoon clearing the terrain Dev had chosen for the fruit garden. Then we had another swim in the river.

When it was time for Dev to leave, he asked me to go back with him, pointing out that the mill was still uninhabitable, that there was not even any bedding in it, that I should stay with him and Kokona for at least a week while we purchased some of the basic essentials.

I told him I'd slept in worse places and in pretty gruesome conditions and that I really wanted to start rooting myself in my first home.

He eventually saw my point. But before driving away, he gave me a few flares. 'If you need anything, fire one. We'll see it. I'll come faster than the south wind.'

After he left, I went to the side of the mill that opened onto the meadow and sat in the shade of the big carob tree. Sipping some of the wine Dev had left behind, I smoked, watched the sunset and faced my demons.

Not long after, Castor came running up. This time he stayed a fraction longer, time enough to snatch the piece of bread I offered him.

Then he sped off back to the meadow.

Soon his master appeared with his train of women and their laundry. I could see that on this return trip, with dusk approaching – a dangerous time for feudists – they were gravely circumspect.

Bostan, holding his rifle pressed against his chest, like cradling a baby, in the incongruous way commandos do, was vigilance personified.

I waved at him.

He didn't wave back. He would not be distracted.

I watched the procession until it disappeared behind the trees. I muttered to myself, wishing them a safe journey home.

8

BOSTAN

After I killed Stefan I stayed on the alert. Every killing turns me mindless, frozen, feeling nothing. But brittle and breakable. So Xenos had disappeared from my head. I'd even forgotten he'd said he'd inherited the water-mill. I should have remembered that. It's on the way to the *lavanderi*. I always walk past the place cautiously. It's a perfect location for a sniper. Of course, I always set out at different times to prevent the Rogosins guessing my movements, but I can never be careful enough. Fortunately, Castor knows the terrain inside out. He can sniff danger leagues ahead.

So I was very surprised to see Xenos again. In Skender we avoid people. Safer that way. Alliances are made and broken all the time. We never know from one day to the other who is a friend and who is a foe. Which means forgetting about Xenos was a mistake. It could have been fatal.

Castor must have smelled him long before. But he didn't give me any warning. Obviously he didn't consider Xenos a danger. The man certainly has a way with dogs. Castor's never fooled. Even so, I don't like him developing a soft spot. It almost makes him human. Dogs are meant to be dogs.

And watching Xenos cavort in the river with the Shrimp rankled me. Like kids. As if life's a festival and all our troubles are bogus.

But what really galled me was seeing him naked. In front of our women! As if that wasn't bad enough, the women shamed me – all of them widowed, needless to say. Giggling and guffawing as if they'd never seen a man's gong.

I was also mad at myself. I waved at him, too. Twice! First when he was in the water. That's acceptable. A courteous greeting. No harm in that. But afterwards when he climbed out of the river, when he stood naked as a snake that had shed its skin, when our women were laughing at him. Why that second time?

As for his scars! Can a man with so many be harmless? I'd better be wary. Now that he's living in the water-mill our paths will keep crossing – certainly every time I take our women to the *lavanderi*.

On the way back, he waved again. That time I ignored him. Sitting in the shade of a tree, like a pasha. Swigging wine and smoking. As if he belonged here.

9

DEV

I don't drive back straight away. I stop the van up the hill in the middle of the track. That way Bostan and the Kristof women can spot me. Seeing me having trouble with the van they'll know it's not an ambush.

I lift the bonnet. Pretend to tinker with the engine.

I don't trust Bostan. Not yet. I want to make sure he doesn't have second thoughts about Osip. Some Skenderis don't believe Osip's story. Some even embroider tales. Say he returned for revenge. For Skenderis revenge is glory. It addles their brains. The obvious is dressed in fantasy. I do that, too. Like thinking Bostan wants to kill Osip because his dog likes Osip. Silly? Yes and no. Kokona says killing becomes an addiction. I must make sure Bostan is not an addict.

I see the Kristofs an hour later. Castor first. He runs up. Sniffs. Allows me to stroke his head. Then goes back to Bostan.

Bostan approaches, ahead of the women. Rifle ready. 'Problem, Shrimp?'

I grumble. 'Carburettor.'

'Can't help you. I'm escorting our women.'

'No problem. I'll fix it ...'

He lingers. 'That man ...'

I look up. I turn this way, that way, as if there's someone around. 'Who?'

'The one at the mill ...'

'Xenos?'

'You've hit it off with him ...'

'He's a good man.'

'Is the mill really his?'

'Yes.'

'Didn't the Gospodins buy it before?'

'No.'

'We only have Xenos' word for it.'

The Kristof women gather round, listen keenly.

I shake my head. 'I saw the deeds. It's his all right.'

'What would you know about deeds? Nobody can understand them.'

'Kokona can. Xenos stayed with us last night.'

'Noticed his scars?'

That shows why Bostan's a great shot. Eyes like an eagle's. 'Yes.'

'How come so many?'

I shrug. 'I didn't ask him. The Peoples' Wars, I think ...'

Bostan grunts.

I go back to tinkering. 'Let him cook in his own fat, Bostan. He's all right.'

'I'll decide that.'

'Even Castor likes him.'

'That dog's crazy! There's a time for liking – it's not now!'

I play with the carburettor. 'I always hope it is ...'

Bostan heaves his rifle and walks off. 'Mind how you go, Shrimp. Tell Xenos the same.'

The Kristof women follow him.
I wait a while to put a distance between us.
Then I shut the bonnet and drive off.

10

TOMA

Anibal's son is settling down well. 'As if he belonged here', Bostan is said to have remarked when he saw him lording it at his water-mill – that's the gossip from the Kristof women. There's more gossip, too: that some of them have eyes for him. They're all widows, of course, craving husbands.

This proves my fears about strangers are prophetic. Soon after they appear, something unexpected unravels and dissimilation begins. I can imagine, before we can blink ten times half our women will try to lure him into their beds and the other half, full of envy and clamouring for more like him, will invite all the riff-raff of the world to this island. Thus the purity of our blood will be a distant memory.

That direful prospect provided me with an inspired thought. Since Anibal's son is a Skenderi, albeit of bad blood, why not reclaim him, make him one of our own again, purify him?

So I searched through my archives. Somewhere, I felt certain, there would be a survivor from among the plethora of families that had been feuding with the Goras. It would be unnatural, almost unknown, for their feuding to have ended. If I could find one forgotten man, I could coax him to rekindle his enmity against the Goras. Then Anibal's son would be forced to become engaged, if only to try and save his life.

And sure enough, I found some survivors – four, in fact. But all of them, as if to spite the Law, had died in quick succession of natural causes, and only within the last couple of years.

Superstition – or is it the Doubter? – lurks here. Did Anibal's son decide to return to Skender after he'd made a pact with the Devil and arranged those deaths?

Naturally, I pity the four departed. No man on this island should die a natural death. There is no honour in that.

So where do I go from here?

I remember a story my uncle told me when I was very young. My father, a devout follower of the Law, but not very good with guns, had just been killed and his brother had become the family paladin.

Because I was mourning my father unduly, though he had died honourably, my uncle took me aside.

He told me that in the early days of the Law, when it was still called the *Kanun*, there were two great paladins, Qerim and Saracino. Eventually, it was their turn to confront each other; so they arranged their affair of honour, late one afternoon, in a secluded place. That morning Qerim went to the market to buy some provisions and, on his way there, he saw his foe, Saracino, sitting in the shade of an olive tree, meditating. As chivalry dictated, Qerim saluted Saracino, but the latter, deep in his ruminations, did not even see him. That encounter unsettled Qerim. Admiring Saracino's single-minded preparation, he realized that, like the bull-jumpers of ancient Crete, a combatant should abstain from all daily activities on the day of an engagement, immerse himself in serious contemplation and then take to the field with a single thought: the instant disposal of his opponent. So, feeling spiritually undermined, Qerim went to his duel at the appointed hour; and, in that disturbed state, he was duly shot dead by Saracino.

Then my uncle asked me: what is the moral of this story?

I proudly replied that honour should be upheld always, as Qerim had done, even though he was spiritually unprepared.

My uncle said no. The moral is that a paladin should never waste an opportunity to kill. Qerim should have killed Saracino while the latter was meditating in the shade of the olive tree. Had Saracino been in his home that, of course, would have been dishonourable; attacking a foe in his home is anathema. But Saracino was out in the open – and Qerim had the right to kill him without tarnishing his own honour.

My uncle concluded by saying that thereafter I must, like Saracino, be single-minded. Opportunities always come, he assured me. That's the nature of existence. But one must always be alert for that moment. A wasted opportunity invariably leads to disaster.

Well, I've never forgotten that story; never wasted an opportunity since. Thus I've empowered myself to become the Law's prophet. I even used my unmanning as the excuse to immerse myself in the exegesis of the Law. Freed of feuds, and fortuitously given a long life, I made myself a man above all men.

So now I'm on the look-out for the chance that will force Anibal's son to take up arms and live and die like all Skenderi men. That will mitigate the pain – still with me after all these years – that his father inflicted on me by constantly challenging me and seeking the abolition of the Law. It will also honour the memory of his mother, Eleanora the Falcon.

To cleanse Anibal's son's bad blood before it has had a chance to contaminate Skender – that's my duty now.

11

KOKONA

Winter could be seen infiltrating the clouds. The winds had Siberian hoar on their breath; for the next four months Boreas would be their charioteer.

But I wasn't at all apprehensive. As some of you know, I have this conviction that I will die in the darkest of days, with a blizzard rolling through the windows and shrouding me. Whereas the sun is the twin of my deity, the Lover of Love, and I'd hate to have coins placed on my eyelids when it's not shining; basking in it would be the proper way to leave life.

However this autumn, the thought that Death might be round the corner rarely crossed my mind. I even looked forward to the winter as do our fishermen who go off trawling in the south, free from feuding for a season.

The fishing folk are the only coastal Skenderis who haven't abandoned their homes because of the troubles. Admittedly, they wouldn't have known how to work the land around the Citadel; but also, fortunately for them, the few coves where they've anchored their villages are not easily accessible either by land or by sea. The odd feuds they've kept up, albeit as bitter as ours, have been restricted to their own communities.

I'm sure the fact that I'd begun weaving figurative tapestries contributed to my good cheer. But the main reason, as Dev and I agreed, was Osip's presence.

He had settled in the water-mill as zestfully as a seed in a forest. Naturally, we had helped him. Dev had laboured like Hercules sorting out the mill, taking him here and there to buy this and that and I had lent a hand with the cleaning. But it had been Osip's obvious contentment at having a place of his own that had made us joyful. He was captivated by the mill and his face shone as if the grotto he'd been searching for all his life was within his reach.

There had been only one sour episode during this period. Toma, who, since his first encounter with Osip, had regarded him as a threat to his authority, had arrived one day towards the end of August: he acknowledged that, having spent weeks examining Skender's records, he could now declare, despondently, that Osip was not heir to any feuding obligations. All the enemies of the Goras had died in the course of time, leaving not even a patriarch, like Toma, whom Osip could engage to reclaim his family's honour. Fate indulges the mollusc, Toma had mocked, adding that henceforth Osip would command less respect in Skender than a snail. Osip, remaining composed, had replied that he desired no more and had sent the old man away, handing him a gold coin partly out of pity and partly in contempt. Toma, brewing his vexation, had nonetheless accepted the money – in compensation for his painstaking investigation, he had claimed.

Nasty as that episode had been, it had uplifted our spirits; we could breathe easily; Osip was outside our feuding culture. Blissful is an inept word to use in Skender, but much of the time after that, that's how Dev and I felt.

I should admit, of course, that our happiness was rooted in the fact – unspoken, yet intensely felt – that we three had become a family. I cherished Osip as the son I'd always wanted.

As for Dev ... Naturally, his paternal instincts flourished. But, although some aspects in a father–son relationship are similar to those between mother and son, I believe the love that grows between men is much more complex. There is, certainly, rivalry – a drive that's innate in the male; this is evident even when the drive is seemingly placid. But more importantly, there is a continuous reversal of identities. One moment the father is the father and the son, the son; the next, it's the son who becomes the father. And most magically, this constant cross-over occurs within a friendship that is infinitely gracious.

That was the kind of relationship that developed between Osip and Dev. And though, on occasions, it made me jealous, I also delighted in it. Except for an older brother who had died when he was ten, no man had ever befriended or cared for Dev. And it seemed plain, too, that Osip, after his father's death, had gone through life without experiencing the affection of a good man. So they felt intoxicated by the treble joys of fatherhood, son-hood and brotherhood.

Osip proved to be singularly generous. He constantly lavished gifts on us. On one occasion, when he went to the mainland to collect a trunk containing the few belongings he had accumulated over the years – he had left it in storage in case he couldn't settle in Skender – he returned with a modern loom for me. As if that weren't excessive enough, he also brought Dev a new gearbox for the van.

By contrast, he was very sparing towards himself. Save for a large iron bed – a restless sleeper, he needed room to toss about – he furnished his home with monkish austerity: coarse-weave linen, a chest of drawers, a bottled-gas cooker, a paraffin heater, a table, six chairs, a few pots and pans, dishes, glasses and cups.

The gardens Dev had bedded down promised a luscious spring. The draining of both the millpond and the wheel chamber had been completed. That had necessitated, initially, hiring Uran, our expert with a dredger, for a couple of weeks. But once the main work had been done, Dev and Osip had toiled for days on end. Osip had insisted on doing the heavy lugging himself. He proved to be a man of remarkable strength and stamina. All that was needed to start operating the water-mill was a new shaft and some wheel-segments. Lefteris, the carpenter, had promised to deliver these well before harvest-time.

However, despite our unguarded intimacy, Osip remained as mysterious as ever. Since our talk on the evening of his arrival – so pregnant with questions and allusions – he had divulged nothing more about himself, although there had been occasions, particularly during some of the tranquil times, when I'd felt he wanted to talk to me. But as if these moments of unburdening carried extreme danger, he had hurriedly retreated into a dense silence.

He had also been reading his father's papers and I'd imagined that from the conflicting emotions these must have produced, he desperately wanted to pursue his new life, at his wellspring, liberated from the debris of his earlier selves.

His previous existence, I surmised, could not have been the cursory one of a drifter. When, on one occasion, he had unlocked his trunk to take out a pair of binoculars and to indulge, once again, in his passion for bird-watching, I had chanced to see the paltry items that made up his belongings: a dozen or so reference books ranging from philosophy to medicine; a hefty canvas briefcase and an even heftier backpack, both surprisingly marked with a Red Cross; but nothing really personal, not even a photograph or two. Against those, some surprising articles: a well-oiled gun, carefully wrapped; a box of bullets; and a bayonet, sharp as a butcher's knife. Both the gun and the bayonet had lost their lustre, prompting me to think that they had been in his possession for some time.

Those items had increased Dev's and my anxieties about him. If a person owns a weapon, sooner or later he'll use it. That's as natural a law as figs are made to melt in our mouths.

And so it happened on that last day of summer.

We had gathered where the mill opened up onto the meadow.

I had prepared the all-wheat Skenderi meal that bids the sun farewell while beseeching it not to forget to return.

Dev and Osip had finished pointing the last of the stonework and were having a swim in the river. They hoped to do so all year round unless, as Osip quipped, the water froze their balls off.

I was facing the meadow and was the first to see the men. They were armed with rifles and approached solemnly. Viktor Mikhail, Urs Eduard and Rustu Nis. We hadn't had any dealings with them so I was surprised to see them. And surprised, particularly, to see Viktor carrying a gun. As the agent of the Gospodins, he had become Skender's wealthiest man; now in his mid-sixties and determined to enjoy his riches – as well as his young wife – he had kept away from conflict.

I called out to them. 'Greetings, Viktor, Urs, Rustu!'

They raised their hats and replied in unison. 'Greetings, Kokona!'

Dev and Osip, hearing our exchange, scrambled out of the river and grabbed their clothes.

The men looked at Dev and Osip, disdainful of their nudity. 'Greetings, Xenos. Greetings, Shrimp!'

Viktor, I noted, was taken aback by Osip's scars, whereas Urs and Rustu, younger men and robust, sniggered at Dev's deformed body.

Osip, unruffled, took a long look at their rifles while pulling on his trousers. 'Two conditions, good folk, before I can greet you. One: my brother here is called Dev; address him so. Two: courtesy demands you introduce yourselves!'

The three men, put out by Osip's commanding tone, held their rifles more tightly, but uncertainly.

Viktor Mikhail, assuming his seigniorial right as their spokesman, pointedly ignored Osip. 'There's been ...'

Osip, marginally raising his voice, interrupted him. 'My conditions first ...'

The men exchanged looks. Urs raised his gun to his hip.

Viktor opted for courtesy. 'My apologies. I am Viktor Mikhail. This is Urs Eduard. And Rustu Nis. We are heads of our respective families. Greetings, Dev! Greetings, Xenos.'

Osip smiled. 'Greetings, Viktor, Urs and Rustu. Welcome to my home. Can I offer you something? Food? Refreshments?'

'Thank you. No. We're here on business.'

Osip put his shirt on. 'The mill's not ready yet. Early next year, all being well.'

'Not that sort of business. There's been a killing ...'

Osip tensed up. 'We've heard nothing around here ...'

I interjected. 'Who got killed?'

Viktor turned to me. 'Anton Kaplan.'

I was shocked. 'Young Anton – the lutanist?'

'The same.'

'But who'd want to kill him?'

'No one, you'd think. But Bostan did.'

'Bostan – are you sure?'

'Yes.'

'That's crazy! Bostan has no quarrel with the Kaplans.'

'He has now. Alas, not with Anton's brother. Marius refuses to feud. So it's up to us. We're related to the Kaplans.'

'I don't understand. Why should Bostan kill Anton? He loved Anton. Loved his singing. He'd go out of his way to hear him!'

'Bostan killed Stefan Rogosin a few weeks back. Stefan was Anton's lute teacher. Anton worshipped him ...'

Dev, grief-stricken, moaned. 'Yes! When Stefan died, Anton cried like a babe. Poor, lovely Anton ...'

Viktor nodded. 'So he took it upon himself to avenge Stefan.'

I felt like tearing my hair out. 'But to challenge Bostan?! Whom everybody fears! How did he manage to waylay him? No one has managed to do that!'

'He didn't waylay him. He went to Bostan's home. As a visitor.'

'To kill him there?'

Viktor looked embarrassed. 'I know what you're going to say. To kill a feudist at his home is prohibited. But Anton was young. Didn't know everything about the Law.'

'How could Marius let him do it? He always kept an eye on Anton.'

'Anton got a sleeping draught from Basil, the apothecary. Claiming he couldn't sleep because of Stefan's death. And served it to Marius. Then locked him up in his room.'

'The silly fool!'

Viktor raised his voice reproachfully. 'Anton was a man of honour! I might have done the same!'

My anger got the better of me. 'You're talking like Toma! You certainly wouldn't have! I know you, Viktor, you're not a gamecock. You're a good man!'

Viktor fidgeted. 'Well ...'

I spewed my fury. 'If you ask me, Toma's the one to blame. Him and his *Morituri*! Teaching all that blood and honour drivel to a bard! What madness!'

Viktor protested. 'Mind what you say, Kokona! Righteous Toma is a great man!'

I responded with all the contempt I could muster. 'No balls. No heart. The greatest of them all!'

Viktor was outraged. 'Kokona, that's ...'

Osip interrupted. 'What has Anton's death got to do with us?'

Viktor paused as if searching for words. 'According to the Law – nothing. But we'd like to propose a deal. We can't, of course, attack Bostan in his home. We stick to the Law word for word. But we know he escorts the Kristof women to the *lavanderi*. We know they take the track by that meadow. What we don't know is when they go. Bostan always decides at the last minute. We can't spy on him. He'd spot us and kill us. But you live here, Xenos. You must see them pass by. So here is the deal: you alert us when Bostan next comes along ...'

'So that you can ambush him?'

'That's right ...'

'And in return?'

'We don't brand you, or Kokona, or the Shr ... Dev, as Bostan's allies, therefore our enemies ...'

Dev and I exchanged looks. 'Us – to act as informers for you? What do you take us for?'

Osip took my hand. 'Teacher, please, let me handle this.' He turned to Viktor. 'Can we have this agreement in writing?'

Viktor looked surprised. 'In writing? What for?'

'A deal is not a deal until it's signed and sealed.'

'That's not the way we do it here.'

'Surely that's how you strike deals with the Gospodins.'

Viktor looked surprised. 'They're from … What do you know about them?'

'Only what I've heard. Absentee landlords. At some point they wanted to buy this water-mill, but I wouldn't sell. You're their agent, if I'm not mistaken.'

'They're just speculators. Of no importance. Anton's killing is of great importance!'

Osip shrugged. 'All the more reason to have the deal signed and sealed. Anyway, that's how *I* make deals.'

I was bewildered. 'Osip, no! Don't!'

Osip kissed my hand. 'Please, Teacher … I know what I'm doing …'

Viktor was exchanging uncomfortable looks with Urs and Rustu. They nodded uncertainly.

Viktor grimaced. 'Yes. Very well.'

Osip smiled. 'I'll get pen and paper.'

Viktor tried to smile back. 'Fine.'

Osip walked into the mill-house.

Dev and I watched him, admiring his composure, yet deeply perturbed that he had so readily agreed to be an informer.

Urs and Rustu looked like portraits of smug bullies.

I turned on Viktor. 'I never expected this of you, Viktor. You've always been a compassionate man. What's happened to you?'

Viktor shuffled uneasily. 'Anton was very dear to me – a nephew, but more like a son …'

What happened next happened very quickly.

Osip burst out of the house and rushed at Viktor, Urs and Rustu. Before the men could react, he hurled Viktor to the ground, disarmed him and, pressing his knee in the small of Viktor's back, poised his bayonet on his neck. With his other hand, he pointed his gun at Urs and Rustu.

He addressed the latter. 'Drop your rifles. Don't try to move. You'd be dead before you could pull the trigger. Then Viktor here can tell all Skender how honourably you died!'

Urs and Rustu, stunned, stared at Viktor.

Viktor groaned. 'Do as he says!'

Urs and Rustu dropped their rifles.

Osip shouted at Dev. 'Get their rifles! Then get some rope!'

'Right!' Excited as a child, Dev collected the rifles and sprinted into the mill-house.

Acutely anxious, I went up to Osip. 'What will you do?'

'I'll offer them another deal.'

Dev ran back from the mill-house with a roll of rope.

Osip pushed Viktor towards Urs and Rustu. 'Tie them up, Dev. Hands at the back! Then their feet!'

Dev did so happily.

Osip stood alert, his gun poised in case Viktor, Urs and Rustu tried to overpower Dev, but the three seemed paralysed by shock.

I nudged Osip. 'What's this other deal?'

'Better than theirs. Don't worry, Teacher. It'll be all right.'

'I'm not worried about me. I'm worried about you.'

'No need!'

'Half the island could turn against you.'

'Maybe. Maybe not.'

'If they do?'

'I'll think of something.'

'And your demons?'

He looked up sharply. 'What about them?'

'They swooped on you the moment they sighted you with a gun ...'

'You saw that?' His surprise turned into a grimace. He looked ransacked by pain like I imagine Prometheus did every time the eagle ate his liver. But he never shifted his eyes from the men.

'Now they're disembowelling you, Osip. I can see that, too.'

'I can survive it. Always have.'

'Survival is a poor substitute for felicity.'

'Destiny is destiny.'

'Destiny can be defied. Isn't that why you came back?'

'Teacher, at this moment, it's your lives I care about. You and Dev are worth the Earth.'

'And you? What are you worth?'

He shrugged wearily.

Dev had tied up Viktor, Urs and Rustu.

Osip went over to them.

I watched him walk. Not with his usual spring, but slow and heavy-footed, shoulders hunched. I felt distraught. Here was a man transformed into a monster yet struggling to cling onto his soul. I had seen such hopelessness only once before – in Dev, when he had broken down after killing those two men who had come after me.

Mercifully, Dev had mended himself. Through my love for him and his love for me. Who or what could mend Osip?

12

OSIP

I hauled Viktor, Urs and Rustu onto the back of the van and sat by their side.

I told Dev to drive to the Citadel.

Kokona came to sit with me instead of on her usual seat next to Dev. Her nearness soothed my forebodings. Unconditional affection is like finding a foothold in quicksand. But exposing my weakness – even to Kokona – had unsettled me. I'd hardened myself to be dispassionate at all times. In a confrontation, a mere shudder can be fatal.

Uncanny, how easily she read me, how immediately she saw me fighting off my demons.

Could it be that I'd wanted her to see me weak, that when I'm with her, I don't want to hide anything from her? After all, she had become the mother I'd longed for so desperately.

And yet, I'd felt that the way the demons had swooped the moment I'd picked up my gun might have meant I was no longer my old self, that, imperceptibly, I had softened. In the past, picking up a gun had been as unconscious an act as blinking; the demons had stayed back. They had pounced only after I'd killed, when the sensation of having discarded mind and body had eventually waned and some sanity had returned. Then sanity – whatever it is – had found me as it had left me: a beast who had fallen into a pit. And, for demons, that's succulent manna.

So the sense of peace of the last months, the feeling of having acquired some softness, had been gossamer. Just handling a gun – not even using it – had shattered the illusion that I had finally climbed out of the pit. Now it was clear. I was condemned to be trapped for the rest of my life, pitifully yearning for a haven. The water-mill would never grind the past into dust. I was cursed for having sent my father to his death. Wherever I'd go, there Death would follow because curses last for ever and the demons who pursue the accursed do so for ever and ever.

I should have stayed in the wastelands, where at least my bones would have blanched honestly.

And yet ... I couldn't have avoided this clash. Even if I had it in me to betray yet again, even if I'd felt indifferent towards Bostan, deserting Kokona and Dev would have been like abandoning my father once more. Past and future fused.

That's all there was to it: destiny is destiny. Unalterable. Inescapable. I had resigned myself to that truth in the past and I had to do so again.

Kokona was nudging me. 'Osip, they're talking to you ...'

I surfaced from my thoughts. 'Who?'

'Viktor, Urs and Rustu ...'

For a moment I was confused. Caught between demons and stark reality. Often indistinguishable. Maybe one and the same. I turned to the three men. 'Yes?'

They burst out in an avalanche of words, threatening me, cajoling me, even offering hefty sums if I'd set them free.

I barked at them. 'Shut up! Just shut up!'

Kokona took my hand. 'Be kind, Osip. They loved Anton. They're angry and laden with sorrow. So am I. I loved Anton, too.'

Dev muttered mournfully. 'And I! This crazy island!'

Moved by their compassion, I calmed down.

I lit three cigarettes and stuck them one by one into the mouths of Viktor, Urs and Rustu. I spoke as gently as I could. 'I don't want to harm you. All being well, I won't. We'll make a deal. And we'll leave it at that!'

I lit three more cigarettes, handed one each to Kokona and Dev.

I inhaled mine deeply. Smoke, the wise say, soothes a burnt forest so that trees can blossom again. A good metaphor for those seeking hope.

Kokona sighed. 'Such a waste, Osip ... Such a waste ... You never had the chance to hear Anton play and sing – or Stefan Rogosin, for that matter ...?'

'No.'

'When you heard those two play, you no longer feared death ...'

'Makes sense – in a grim way. Spurn Death – and he kills you.'

'Death is not a killer. Just an undertaker. An overworked one at that. It's we who killed Stefan and Anton. The Law killed them.'

'I agree, Teacher. I'd go further. If there is a Last Judgement we'll all be judged killers.'

'Is that meant to console me – or you?'

Foiled by her acuity, I smiled sheepishly. 'Me.'

'Doesn't become you – self-pity. More to the point, you're wrong. We're not all killers. I can't help thinking: if Skender can produce lutanists like Stefan and Anton, surely it can also reclaim its faith in life – in Creation.'

Blessed Kokona, purveyor of hope. But then that's her destiny.

'If ... When ... Teacher ...'

Kokona looked at me sternly. 'There you go again! Who's speaking? You or the demons?'

'Maybe both.'

'Well, let me assure you, one day Skender will reclaim its faith in life. Sooner or later everybody here will want to live in peace and harmony. As I said, we're not all bad. In fact, Stefan is the perfect example that no person is entirely bad. Yes, arrogant and bad-tempered he was, but, like Amphion, the moment he touched a lute, he charmed the stones and they happily became walls. He could send the most cold-blooded men into spasms of tears. Best of all: he loved Anton – believed, without a mite of jealousy, that Anton was a better musician than him. And taught him everything he knew.'

'Was Anton really better?'

'He would have been. Anton was the other side of Stefan. The perfect example that there is evil even in the best of men. A gentle, loving boy – a god out of nowhere who could have healed all Skender with his music. But what does he do? He willingly dives into Skender's maelstrom. Like his mentor, Stefan, he sacrifices his life for the Law – of which, as it turned out, he didn't even know the fundamentals. Like Stefan, he sins against Creation!'

Her outburst had brought Viktor, Urs and Rustu to tears.

And it had inspired me. By the time we reached the Citadel, I'd persuaded myself – hopeless seesawing creature that I was – that, cursed though I might be, some goodness had again flowered in me. I even thought I could strike a blow at Skender's feuding culture.

At the Citadel I bundled Viktor, Urs and Rustu out of the van, untied their feet, herded them into the main tavern and seated them on stools in front of the bar counter. I stood behind them within easy reach.

I told Jiri, the taverner, to squeeze as many rows of chairs as he could into all the available space in front of the bar.

I sent Dev and Kokona to ask Toma and all heads of families to come to the tavern.

Then, as I waited, my eyes drifted to the portraits of Skender's famous feudists hanging around the tavern.

And there was my mother, Eleanora the Falcon. Prominently exhibited. Skender's most famous designated man. Even in an ageing photograph, a beautiful woman. A beauty unspoilt by the false moustache she had chosen to wear, but a face breathing fire like Chimera.

As Toma had taunted me, no picture of Anibal, my father.

Now, having immersed myself in my father's writings, I felt pleased. This gallery of killers was not the right berth for my father. His place was with the generations of just men.

Soon a crowd started gathering. Exceptional news travels very fast in the Citadel.

Toma came shuffling from the Palladion. His retinue of *Morituri* followed him.

A middle-aged couple – Kokona identified them as Nexhat and Mimoza Kaplan, Anton's parents – were among the last to arrive. Accompanied by Anton's brother, Marius, their faces swollen from weeping, they shuffled in as they supported each other.

I asked Jiri to seat them and Toma in the very front row.

When the tavern was packed with the islanders, Kokona and Dev came over to stand next to me.

I turned to the people. 'I'm not one to sermonize. But today I must. I'm going to talk to you about honour ...'

I pointed at Toma, seated in front of me. 'You all know by heart the Law this man promotes. Now, you'll hear mine.'

Toma gave me a derisive look.

The gathering murmured, distrustfully.

Anton's parents and brother looked up, perplexed.

I waited until there was complete silence and all eyes were on me. 'Let me tell you straight away I don't give a mullet's piss about honour!'

Toma jacked up from his chair. 'What did you say?'

'You heard me!'

'You're vomiting offal – same way as your father!'

'Sit down, Toma!'

'I'm not going to listen to you! You're a heretic! An unbeliever! A heathen!'

I bellowed. 'Call me anything you like, but you will listen! And when I finish, I expect you, as the authority on the Law, to pass judgement! Maybe even show us that somewhere in your tortured mind, there's still a memory of right and wrong!'

Toma was outraged. 'That's it! I'm leaving!' He turned round to the *Morituri*, seated at the back. 'Come, my paladins ...'

I shouted him down. 'Stop your charade, Toma! You won't leave! Your curiosity won't let you! You want to hear me! So sit down!'

Toma, in two minds, looked around him.

Some of the people, among them Anton's parents and brother, coaxed him to sit down.

'Let's hear what he has to say!'

'He said you'll be the judge, Righteous Toma. So stay!'

Kokona went over to him and gently eased him onto his chair.

'Sit, old man, sit! A leader must face everything that comes his way.'

Finally, shaking with fury, Toma sat down.

I waited until the people had quietened down. 'As I said, I don't give a mullet's piss about honour – though even a mullet's piss contains life! Whereas honour kills! Whether in pursuit of tribal disputes or ethnic clashes or religious conflicts or nationalist wars or, as you have it here, blood feuds, it kills! Always! Honour is an excuse for power, for oppression, for evil-doing! It has been killing us for thousands of years and it has killed us in billions! I've seen some hundreds of those billions die! And they died horribly! And I realized that taking lives is the basest human pursuit! I now protest against any killing – anywhere!'

I watched their faces. I could see they were shocked, uncertain as to what I would say next.

Toma had his eyes shut and was grimacing as if suffering torture.

Anton's parents were weeping.

Marius caressed their hands.

I went on. 'But since here, in Skender, honour has become your most cherished faith, a faith superior to any religion, I've decided to abide by your tenets. Today I'll submit to the Law!'

Toma opened his eyes in surprise. 'What do you know about the Law? You're a *xenos*.'

'In fact, Toma, I know the Law chapter and verse.'

'Impossible. How can you?'

'I've read it – every word of it.'

'You're lying! There are no texts in existence. Only the Scroll in my possession – and I've certainly not given that to you – or to anybody.'

'My father copied down the Scroll – before you took sole possession of it.'

'Another lie!'

'Want to test me?'

'Why should I? You're lying! We burned your father's books!'

'But not the trunk containing his writings. That's still at the water-mill.'

Toma was stunned. 'The trunk ...?'

'Didn't think it worth burning, did you?'

Toma, dismayed and confused, muttered. 'No.'

I scowled. 'Of course not. Why should you be interested in a bird-watcher's writings?'

Toma spluttered. 'I ... I ...'

I grinned. 'But let's put that aside. Let's get back to the present – to Viktor, Urs and Rustu.'

The gathering watched me, mesmerized.

'For a start, let me point out that Anton contravened the Law – violated its most incontrovertible prohibition – by going to kill Bostan in his own house. That offence in itself should absolve Bostan of Anton's death and spare him for having to feud with the Kaplans or their allies.'

A few voices supported me.

'That's true!'

'What Anton did was wrong!'

'He transgressed abominably!'

I sighed. 'Alas, yes. But let's leave that to the Kristofs, the Rogosins and the Kaplans to sort out. My only advice to you is to take into account Anton's youth, his lack of knowledge of the Law, his deep love for Stefan and assume that he momentarily lost his mind.'

Many in the audience, all obviously great admirers of Anton and still mourning him, shouted agreement.

'Yes!'

'Good advice!'

'Forgive Anton!'

'Absolve him!'

Nexhat Kaplan joined in, wailed. 'He didn't know what he was doing!'

His wife, Mimoza, whimpered. 'He was a boy! Just a boy!'

Marius remained silent.

Toma, having tenaciously regained his composure, hit the floor several times with his mace and shouted above them all. 'We've discussed all that! The families will do what they have to do!' Then he turned to me. 'Come to the point!'

Speaking directly to Toma, I pointed at Viktor, Urs and Rustu. 'These men came to my place to offer me – and to my friends, Kokona and Dev – a deal. They asked us to spy on Bostan – to be informers. In return, they said, we would not be targeted as enemies.'

The gathering started murmuring.

Anton's parents gaped at me.

Marius waited, paying full attention.

I continued. 'Now, informing is generally condemned in every code of human affairs. I'll admit, of course, on certain occasions it might be admissible. But in order to decide the rightness of that act, people must be given the reasons for it so that they can judge for themselves. Even then, the judgement may be wrong. Today, Kokona, Dev and I were not given the chance to judge. So, naturally, we refused.'

I stopped and watched them as they murmured among themselves.

Toma sat like the Sphinx.

Anton's parents, their faces distorted by conflicting emotions, looked bewildered.

A twinge of a smile appeared on Marius' face.

I brandished my bayonet and gun. 'I had the option of killing Viktor, Urs and Rustu. You can ask them. They don't look like liars. I'm sure they'll tell you.'

The gathering turned to the three men.

The latter averted their eyes in shame.

I pointed my gun at them. 'I can still kill them. Before any of you can move!'

The gathering stared at me, spellbound by my weapons.

I drew back my gun. 'But I won't. Instead, I will offer a deal in return. To them. And to you all.'

The gathering fell silent.

This time I addressed Toma directly. 'As you must know, Toma, there is a stipulation in the Law that says if someone spares a life, he is, in turn, owed a life. Right?'

Toma maintained a long silence then nodded. 'Yes.'

With my bayonet, I cut the ropes binding the men's hands. 'Here, in front of you all, I'm sparing the lives of Viktor, Urs and Rustu.'

A great tumult arose.

The families of Viktor, Urs and Rustu went over to them, perturbed but relieved. Yilka, Viktor's wife, burst into tears as she hugged him.

I shouted above them. 'That means I am owed three lives.'

The commotion subsided.

Again, I addressed Toma. 'Right, Toma?'

Again, Toma nodded.

I turned to the gathering. 'I now claim the three lives owed to me: Kokona's, Dev's and mine.'

Silence ruled.

I went up to Toma. 'You are the judge. Can I claim that?'

Toma looked tormented, but finally spoke. 'Yes. You can.'

I faced the gathering. 'Did you hear that?'

Some people applauded in agreement; others shouted. 'Yes!'

Anton's parents, now weeping openly, were, nonetheless, nodding.

I patted Toma's shoulder. 'My congratulations, Toma. You've judged fairly. Maybe you've even accrued honour – true honour, no matter that it has no substance.'

Then I handed Jiri, the taverner, some gold coins. 'Serve everybody whatever they want – and as much as they want.'

I put my arms around Kokona and Dev and we walked out.

As we were about to get into the van, Marius darted out of the tavern and ran to us.

He grabbed my hand. 'Thank you, Xenos. You've given me – and the people here – hope. You've shown there is a better way ...'

'Better way to where?'

'To avenge Anton.'

I looked at Kokona and Dev. I could see they liked Marius, but they were equally puzzled.

Marius offered a lame smile. 'I'm his brother.'

'I know.'

'I owe it to him.'

'Revenge? I was told you didn't believe in the Law ...'

'I don't.' He turned to Kokona and Dev. 'They'll attest to that.'

Kokona and Dev nodded, still puzzled.

Marius continued heatedly. 'When I say avenge, I don't mean by feuding. I mean by fighting the way you did. With reason. That's how I intend to fight Toma. Will you help me?'

I put my arm around his shoulders. 'Sorry, Marius. I don't want to fight Toma or anybody. I just want to retire to my water-mill.'

Marius became tearful. 'You don't understand! Anton would have been alive if he hadn't drugged me before going after Bostan. I'd have stopped him! Even more importantly, he'd have been alive if I, as the elder brother, hadn't declined to join the *Morituri*.'

I felt sorry for the young man, but I refused to weaken. 'I understand your feelings, Marius. But I don't have it in me to help you. You'll have to fight your own battles.'

Marius almost wailed. 'Anton died instead of me. Are you saying I'll have to turn into a lonely and maddened prophet, like Toma, but his opposite, so that Anton – and our people – can live?'

'Yes.'

'That's a cruel fate!'

'Fate is Fate, Marius. Nothing we can do about the way she manages things.'

Marius nodded, then started walking away disconsolately. 'Thank you for today, anyway.'

I looked at Kokona and Dev. I could see disappointment in their eyes.

I growled. 'I can't save myself! How can I save Skender?'

13

BOSTAN

I stole in through the mill-room. Castor went ahead. He'd already scoured the terrain and not sniffed danger.

As I went up to the ground floor, I could hear Castor breathing – contentedly.

I had expected it. He had come across Xenos. He's so taken with the man he no longer bothers to alert me. Were he a cat, he'd be purring.

I remained cautious, lit my torch and quietly slipped into the main room.

Castor was not with Xenos, but with the Shrimp.

And the Shrimp was crouching behind the door, ready to strike with a sword – one of those curved Turkish ones.

I nearly shouted. 'Shrimp!'

He pointed his sword menacingly at me. 'I didn't expect you, Bostan!'

I replied just as tersely. 'What are you doing here?'

'Keeping watch ...'

'What for?'

'In case someone comes for Osip.'

'What someone?'

'Like you ...'

'Me?'

'You crept in ...'

'I came to thank him. For refusing to inform on me.'

'In the middle of the night?'

'Safer for me – the middle of the night.'

Suddenly Castor jumped up and ran to the other room.

And there was Xenos, barefoot, wearing only his underpants, watching me and the Shrimp.

He stroked Castor, then lit the oil lamps. 'Visitors are always welcome, whatever the time. What can I offer you?'

Seeing the scars up close on his chest – like a map – I was shocked. How could someone stand upright after so much stitching? Yet somehow the scars made him look larger.

My voice lost its usual edge. 'I came to thank you.'

The Shrimp muttered. 'And I ...'

Xenos hugged the Shrimp. 'Yes, I heard you two.' He turned to me. 'No need to thank me. You'd have done the same.'

I nodded. 'Even so ...'

He pointed at the chairs. 'Sit down.'

He put some cigarettes and matches on the table. 'Help yourselves. Dev, you know where the *rakiya* is. I'll put some clothes on ...'

I watched him walk into his room.

Again Castor followed him.

I lit a cigarette.

The Shrimp brought a pitcher of *rakiya* and filled up three glasses.

I took a hefty gulp. 'Thanks, Shrimp ...'

Xenos came in, with Castor in tow. Dressed in shirt and trousers, he didn't look as attractive as when he was almost naked.

He sat next to me. 'His name is Dev, Bostan. And a very apt name, believe me. He's a true giant ...'

Dev, embarrassed, muttered. 'I don't mind Shrimp ...'

When I'd heard about Xenos trussing up Viktor, Urs and Rustu, I'd also heard that Kokona and the Shrimp had helped him. So I took the Shrimp's hand. 'Of course: Dev. Thank you too. And thank Kokona.'

Dev shrugged shyly. 'It's nothing ...'

Xenos smiled and raised his glass. 'As I once heard Teacher toast: may we all die tending roses.'

We drank to that. 'Amen!'

Xenos lit a cigarette.

I felt I should go, but didn't want to.

Xenos must have read my mind. 'Stay. Stay. We're too awake to sleep.'

Dev was fidgeting.

Xenos noticed it and turned to Dev. 'Worried about Teacher?'

Dev shook his head. 'No ...'

Xenos took Dev's hand. 'Your friendship is my blessing, Dev. But go to her. She'll be worried.'

'Yes, but ...'

Xenos turned to me. 'You're not going to kill me, are you, Bostan?'

That offended me. 'No!'

Xenos smiled. 'See, Dev. I'm perfectly safe.'

Dev sighed, got up and hugged Xenos. 'See you.'

He stroked Castor, shook hands with me, picked up his sword and left.

Xenos poured more *rakiya*, offered me another cigarette and took one himself.

Then he watched me, not saying a word.

This time he was actually looking at me – as a person. And with interest. But his gaze was changeable. Eyes as I'd first seen them: one moment peaceful, next murky.

I began to feel uneasy. Usually, I'm not bothered by scrutiny. Not since I made myself Skender's best feudist. But now I wondered what sort of things he was imagining about me.

When I'm annoyed, I become talkative. 'I didn't want to kill Anton ... I – I had to ...'

He made no comment, but looked as if he believed me.

'I loved him – like everybody else. Beautiful lutanist. Beautiful voice. When he came to my house, I thought he'd come to see my son, Zemun. But he said no, he knew my son was at the Palladion, taking an elocution lesson from Toma. I came for you, he said. That made me very happy. It's a blessing to have a visitor. I invited him in, offered food and refreshments. He refused. He said: "This is not a social call. I came to kill you because you killed Stefan." I tried in every way I could to talk him out of it. Don't try it, I said, go home, this isn't your fight. This is between the Kristofs and the Rogosins. I even begged him: "Go and play your lute. Your music gives us the strength to live."'

Xenos was listening intently.

'But he wouldn't leave. He loved Stefan and Stefan loved him – we were like two bulbuls in the wilderness, he said. Then he drew his gun. His hand was shaking. For a moment I even thought he'd probably miss me so I should let him fire. But he was too close. When he steadied his hand to fire, I reacted instinctively. My gun was on the table. I'd just cleaned it. I grabbed it – I'm pretty quick – and fired ...'

Xenos drank a big mouthful. 'How did you feel?'

'Terrible. He was even younger than my son. And it wasn't his fight.'

'The others you killed ... How did you feel then?'

'Oh, fine. Really fine. I killed them for good reasons.'

'As a man should.'

I didn't like his tone, it sounded offensive. 'What do you mean?'

'That's what Skender demands from its men ...'

'What else?'

'You mentioned your son ... You expect him to be like you, too?'

I hesitated. I certainly didn't want Zemun to be a feudist. So I wanted to say no. But how could I? 'Yes.'

'Do you have other children?'

'No.'

'How old is your son?'

'Almost seventeen.'

Xenos' eyes misted. 'Not much older than when I ...'

'When you what?'

He shook his head sadly. 'Nothing. A passing thought.' He poured us more *rakiya*. 'What about Zemun's mother? Does she think as you do?'

'He doesn't have a mother. Not any more.'

'I'm sorry.'

I shrugged. 'But yes. She'd have thought the same ...'

'So who looks after him? I mean, with you always on the alert.'

'The Kristof women ...'

'He doesn't mind?'

Again I felt he was getting at me. 'You've been away too long, Xenos. Skenderi boys become true men when they're still suckling.

Not like mainland wimps. Besides, Zemun's a member of the Paladins of the Law. As I was some years back. He's Righteous Toma's best student, in fact. He's now studying elocution. To be a leader like Toma. That's why he wasn't at home when Anton came. Had he been, he might have held Anton back.'

Xenos' expression had darkened. He seemed more remote. 'True man, you said.'

'Yes.'

'What's a true man?'

I could fence with words, too. 'You're a true man. You refused to inform on me!'

'That's all it takes?'

'And everything that goes with it. Being a mass of strength, an ever-present presence – like the mountain guarding the Citadel. Doing what needs to be done. Acting honourably. Free spirit! No ties! No weaknesses!'

'Not like a woman ...?'

'You said it ...'

'I said it sadly. I like women ...'

For some reason, his comment made me flinch the way jealousy does. What did he know about women?

I laughed lewdly. 'Yes, women are fine. They do everything we ask. Cook for us. Open their legs whenever we want. Bear children. Bring them up. Keep the family on its feet. Faithful slaves! Thank God for them! But honestly, who'd want to be a woman? Would you?'

'No.'

'Nor I! Nor anybody in his right mind!'

Xenos sighed and swallowed the rest of his *rakiya*. 'A bleak world ...'

The way he kept looking at me was troubling.

I decided to go. 'Yes, well. That's how it is ...' I got up. 'I must go. Thanks for the hospitality. And thanks again for what you did.'

'Part and parcel of being a man.'

I had a feeling he was mocking me. I decided to be crusty, too. 'A true man. Not many around.'

I whistled at Castor, who immediately came to my side. At least my dog knows I'm a true man.

I walked out.

As I stomped away, I could sense Xenos' eyes on me – just like when we first met.

14

DEV

I don't like leaving Osip with Bostan. Not because I fear Bostan will harm him. The Law says Bostan owes his life to Osip. Bostan never goes against the Law.

I worry because of Osip's interest in Bostan. Very plain now. Tonight's the first time they've been alone. But they've met many times already. When Bostan takes the Kristof women to do the washing, Osip always greets him. Offers refreshments. That's how Viktor, Urs and Rustu heard of Bostan's route. The Kristof women blabbed. They find Osip's interest curious, too. So word got round ...

More than an ordinary interest, this. Take tonight. Osip sends me away. Says he doesn't need me. Harsh. Not like him to leave me out. He wanted to be heads together with Bostan more than with me.

Maybe I'm being stupid. Maybe Osip feels fatherly. He has no children. We know. He told us, life prevented that. A great sadness for him. Maybe Bostan's obsession with honour makes him feel sorry for him. Makes him see Bostan as a son needing protection.

Fatherly feelings ... Very strong. I feel the same for many young feudists. But to them I am only a dwarf. So I keep away.

Something else: Bostan's secret.

Makes me think ... Is it possible Osip knows? The Law says such secrets must stay secret. Especially from strangers. And for Skenderis, Osip is a stranger for ever. A wreck the currents brought. I thought maybe Kokona and I should tell him the secret – we don't believe in the Law – but then we'd be excommunicated. I can cope with that. I've lived half my life ostracized. I know how to survive. But Skender is Kokona's soul. Cut her off from the people and she'd die in no time.

Does Osip like Bostan's flesh? Does he want him? If so, it's the wrong time. And Skender, the wrong place. Nothing can come of it.

I could ask Osip. We're close. But I don't dare. Never will. Even friends like us must keep some passions locked up. That way we don't hurt each other.

15

TOMA

When a tree threatens the foundations of your house, you don't just chop it down; you deal with its roots, treat them with poison to make sure it dies.

That's how I must destroy Anibal's son. Wise of me to recognize he'd bring trouble the moment I laid eyes on him.

Now that he and I have had our first clash, I can see how much like his father he is. Worse still, and I don't imagine he is aware of it, he fights exactly as Anibal did.

He discards his own weapons and fights me with mine. He has studied the Law, My Law, and wields it against me.

How come it never occurred to me Anibal had transcribed my Scroll? What an aberration on my part to disdain his trunk. And why didn't Eleanora the Falcon let me know Anibal had a copy of the Law? No wonder he could challenge me at will!

No, I mustn't blame Eleanora the Falcon. She wouldn't have known. She had little to do with Anibal.

The fault was mine. I can only think I must have fallen prey to the Doubter. He must have clouded my mind.

I can easily neutralize the alien's weapons of logic, reason, mitigating circumstances and pleas for mercy. I immediately confront those with the Law and that's the end of them. There are no terms for argument.

But when I have to dispute the Law, My Law, against You, the Law, My Law, my hands are tied.

The result is defeat. A personal defeat. And gross humiliation.

That's what happened the other day in the tavern.

And after every defeat I suffer, there is disorder, confusion, chaos.

That's what's happening now.

We have deranged youths running around, like Bacchae, screaming for a better *modus vivendi* without knowing what *modus vivendi* means.

That's right, our delinquents have ganged up with Anton's befuddled brother, Marius, and trouble is fomenting. *You* know them well: our vermin, our rootless ones, the dregs of the new generation, the absconders from the Law!

A better *modus vivendi*!

Have You heard anything more outrageous?

What humiliation!

And what a threat to me!

Can You imagine the dilemma I had to face having to judge in favour of Anibal's son?!

What else could I do?

I hold You, the Law, My Law, sacred.

It must not be bent!

Never ever!

Even if it means, on occasion, I have to lose ground and face humiliation!

Or start thinking maybe the Law has some fine print, some escape clauses that I've forgotten.

Or that maybe I'm losing my mind.

It eats me up.

That's exactly what Anibal used to do. No matter how clear-cut a decision I had taken, he would find an obscure passage in the Law – and alas, as *You* well know, You, the Law, My Law, abounds with obsolete exegeses.

And then, he, Anibal, went on to interpret that obscure passage, I must admit, so brilliantly that his explication became more pertinent than the commandment he had challenged.

You will no doubt remember there were times when I doubted the incontrovertibility of the Law and wondered whether the pursuit of compassion, Anibal's basic tenet for discourse, offered a better code for dignity and honour.

But that, of course, meant enslavement to conscience, that straitjacket from Europe.

I'm proud to say I managed to wean myself off it. Despite the Doubter You kept sending me to test me – even trick me – whenever I showed signs of weakness. As in the case of Anibal's trunk.

Anibal's main objective was to abolish the Law. He found many supporters among the Skenderis. Particularly among those of doubtful lineage.

I triumphed in the end, but his ideas linger. You can hear it travelling subterraneously, sometimes even on the wind.

Where else would Marius and his delinquent entourage have got the idea of a better *modus vivendi*?

In fact, and I've never told You this, Anibal might have defeated me had I not hastened his killing.

I had no other option.

His enemies didn't discover the day and time he had decided to go bird-watching from schoolchildren. That's the story I concocted when I heard, from one of Anibal's son's classmates, how excited young Osip was about the outing.

But it was me, Your unflinching prophet, who actually informed Anibal's enemies when and where to find him.

Eleanora the Falcon, who hated her husband's meekness as much as I did, who felt demeaned by his love for books and birds instead of a passion for honour, used to complain to me constantly about him.

And so, vituperatively, she disclosed Anibal's movements.

Informer I certainly was, but no more than she.

On the other hand, my strategy was that of a true leader. It saved You, the Law, My Law.

It saved Skender.

It brought back honour and order to this island.

In retrospect, that episode's only misfortune was that Anibal's enemies didn't also kill his son. They could have done so easily and claimed that the boy had been caught in the crossfire.

It would have spared us all the present problems.

So you, Anibal's son, you who hate informers, listen well.

I fight ruthlessly when what I hold sacred is attacked.

I have no alternative.

So, by all means fight me with Anibal's ways; pit the Law against the Law, My Law; impress confused youths like Marius.

I'll bide my time.

And one good day, the Law, My Law, will triumph.

As it did over your father.

16

KOKONA

It was the Day of Persephone, our hallowed festival. Some scholars link it to the spring equinox; others to the ancient Greek bacchanal celebrating the reappearance of Dionysus after he had hidden, all winter, under the sea. Through the ages, Skenderis developed their own beliefs. For our Christians, this is the day when saints receive thanksgiving from their adherents for achieving martyrdom. For our Muslims, it is the day when Allah's angel, Jibril, guided Ibrahim to the Black Stone, the foundation of the Ka'aba. For our Jews – yes, Skender has some Jews, too, though ours, in the main, are visible only on festive days – it is the day on which Noah's messenger, the dove, returned to the Ark with an olive twig and announced the end of the Deluge. For those converts to various religions whose real faiths, if any, remain secret – the islanders call them *turnabouts* – it's the seventh day of Creation, a time of respite and integration, no questions asked. And for the irreligious like me, it celebrates the time when the Lover of Love ruled the Earth and hatred was kept at bay. Yes, there was such a time. I know it in my heart. And, I believe, so do we all.

But for all of us, it is the day when the sun comes back to earth bearing the gift of greenness.

Every Skenderi, except the bedridden, had congregated in the Citadel. Of course, another reason that makes the Day of Persephone so important is that on this day all feuding stops and a week's truce prevails.

The centre of the Plaza had been cordoned off for musicians and dancers. The perimeter had been sectioned off for family stalls where home-made food and handiwork were on sale. The shops, of course, were closed, but the tavern and the *rakiya* distillers were open and doing a roaring trade.

I had settled in the tavern, at a table where I had a good view both of the dancing in the Plaza and the revellers around me.

As always happens with me on the Day of Persephone, I was happy. I had lived through another winter and felt I could stretch my days further still.

The ferry service, normally atrocious in winter, had been mostly reliable. The islanders had bartered well in Turnu with the few goods they could produce and we hadn't suffered shortages of fuel and food. I had completed two tapestries – both figurative – and the Handwork Cooperative, having sold them quickly and for a good price, had urged me to weave many more.

Another cause for my contentment was that, by Skenderi standards, the last few months had been relatively peaceful. We had suffered only nineteen killings: among the Popov, Gjorg, Dardan and Abraham families and their various allies.

Against that there had been forty-one births. A good ratio, the islanders had decided. It had reduced the ever-present risk of critical population depletion. In other words, we had produced enough new fodder to feed our Moloch.

The dancing, a jumble of different ethnic gambols, had started in earnest. First to take the floor were the old folk, in costume, for the traditional Skenderi terpsichores. I watched them for a while, trying to curb my envy. Not too long ago, I was the best dancer in Skender; I could perform those twists and turns with such flair that my skirts swirled like racing rainbows. And my thighs weren't flabby like some of the women's out there. But these days what strength I have I devote to making love with Dev. Much more pleasurable than dancing.

I turned my attention to the people in the tavern.

According to tradition, the head table was occupied by the Steward of the Archipelago and the trio of so-called spiritual leaders of offshore communities. I have no respect for any of them. Neither they, nor any of their predecessors, have ever spoken out against the feuds.

We might perhaps make allowances for the Steward. He serves in absentia. Since many of his forerunners, while trying to set up office in Skender, were killed in one feud or another, the despairing Ministry of the Interior decided to install the post in Turnu. Thus he visits us once a year on the Day of Persephone. This commitment, giving the impression that we happily put up with an official, bolsters our government's pretence that it has authority over us.

But I can't make any excuses for the religious charlatans. They, too, live in Turnu, claiming it is a safer place, though neither they nor any of their precursors have ever been harmed. Way back when the Law was formulated, it exempted people of the cloth from feuds on the grounds that they would be needed to bestow greater sanctity on honour by conducting the burial services. So they visit us more often than the Steward – on important religious holidays – but for very brief spells. Since a truce always reigns during the holidays and no one gets killed, these worthies return to Turnu without having officiated at a single grave. Even so, I go on hoping that these spurious learned men, cascading piety down their sleeves, will challenge our worship of slaughter if only by paying lip service to the commandments. Never! The priest maintains that each killing sends the departed to heaven or to hell – depending on the life he has led – ahead of his time and that this is a blessing in disguise. The imam accepts the bloodshed as part of Allah's immutable will. And the *haham* justifies the deaths as retribution from Yahweh for a transgression that mortals still cannot comprehend.

I watched, in disgust, as the three conversed animatedly. I knew – because I hear the same refrain every year – that instead of discussing moral issues, they were either moaning about the meagre stipend they received for their ministry, or about the shortcomings of their wives' cooking, or the limitations of this and that remedy for this and that ailment. I prayed to the Lover of Love that these bogus servants of God should never have a sniff of paradise.

I'm being harsh, I know. If you ask Dev, he'll say we could have been worse off, that the religious leaders could have been fanatical fundamentalists instead of these ineffectual pretenders; then, in addition to honour feuds, we would have had ethnic and religious conflicts – like the Peoples' Wars they keep having on the mainland – and, in no time at all, Skender, bloated to the gullet with blood, would sink to the bottom of the sea.

Dev is right. Though this island is the last place on earth where wisdom can flourish, we Skenderis are light years ahead of the world in the way we keep religion out of our lives. Even those who claim affiliation to a faith do so with scant respect or interest or acknowledgment of it. For the Skenderis, creeds serve as the validation of their cherished Law; it endorses the tenet that killing for honour is not only superior to all commandments, but also, and more importantly, a God-given natural function like eating, drinking, shitting and pissing.

The so-called government on the mainland attributes this unorthodoxy to the island's geographical isolation; a myth substantiated by the warlords who codified the Law.

According to this myth, when God sought to punish Satan, Satan tried to appear innocent by spitting the evil in him far out to sea. That spittle duped God and saved Satan's life. And Satan, in a rare act of gratitude, transformed the spittle into the island of Skender. Leagues out at sea, as we are, and the way we continue to whip up the evil in our souls with our feuds, are given as proof of the myth's veracity.

Dev and I have spent our lifetimes ridiculing such nonsense. Having to live so close to Nature, we see little sense in man-made piety. What Osip said about honour is true for religion also: it, too, is designed to rule and kill. Whereas Creation has sublime objectives: to create every being equally and, after that, to bless them, also equally. That's why Dev and I revere the Lover of Love. That's why we try to bring the killings to an end.

Dev, being Dev, was helping Jiri, the taverner, serve drinks.

As usual, groups of men had pulled tables together and were talking, for a change, not about feuds – a taboo subject on the Day of Persephone – but about island business and husbandry. Some, already drunk, were trying to outshine each other with inflated hunting and fishing exploits.

The women were sitting separately and, also as usual for them, were discussing pregnancies and baby lore and how to make ends meet and, for those with marriageable daughters, talking about eligible men and the advantages or disadvantages of hiring matchmakers.

The marriageable daughters themselves – twenty-four in all – were seated in their special corner, eyeing the bachelors who, in turn, had clustered at tables in the opposite corner.

Next to the girls, though sitting slightly apart, were the widows who, having lost their husbands in feuds, were hoping to find new ones. Among them were several Kristof women. Having had, in Skenderi parlance, their 'heavenly estuaries trawled' by their departed husbands, these widows knew that, irrespective of their ability to work, they would have to make their *amatas* sweeter than raisins in order to compete with virgins. Some do manage that. Last year, no fewer than five widows found new spouses.

Traditionally, on this day, a marriageable female has the right to approach a bachelor and ask for his hand. If the man refuses, she can try someone else. Indeed, she has the right to ask every man in the bachelors' group. But that's something that has never happened. What woman would risk a bilge of rejections?

Also, traditionally, if a man accepts the proposal, he is obliged to marry the woman come what may – even if the two families have an ongoing feud. I know of several such alliances that instantly ended their families' enmity. Indeed, insisting that what our people really yearn for is peace, hard work and enough food to feed their households – the ordinariness of life, in effect – I once proposed that the only way we would stop the killings would be to impose marriages between the feuding families. Needless to say, people laughed at me.

I surveyed the bachelors. They were nervous and drinking heavily: some, no doubt, because they were impatient for a proposal; others, in trepidation that they might not be able to resist a request from the daughter of an enemy family and thus bring about the very outcome I'd suggested.

Toma, wearing his best purple cloak, sat prominently among the bachelors. In olden days, when he had so presented himself, he had incurred both mirth and admiration from the Skenderis. What woman would want to marry a man without a tackle, some had mocked – and indeed in all these years, he had not had a single proposal. But others, particularly his disciples and, not least, the successive generations of *Morituri*, had praised his courage. Who but an exceptional man would audaciously defy the Fate that had unmanned him? The latter, I always thought, had a valid point.

Since talking about feuding was taboo, Toma, for the only time in the year, was silent. He was very drunk. Some of the *Morituri*, among them, Gavril Rogosin and Bostan's son, Zemun – though neither was included in the bachelors' group – were making sure that his goblet – putatively Skanderbeg's – was never empty.

I had hoped that Marius would offer himself for marriage. A woman would have eased his mourning for his brother, Anton; but he had sworn never to sit at the same table as Toma and not even the prospect of a good wife would change his mind.

Bostan and Osip completed the group of bachelors.

Some of the women, surprised to see Bostan blithely drinking and bantering, were muttering in undertones.

They were our amnesiac women. They always forgot that, invariably in the past, the bachelors' corner had accommodated the likes of Bostan unquestioningly. On the Day of Persephone every single man was entitled to seek marriage. Irrespective of what they were, Bostan and Toma had the same rights. And their motivation was plain to see. Both wanted to prove they were men moulded in the Skenderi image.

I concentrated on Osip. He was talking to Bostan, judging by his gestures, about the workings of the water-mill, while stroking

Bostan's dog. With Lefteris having delivered the shaft and all the other woodwork on time, the water-mill was now running and looked as good as new.

Osip had been placed in the bachelors' corner by Dev. Who else? My Dev, the Lover of Love incarnate, was determined that Osip should not sleep on his own for another season.

Dev had talked to me many times about Osip's attraction to Bostan. He believed that Bostan, too, was attracted to Osip. For some time now, whenever he escorted the Kristof women to the *lavanderi*, Bostan happily accepted Osip's offer of refreshments. Naturally, nothing untoward had happened – not with the Kristof women standing around like a colony of buzzards. But Dev was afraid that if their meetings continued – particularly now with summer on our doorstep, the Kristofs' excursions to the *lavanderi* would increase – Osip might well become infatuated with Bostan. The Devil alone would predict what might happen then. Therefore, Dev believed, it would be prudent, not to mention safer, to get Osip bedded down with a wife as soon as possible.

I must admit that, I, too, had been troubled by the chemistry that had so drawn Osip and Bostan to each other. And Bostan, I imagined, was the more captivated. He had started borrowing many more books from me, not manuals and brochures that might help improve his farm work, but 'good books' as he put it. Once I asked him whether he wanted to teach some of the Kristof children to read and write – as his mother, a truly maternal woman, had taught him. He said no, the learning was for him, he wanted to be able to talk to people about this and that. I felt tempted to ask him who those people were since I only knew of three – Dev, Osip and myself – who'd give him the time of day. But I didn't. Maybe I should have.

It stood to reason: since Bostan had never been gregarious before

Osip's arrival, the only person he'd want to impress had to be Osip. Osip is quite learned, that much I'd found out. Though he never shows off his knowledge, sometimes, without being aware of it, he says things that even I know nothing about.

Osip, however, had shown no interest in marriage and had resisted the idea of joining the bachelors. He kept arguing that he was too old for wedlock, that, in any case, he hadn't had much to do with women – which is hard to believe – and, consequently, wouldn't know how to live with one under the same roof, let alone in the same bed. I felt certain the reason for his resistance stemmed from his fidelity to Sofi's memory and, perhaps more importantly, from his fear that, like Sofi, his new woman might die instead of him.

But once Dev gets an idea into his head, he pursues it all the way up Hephaestus' arse. So, finally, partly to please Dev and me, and partly because, given his low self-esteem, he felt convinced he wouldn't get a proposal, he had agreed. I didn't doubt that he wanted to please us, but within that indulgence, I could see a deeper reason. Having sensed our concern over his attraction to Bostan, he had wanted to reassure us that his interest in Bostan was basically fatherly and that should a good woman seek him out he'd be delighted.

Grey-haired he might be, but, as everybody could see, the girls, not least the widows, couldn't keep their eyes off him.

One, in particular, Lila, by far the prettiest girl in Skender, looked the keenest. While all the bachelors were trying to catch her eye, she was cannonading Osip with enticing looks; and getting flustered because Osip, quite unaware of her, was talking animatedly with Bostan.

Finally, Lila got up from her chair and glided loftily, like a swan, over to Osip.

She sat between him and Bostan, turning her back disdainfully on the latter.

She placed her hands on the table to indicate that she had made up her mind and addressed Osip – loud enough for everybody to hear. 'I am Lila. Almost seventeen. A virgin. And ripe for marriage. I'm in good health. I can give you many children.'

Bostan, baffled and annoyed at first, soon regained his composure. Smiling, he rose from his seat as would be expected of a gallant bachelor and, calling his dog, moved away. But instead of moving to another seat at the bachelors' table, he joined one of the men's groups near the bar, thus declaring he was no longer available for marriage.

Some of the mothers, I could see, were relieved by this move. Bostan, irrespective of his secret, was a condemned man, like all feudists; he would be killed sooner or later; no mother, even the most open-minded, would have wanted her daughter attached to someone with such an obviously brief span of life.

But Toma, incensed by Lila's proposal to Osip, started shouting. 'Lila, no! Not Xenos! He's an unbeliever! A heathen! Bad blood!'

Bostan's son, Zemun, also looked distraught. It was common knowledge that he was very keen on Lila, and that since she had joined the *Morituri*, he followed her everywhere. He had even confided to some of his comrades that one day he would marry her.

Wishful thinking. He was the same age as Lila – much too young for her.

Toma's voice rose to a screech. 'No, Lila, no! He's Anibal's son! Bad blood! His father was a bird-watcher! Look around you! Where's Anibal's picture? Nowhere! Bad blood, I tell you!'

Ignoring Toma's outburst, Lila pushed her chair closer to Osip.

'Also I'll leave the paladins. I'll work day and night to make you a good home.'

Toma howled. 'No, Lila! No! Choose a real man!'

Some in the gathering laughed and teased Toma. 'You mean a real man like you, Righteous Toma?'

Toma defied them. 'That's right!'

I was amused, too.

I watched Osip to see how he would react.

He didn't seem to have heard Toma. He was flustered. Had he really believed he wouldn't receive a proposal?

Scarcely managing to look at Lila, he muttered. 'You ... want ... *me* ...?'

Lila smiled pertly. 'Yes.'

Osip offered her his cigarettes. 'I – I'm ... Do you smoke?'

Toma was still shouting. 'Not him, Lila! Not Anibal's son!'

Lila took a cigarette. 'How can I refuse?'

I could see, as he lit her cigarette, that Osip's hand was shaking.

Then he lit one for himself.

Lila inhaled deeply, her eyes fixed on Osip, and exhaled slowly. Then, smiling as if she had passed a test, she took a good swig of Osip's *rakiya*. 'Now, I've also drunk from your glass ...'

Once again, Toma's voice turned into a screech. 'No, Lila, no!'

Osip looked dazed. Dev had instructed him that should a woman drink from his glass it would mean she was prepared to drink his seed for ever. In Skender, for a marriageable girl, this was the boldest proposal.

Everybody watched Osip intently – some of the bachelors with unbridled jealousy.

Zemun glared as if he wanted to kill Osip.

Toma's desperate incantation hit a higher pitch. 'No, Lila! No! He's bad blood!'

Osip finally managed to face Lila. 'I – I'm ...'

Lila gulped down the rest of his *rakiya*. 'I drank – all of it.'

Osip rose from his chair as graciously as he could. 'I'm sorry, Lila ... I'm really very sorry ... I shouldn't have sat here with the bachelors ... Stupid of me ... I ... I'm ...'

Lila seemed stunned. 'Don't I please you?'

Osip could barely speak. 'You're lovely ... Beautiful ... you really are ... And I'm sure a very good person ... But I – I can't marry ... Don't know how I can explain ... But I can't ... I – I shouldn't have sat here ... I – Stupid of me ...'

Lila, mortified, was on the verge of tears.

Osip grabbed his cigarettes and lighter. 'Toma's right ... I'm bad blood ... Believe that ...'

Lila's dismay gave way to indignation. She grabbed his arm angrily. 'You're the man I want. I'll have you. Come what may. And I'll still be a virgin.'

Osip gently extricated himself from her grip. 'No ... No ... Choose a good man ...'

And he tore out of the tavern.

Dev and I exchanged looks; then, as if prompted by each other, we watched Bostan.

He had witnessed the scene and was casually stroking his dog. He had a strange smile on his face.

A number of the bachelors, hoping that Lila might propose to one of them instead, tried to catch her eye.

But she ignored them. Then, purposefully, though still trembling with rage, she went over to Toma.

People looked at each other in amazement.

Lila's mother started wailing.

A hubbub of disbelief engulfed the tavern.

Toma stared at Lila, more incredulous than the rest of us.

Lila sat by his side. 'Will you have me, Righteous Toma?'

Toma went wild. 'Yes! Yes! Yes!'

Lila lowered her eyes. 'I'm yours.'

Toma, almost delirious, turned to the gathering. 'See! See! See! She knows a real man! She can smell bad blood instantly! She knows who has good blood! She knows! She knows!'

17

OSIP

I waded through the people in the Plaza.

I had to get away.

Where to?

Skender is my last stop. There's nowhere else.

I ran out of the Citadel.

But to panic?

Me, of all people?

Remember how I stood, insensate, while comrades around me fell like blossom in the wind?

Remember how I sped through torched villages, never looking right or left?

I didn't panic then.

Yet I panicked in front of a wisp of a girl.

Because she reminded me of Sofi?

No, there will never ever be another Sofi.

Sofi was the only hope I've had for another existence.

She was so intent on reclaiming life for me.

Save yourself, she said, there's a god in you; there's a god in each of us.

Then, as she died, she begged me. 'Live!'

I promised I would.

That's why I came here.

That's why I offered myself for marriage today.

Yet I knew in my guts that should a woman be naive enough to want me, I'd flee.

Lila could have given me a sort of life.

She offered to drink me for the rest of my days.

Me! This pathetic man who pleads night and day: women, women, one of you, find me, love me, take me, house me in your grotto.

I panicked.

A woman is the sublime grotto, Sofi once said. Inside her all the ills of the world are soothed. Where else can a man breathe freely? Where else can he be taught to live?

I panic before life.

I panicked when Sofi loved me.

She never told me she did.

But I knew because she loved everybody.

I never touched her.

I didn't panic when she was killed.

I don't panic before death.

I panic only before life.

What made Lila want me?

Couldn't she see Sofi's ghost warning everybody like a bird of ill omen: he brings death; don't touch him, he's dead himself; save yourself; or you, too, will die!

Couldn't Lila see what my mother saw when I was born?

My mother cast me away after my birth.

My father took care of me.

Had I felt my mother's hatred of me at my birth? And her hatred of my father?

Is that what she saw when she first looked at me – a homunculus forced on her?

A life unworthy of life?

My mother didn't know about life; she only knew about death.

But if I was unworthy of life, why didn't she love me?

Those who know death love the living dead.

My mother was a man.

The best designated man in history, Toma said.

I ran until I collapsed.

A strong wind revived me.

I was on the cliffs, between the cluster of rocks where I'd hidden when they killed my father.

I had run here without thinking.

I'd been meaning to come back, but kept putting it off.

I lurched towards the cliffs.

I gazed at the Earth's curvature where the sea meets the horizon.

So welcoming ...

So peaceful ...

One step forward.

Arms stretched out like wings.

Into the air.
Osip, Eleanora's Falcon.
Flying off to Madagascar.
And beyond.

But I couldn't move.

I had become a little boy again.

A trembling little boy who had finally crawled out of his hiding place.

I was holding my father's corpse.

Still warm.

My hands sticky with his blood.

His spent blood still full of his love for me.

That's how I held Sofi, too.

And her spent blood was also full of love.

For everybody, for everything.

I want to be with my father again.

One step over the cliff and I'd be with him.

And I'd tell him: I love you, my bird-watching father. Forgive me. It was my fault they killed you.

Forgive me!

Then I heard her voice.

Not my mother's.

Teacher's. Kokona's – Maro, as she was then.

The almond blossom. The softest of voices. Rising above the waves. 'Osip, my boy, listen to me ...'

I listened.

'We must live in order to achieve at least one decent thing ...'

'But, Teacher ...'

'Listen, my boy, listen ...'

'I am listening ...'

'It may take a lifetime ...'

'But, Teacher ...'

'Even then we may never achieve it ...'

'I loved my father. I love you. Don't you and he count as decent, Teacher?'

'Love is where we start from. And where we should end. But there's a long journey in between. We have to endure it. No matter how difficult. Understand?'

'No, Teacher, I don't ...'

'Yes, you do.'

'No, Teacher ...'

'Yes, you do, my boy.'

I lay down by the cliff's edge.

A fledgling falcon.

I waited for Father to tell me my wings were strong enough; that I was ready to fly.

I fell asleep.

I woke up.

Teacher's voice was still swirling in my ears. The descant of unfailing love.

I'd heard her all my life; through all my years of brutality; when I'd been Death's instrument; when I'd most needed it.

But I'd ignored it.

Why can't I ignore it now?

I started thinking about Bostan.

I cared for Bostan.

He reminded me of myself during those years when I was stranded in the void. When my eyes were forever at the back of my head searching for a mother that never existed and a father that I had led to death.

Full of anger because everything good in the world was unattainable.

Contrite because evil had offered itself without demur and provided me with men's favourite accessories: guns, power and ersatz moments in the sun.

That's how I became a killer.

Yes.

But somewhere inside me I kept believing that the hand that pulls the trigger does not really belong to the heart because the heart is as soft as a woman's breasts.

So I shut out the heart.

Which makes it easier to live as the living dead.

And easier to kill.

Bostan, I'm sure, also has a soft heart.

So I want to help him redeem himself, to stop killing.

Be like a wing for him, yes.

Maybe then I could save him from getting killed – though that's wishful thinking; feudists never reach old age.

There's something else about Bostan.

It's facing me.

But I choose to disregard it.

Safer that way.

There's no denying he's handsome and delicately featured.

Both masculine and feminine.

Therein lies the attraction.

Much as I accept the paradox, intellectually I must resist it.

As I said, safer that way.

Yet the question remains.

Do I want to be with him differently from the way I am with Dev, whom I have come to love as a brother?

Put bluntly – whereas I can horseplay like a kid with Dev, do I want to touch Bostan?

Strange question, considering I've billeted with many men far more attractive than Bostan and none of them interested me.

Many, in fact, propositioned me, forcing me to reject them. At times openly, other times, brutally.

I had calmed down.

I strode up and down the cliffs looking for Eleanora's Falcons.

But it was too early for them.

They would start arriving in a month or so.

18

BOSTAN

I left the tavern soon after Xenos.

I used to enjoy the Day of Persephone. The celebrations. The way people got paired.

Not any more. When you're young you always think love is peachy and for ever. But once the years go by, you see it's short-lived. Like damsel flies.

Besides, no sense in setting up house when you've got to feud. Honour's more important than having someone in your bed.

The likes of Kokona and Dev don't agree with that, but they're lucky. They're able to live in their own world. The rest of us must do as the Law says. Though I'd bet many, like me, secretly curse honour and yearn to return to living.

I went straight to my den. Castor, as usual, scouting ahead of me, even though on the Day of Persephone everybody would be in the Citadel and no one beyond it.

My den's a complex of Hellenistic catacombs.

It's dug into the rock on the east coast. Not a soul goes there. The Germans mined the area during the World War. They set up Skender as a supply base for their troops in the Balkans. They feared partisans might use the catacombs as a hideout. They didn't know Skenderis are superstitious of ghosts and unquiet spirits. They'd never dare enter a burial site. Particularly one that's thousands of years old.

In any case, during the War, people, as ever, were busy with their feuds. They left the Germans to themselves. They knew they'd leave eventually. Invaders always do.

Nowadays the whole area – hectares and hectares of it – belongs to the Gospodins. It's said they're waiting for some country to buy the land and build a military base. But that's of no concern to me. The Gospodins are the best of absentee landlords. They've never been seen. And when they come – if they ever do – I'll be long dead.

After I became our family's feudist, I started pining for a place where I could be alone, where I could be myself.

I thought of these catacombs. I overcame my fear of spirits. Guided by Castor – he has an excellent nose for anything dangerous – I plotted a path through the minefields.

I've come to love this place. It keeps me sane.

It's safely underground.

The entrance is a narrow opening heavily covered with thistles. It can't be seen except from close by. Even so, I make sure it's well camouflaged.

The interior is huge.

Tunnels in every direction. All with burial chambers. I haven't explored the whole place. But I bet there's enough room for half of Skender. You can understand why the Germans thought it'd be ideal for partisans.

I go there whenever I can.

I've taken over three of the empty chambers.

I brought clothes, sewing things, make-up, a mirror, a battery-run radio, some boxes to sit on, plates and cooking utensils.

There's lots of brushwood around to make a fire.

I use one chamber to sit in and cook and the other to sleep in.

The third is the toilet. It never smells. I always bury my piss and shit. Like a cat.

I reached my den in no time. As I knew it would be, the countryside was deserted. I didn't waste time contorting myself to keep out of sight.

I slipped down.

I greeted the skeletons.

I've great respect for them. I haven't touched them or shifted them. Not even when I was making the place homely.

I've curtained off their chambers. That way we all have privacy.

I think they're happy with this arrangement. I've not been haunted. That means I haven't upset them.

At last time was my own. In a place where I didn't have to pretend. Where I could be myself.

I put the radio on.

Music from the mainland filled the chamber. Reception was fine. I'd extended the aerial all the way up to the entrance.

I undressed.

I stood before the mirror and gazed at my body. I took my time.

Still a desirable body. But a sad body. A hungry body. Worse, a body that was going to be hungry for ever. A body I'd had to sacrifice.

I sat down.

I applied my make-up. Lipstick, mascara, eye-shadow, blusher.

I put on pants and a brassiere.

I went to my dresses.

I chose the flimsiest. Since I got talking to Xenos, it had become my favourite.

I started dancing.

Western music – a foxtrot, now a classic, the announcer said.

The next song was a loud caterwauling from a new group.

I stopped dancing. I wanted a soothing melody. Not something wild and jangly.

I picked up my sewing. Again I didn't feel in the mood for it.

I lay down.

I started thinking about Xenos.

When I'm in my den I always get stirred up. Today I was even more aroused.

I knew why. To my relief, Xenos had rejected Lila. I'd felt jealous when she'd proposed to him. Strange to feel like that again.

I can't have feelings for Xenos. Whether he marries or not makes no difference to me.

Yet I felt happy. No woman would touch him. Not for a while, at least. Maybe not until next year's Day of Persephone.

I pulled up my dress.

I yanked down my pants.

I masturbated.

Relief brought sadness.

It always does.

I couldn't stop thinking about Xenos; that time I'd seen him with only his underpants on seemed branded on my eyes.

I decided I must avoid him.

My enemies – they were the people I had to think about. Nobody else.

Not much of a life. But that's how it is here.

19

DEV

Bostan is now a recluse. He still takes the Kristof women to the *lavanderi*. But he uses routes that bypass the water-mill.

His charges complain. The new routes are more difficult. Longer and rougher.

My respect for Bostan has increased. Osip's rejection of Lila made him see Osip is interested in him. So he's keeping away.

It's the right thing to do.

Life is tough for poor Bostan. Kokona and I agree.

Loneliness is not fair on anybody. For feudists, even less fair. Their days are always so few.

And Bostan is a good person. Bears his secret like a true man. Skender's madness is not his fault.

So he runs to the catacombs when he can? Good. Free there to do what he wants.

So he dresses as a woman. And puts on make-up. Why not – if it makes loneliness less painful?

Maybe ancient spirits haunt him? So what – he's brave.

Anyway, where else can he go?

The place is homelike.

I've sneaked in. Saw the furniture, the curtains, the dresses, everything. Really snug.

I don't snoop on people. But when, one day, I spotted Bostan going into the catacombs, dare-devilry took over. If he has the guts to go in there, I said, so have I.

And that's what I did. Followed his trail. When he wasn't around.

So Bostan doesn't know I know about his hideout.

The dresses ... Sad things. Old. In tatters. What pleasure can they give him?

As I say, Kokona and I understand him. We are sorry for him. We know what he is. We know his life is hard. That he stays sane is amazing.

So it's very decent he keeps away from Osip. Gives his feelings time to wane.

I will urge Osip to court Lila.

She's been very glum since the Day of Persephone. If Osip asked her to marry him, she'd drop Toma like an electric eel.

Of course that would be a perfect excuse for a feud. But Toma and Osip have no families. Ball-less Toma can't be a feudist. And Osip won't. So a stillborn feud.

Anyway, Bostan will be killed soon. That's how it goes.

We'll mourn him. As a good person. Fodder for the Law.

Then we'll forget him.

Osip will forget him too.

Especially if Lila's flesh is as tasty as it looks ...

20

TOMA

I have a wife! I am *a husband*!

The tavern is still buzzing after my nuptials. Jiri tells me that drunkards guffaw and call my betrothal a shot-gun wedding; others respond by asking: Lila's loins are unploughed; so why the shot-gun?

Let them laugh!

Do I care?

Not at all!

Because it is me walking around with Lila on my arm! Me – *me* – who has as his *wife* the most beautiful girl in Skender.

Imagine what bliss that is for a man whose balls have been slung into the ether, whereabouts unknown.

Actually, they're right about the shot-gun wedding.

It was – metaphorically speaking.

But *I* was the one who held the gun.

At my age, you have to move faster than Death. So, after Lila's proposal, I dictated that we marry straight away. I knew Lila wouldn't object or make silly girlish excuses like needing to prepare her dowry and so on.

No, Lila is wise in many ways. And ambitious.

Choosing me as her husband proves that.

Judiciously, she realized that marrying me immediately – instead of tomorrow when, she would have thought, I'd be pushing up poppies in the graveyard – was in her interest. It would secure for her the status bestowed by being my wife, a status superior even to that of a designated man.

What Lila doesn't know – nor does Death, for that matter – is that no matter how often the Black-draped Skeleton sharpens his scythe as he eyes me, I'll go on until I'm a hundred or more.

What better incentive for that than Lila in my bed?

I know that, sooner or later, Lila will have carnal desires.

I understand that.

After all, despite my condition, I still lust after flesh. Testicles might die, but desire doesn't. The castrato's torment is equal to that of Tantalus. The fruit is always at hand's reach, but never within grasp.

I remember Eleanora the Falcon saying genitals are disgusting. Particularly those of a woman because they smell.

Righteous woman as she was, she was mistaken there.

Much as I hate to sound like that old witch, Kokona, a woman's vagina is lovely both to look at and to touch; and it has the fragrance of myrrh – I've never forgotten that.

Whenever I ask dear Lila to undress for me, she does so without demur.

She even lets me touch her, but not her breasts and vagina; if I did that, she says, it would arouse her and we'd both end up frustrated.

I don't think I'd be frustrated.

On the other hand, vexation *is* agonizing. I know.

So I've accepted her condition that she'll share my bed only if I allow her to wear those European nightclothes called pyjamas.

As her husband and master, I could have forced her to sleep unclad. But to what end?

As long as I can see her naked whenever I want, as long as her face is the first thing I see in the morning, I'm happy enough.

There's another blessing marriage has given me. Maybe You have noticed. My mind doesn't wander as it used to. Or only occasionally.

Apart from her insistence on wearing pyjamas, Lila doesn't ask much.

She's very clean and keeps the Palladion as the temple it is.

Her cooking leaves much to be desired, particularly for me who receives sumptuous dishes every day from families who worship me.

But she's learning. I need only remark that this dish is not well braised or that dish is overcooked or that the soup lacks salt and she immediately prepares it again. Perfectly. I expect in a month or so she'll be the best cook in Skender.

That said, I still have to find a way to curb her desires.

For her sake, too.

She may not be seventeen yet but she's already as female as Eve. No denying that.

Otherwise how would she know that women get aroused when their breasts and vagina are touched?

Also, I suspect she has aberrant tendencies.

There are women like that.

Eleanora the Falcon told me she had two nieces who craved all manner of deviant intercourse.

I think that's why, on the Day of Persephone, Lila went for Anibal's son.

The way she drank his *rakiya* showed she was ready to be ravished in unnatural, barbarian ways.

And don't think I didn't hear her tell Anibal's son she'll have him, come what may, and still be a virgin.

Was that a challenge to me?

There You go again, sending the Doubter to stalk me!

I can tell You now, she won't havc Anibal's son!

I'll see to that.

She's mine and will remain mine!

Anibal's son has become my hidebehind. Just like his father.

He appears to be in front of me always, but really he's behind me where I can't see him. Manoeuvring to strike.

But he, too, will go the way of his father.

That's already decided.

All I need is to wait until I catch him.

As for Lila, I'm still the sublime schemer I was when I jousted with Anibal.

I have the perfect plan.

I've noticed that, since our marriage, Lila is elated by her status. She walks around as if she's the Virgin Mary.

And people now think she has ripened as an authority on the Law and ask her for elucidations.

So – and I'd wager my life on this – Lila would never jeopardize her present eminence to satisfy her aberrances. She'd rather die with her hymen intact than let herself be dethroned as Skender's queen.

Consequently, my course of action will be to bolster her status.

I'll indoctrinate her with the Law, My Law. The fact that people have already consulted her as if she were its expositor has kindled her interest in it. Hence she is ready for my induction.

I'll instruct her in my inimitable way. And, within months, I'll make her the prophetess of You, My Law, Toma's Law.

One last word: women have this predisposition for motherhood – or so it is said.

But Eleanora the Falcon was adamant that children are for the masses. Cherished by them as a blessing, but always a burden. And like Anton's brother, Marius – not to mention his followers – they more often than not take the wrong path.

I have the wisdom to know Eleanora the Falcon was right.

The only good thing about children is that when they grow up, boys become paladins and girls, wombs for a new generation of them.

Well, Lila will be spared the burden of motherhood.

And by the time I die, Lila, *my* Lila, will have shed all thoughts of carnality as disgusting – just as Eleanora the Falcon had – and will rule Skender, as I do, with You, My Law.

She might even go further. She might realize our aspiration to impose our order on the mainland.

Maybe even on the world.

That has been my aim always.

If I've failed all this time, it's only because a man without nuts is condemned to search for his seed in the wilderness.

Now I've found my seed: Lila!

21

KOKONA

Soon after the Day of Persephone I started having nightmares. Always a different one, but always on the same subject. One of the most disturbing went as follows:

I am a stork. Flying away from something or somewhere. As in the old tales, I'm carrying in my beak a baby wrapped up in a bundle.

Dev is flying alongside me. He has neither wings nor winged sandals. He is an African pygmy and wears only a loincloth. He is armed with the yataghan with which he killed the two men who had come after me all those years back.

Suddenly a female falcon with huge talons charges at me. Storks can kill predators, so I am confident I can defend myself. But if I use my beak I'll drop the infant I'm carrying.

I try to beat off the falcon with my wings. Dev lunges with his yataghan, but misses.

I spot a cluster of trees below. I dive and leave the bundle under a tree.

Then as the falcon returns to attack again, I spear her with my beak. At the same time Dev strikes her on the head and splits her skull. She drops from the sky, dead.

We go back to the trees to retrieve the baby. But he has gone.

We spot a woman on the horizon, running. She has the bundle clutched to her bosom. We can't see who she is. Nor can we chase her. My wings have been clipped. And Dev has lost the ability to fly.

As I said, I kept having many versions of the same nightmare. I am either some animal or a faceless person. Always fleeing and always carrying something very precious – a magical stone, a seraph, a curative herb and so on – and always being assaulted by murderous creatures. Dev, in various guises, always escorts me and sometimes gets killed trying to protect me.

As most Balkan peoples, we Skenderis know that dreams either foretell a blessing or give warning of an impending disaster. So we're adept at interpreting their meanings – and none better than me.

But I couldn't shed any light on these nightmares. I didn't even try. Their desolation urged me to ignore them. Like a Sybil who refuses to divine her own fate, I preferred not to know what they boded. Sometimes it's best not to look into the future.

Then suddenly it was summer. Glorious, like all our summers. Our impish winds allay the heat. It's that combination which makes our produce the best in the world.

It was also a purgatorial time because, for generations, our summers have been the season when the feuding becomes relentless. Throughout these months, men forsake home and family and roam the island either chasing or evading enemies. They sleep wherever they can find cover and live on whatever they can scavenge or hunt. Though the women and children put something in the pantry by tending to the husbandry, it's the undertaker who reaps the richest harvest.

By June there had already been over a dozen killings. Bostan, in particular, had disposed of two of his new enemies, Urs and Rustu.

The third of that trio, Viktor, by that time running for shelter whenever a cricket rubbed its forewings, had hired, with complete disregard for tradition, a couple of mercenaries – veterans of the Peoples' Wars – from the mainland. According to rumours from the tavern, where they've been lodging, the wages of these bashi-bazouks will dent Viktor's great wealth. Well, Victor is unlikely to cry over that: dented great wealth is still great wealth.

Given that the mercenaries were seasoned killers, Bostan, people wagered, would not live long enough to pick the grapes for this year's wine. This assumption became a conviction as Bostan's son, Zemun, Toma's blue-eyed *Morituri*, increased his target practice in order to be ready to take up the feuding after Bostan's death. Dev, who watched him shooting on a number of occasions, said the boy was almost as good as Bostan.

I had seen Bostan only once since the Day of Persephone. Early in May, he came to us, in the middle of the night, to borrow some books. He still took the Kristof women to the *lavanderi*, but never by way of Osip's water-mill. No one knew which route – or routes – he took, or when they'd set out. This time, the Kristof women, remembering how their gossip had prompted Viktor, Urs and Rustu to coerce Osip to inform on Bostan, were keeping their mouths tightly shut.

But islanders live on gossip and Skenderis are particularly prone to this pastime. All that is required is a remark – spoken innocently or spitefully or even out of sheer boredom – and within hours the word inflates from fable to assertion and then to folklore.

And folklore, as we know, whether based on reality or not, becomes incontestable.

Thus we kept hearing that Bostan had plunged into a murderous mood, that he would take offence at anything, and that, if we valued our lives, we should keep out of his way, certainly out of range of his gun.

And whenever Dev went to help with the work at the water-mill, he returned troubled; Osip, he said, much as he worked diligently, spent his free time drinking himself into a stupor or bird-watching on the cliffs. Dev is not one to exaggerate. Since the Day of Persephone, Osip had seldom smiled or laughed. The only activity that seemed to give him any pleasure was when he did spend some time with Dev, either working, swimming or playing backgammon. But even those moments were rare because, for people of the soil, like those two, summer means working night and day.

And so, in no time at all, gossip evolved into truth. Skenderis decided that Bostan's and Osip's moods, so mirroring each other's, had a common source. Theories abounded – ranging from an old and forgotten vendetta between the Kristofs and the Goras to a profane or unrequited love on the part of one or the other. The latter gained greater ground when it was noticed that Bostan's dog, Castor, would periodically turn up at the mill and gambol with Osip. Some people even suggested that Castor might be acting as a go-between, carrying messages.

I cared for Bostan, of course. But I could do nothing to save him from the feudist's fate. Whereas Osip had become family: I had to protect him. I was prepared, if need be and against tradition – indeed, against my instinct – to reveal Bostan's secret to Osip. If that would bring execration upon me, well, so be it.

So I asked Dev to take me to the water-mill.

We went in the afternoon of 22 June.

As the summer solstice is a time of festivity, I knew Osip wouldn't have any customers staying late.

We found him sitting in the shade of the carob tree that commanded the view onto the meadow. He and Dev had embellished the spot by laying a flagstone patio in front of the tree and furnishing it with a table and chairs. There was even a pallet where Osip slept on hot nights.

He was drinking *rakiya* from a large flask and, as usual, smoking. His eyes were closed – an inclination he'd always had but which latterly, Dev had told me, had become set: shutting out the world even, after each move, when they played backgammon.

When he heard our footsteps, Osip jumped up. 'Teacher! Dev! Welcome!' He ushered us to the chairs. 'I'll get some food.'

Dev put our basket on the table. 'We've brought a picnic.'

'Some wine then?'

Dev took out a couple of bottles and some glasses. 'We've brought that, too ...'

Osip sat down, shut his eyes and smiled. 'Treating me like a waif, eh?'

I didn't like his sarcasm. 'I hear self-pity.'

He opened his eyes and looked at me searchingly. 'No.'

'Is that what you'd like to be – suddenly? A waif?'

Dev had poured out the wine.

Osip became solemn. 'Maybe – once upon a time. But it's too late now.'

'Good. Have some wine. I want to talk to you.'

He nodded, took his glass, sipped and waited.

'Dev has offered to sit in the van in case you don't want to talk in front of him.'

He looked at me intently. 'This sounds more than a talk.'

'It is.'

'I see.' He shook his head. 'There's nothing I'd hide from Dev. Or from you.'

He brought out his cigarettes, lit them for us and then lit one for himself. He faced me and waited.

I felt unnerved by his scrutiny. I wished I didn't have to speak. 'I'm not one to wear gloves when pruning roses, Osip. So I'll come straight to the point. We're worried about you.'

He seemed surprised. 'Why?'

'Why do you think?'

'I don't know ...'

'You haven't been yourself – not since the Day of Persephone.'

He laughed, but it sounded forced. 'I'm fine ...'

Dev took Osip's hand. 'You're keeping yourself to yourself – even from us ...'

'I'm fine. Truly!'

I blurted out my question. 'Is it Bostan?'

That startled him. 'Bostan? What about him?'

'You haven't been seeing him.'

'He hasn't been coming by ...'

It was time to break the taboo. My voice came out in a whisper. 'I should tell you. Bostan has a secret ... He's ...'

'I know his secret.'

That took me aback. 'You do?'

He gave me a long look, then shut his eyes. 'Not difficult to figure it out.'

'How?'

He didn't open his eyes. He just shrugged. 'I was a doctor once.'

'A doctor? I should have known. I more or less guessed.'

'Long time ago.'

'Aren't you still? I've seen your medicine bags. In your trunk.

Both marked with a Red Cross. Why would you keep them if you had given up practising?'

'Souvenirs of a bygone identity.'

I sighed. 'I hear self-pity again.'

He didn't respond, just kept his eyes shut.

'Does Bostan know you know his secret?'

'No.'

'Were you tempted to tell him?'

'Yes.'

'Are you still?'

'Yes. But I won't. So don't worry about me.'

We sat a while, not knowing what else to say. We sipped our wine and ate some cheese and olives. Osip's eyes remained closed. He was trying to block us out. That made me angry.

I took another of his cigarettes. 'You once mentioned a young woman – Sofi ...'

He stiffened. 'What about her?'

'Tell us about her ...'

'There's nothing to tell.'

'There must be – if she's still haunting you ...'

'That's because I failed her.'

'How?'

'Teacher, you know better than me. People fail people. All the time. And very often they fail those most important to them. How is immaterial.'

My concern propelled me. 'You deserted her?'

He'd kept his eyes shut. Now he opened them in protest. 'No!'

'Of course not. You're not one to desert.'

He closed his eyes again. 'Oh, I am ...'

'I can see you deserting armies. But not people ...'

He shrugged, keeping his eyes shut.

'So how did you fail her?'

'I couldn't protect her. I should have! She was killed – in front of me. I couldn't protect her.'

Dev and I exchanged looks. We knew there's no greater anguish than the failure to protect. Which is why being a mother or a lover is more of a curse than a blessing.

Tears started running down his cheeks. 'Even so ... I haven't betrayed her. Not altogether. It took me a while, but finally I did what she told me to do.'

'What was that?'

'To free myself from men's delirium. To find a clement world. She assured me I'd find it one day. That's what I'm trying to do ...'

'Your grotto?'

'And what that grotto means.'

'What does it mean to you?'

He opened his eyes. 'What you and Dev have ... And what you and Dev believe in ...'

Dev and I looked at each other, moved by the simplicity – and the sincerity – of his words.

'Anything else you want to know, Teacher?'

I wiped his tears with my sleeve. 'Plenty. All the details. But this is enough for today.'

His eyes closed again.

After a while, Dev and I, too, shut our eyes. We knew this was a silence like communion and should not be disturbed.

Later, as dusk began to fall, we opened our eyes. Osip had gone. We spotted him in the meadow, pacing slowly, his solitude an inescapable cage which he had to carry everywhere.

Dev and I left quietly.

22

OSIP

Balmy May night. Soft breeze like a mother stroking her son's brow.

People harvesting roses for jam and attar.

Inebriating fragrance.

Lanterns mimic the stars. Bawdy ballads throb lustily.

When the wagons overflow with petals, the people stop for a round of bread and rakiya.

Suddenly the stench of scorched earth.

Napalm devours plant, soil and sky.

Men hacked to pieces.

Women shot through their vaginas.

Wagons collapse under the weight of corpses.

I'm too late.

Children huddle by the armoured carriers.

One is blind, but she is a young woman, not a child. Spared because she looks small.

The toddlers cry and ask for their mothers.

Their brothers and sisters, barely stifling their own tears, try to keep them quiet.

The blind girl also tries, muttering senseless words of comfort.

They ignore her. They assume she can't see the devastation that has descended upon them.

But she can. Blind though she is, she sees in many ways. I'll discover this later.

She can even see the future.

She foresaw this carnage. She tried to warn family, friends, anybody. Nobody believed her. They thought she was crazy. But that's Peoples' Wars. The sane are called crazy; and the crazy, sane.

The previous year, wanting to shut her eyes to the brutality around her, she blinded herself. It did not help. She began seeing from deep inside her head. She couldn't dim her sight to that.

I've arrived too late.

I, Osip Gora, erstwhile medical officer, have been impressed by a decimated army to join the fighting rather than save lives.

Now the generals are with the Mediators, signing the ceasefire. That makes me, a major, temporarily the most senior commander in this sector.

Having received news that Dušan intends to greet the impending ceasefire with a flourish of ethnic cleansing, I've chased after him.

But it's too late.

It's always too late in wars.

Dušan is surveying the children with excitement. In ethnic cleansing, children are like fish-heads, good only as animal feed. He keeps fondling his flame-thrower as if he is masturbating.

Dušan is not pleased to see me. 'What brings you here?'

I finish my cigarette in one drag. 'To stop you.'

He grins. 'Too late ...'

I'm not much older than Dušan. But I look and feel ancient. According to a nurse when I was still running a field hospital, I'm like a statue in a museum: eyes empty of pupils; skin like unpolished marble.

That's what happens when a mother gets rid of her young one because she wants to be a man and a killer.

I light another cigarette. 'Let the children go, Dušan.'

'You being funny?! No prisoners, no witnesses – that's our rule!'

'The war is over.'

'This war will never be over. We'll have a brief ceasefire – then back to business.'

'They're children!'

'There are no children in the Balkans, Osip. There's only hate. And hate grows up between two blinks of an eye, picks up guns and starts a new war. Best to torch them.'

Dušan loves flame-throwers. We've lost count of the villages and valleys he has set on fire.

'Let them go!'

'Come on, Osip!'

'That's an order!'

Dušan squares up to me. He is much the bigger man. Probably much stronger, too.

But I stare him down. I don't care whether I live or die. That's what intimidates Dušan. He can't understand people like me; we unnerve him. He's also the sort who considers his own life very precious. But that's typical of mass murderers.

'This is crazy, Osip! Against our principles ...'

'Muster your unit! Return to base!'

'Why should I take orders from you? You're only a medic!'

'Formerly a medic. Right now, I'm the commanding officer of this sector.'

'I'd be within my rights to disobey ...'

Casually, I point my pistol at him. 'Try.'

Unlike Dušan and the other men who harness themselves with sub-machine guns, automatics, grenades, bayonets, cartridge belts and, not least, flame-throwers, I carry only a pistol. But I've never hesitated to use it.

'You're bluffing!'

There've been many who thought doctors wouldn't have the spunk to shoot, let alone kill. I proved them wrong. 'Get going!'

Dušan hesitates, then starts walking away.

He stops and turns. 'What about you? Aren't you coming back to base?'

'I'll make my own way.'

Dušan grins and points at the children. 'After fucking their guts out, eh?'

He pulls the blind girl forward. 'This one's not as young as she looks. I know the family. Once upon a time, her father and I were neighbours. Wouldn't mind shafting her myself! Make her day ... and mine!'

'She stays with the kids.'

Dušan, shaking with anger, snarls. 'Not thinking of decamping, are you, Osip?'

'Decamping?'

'Once they sign the ceasefire, we'll be wanted men. War crimes and all that. Not even medics will be safe.'

'I'm not one to hide.'

'You might have to! Better stick with us!'

'Get going!'

Dušan gathers his men.

As they scramble into their armoured cars, some ask why they're not carbonizing the children.

Dušan barks at them to shut up.

I wait until the vehicles disappear into the night.

Then I address the children. 'Go! Knock on doors! There are still some good people about. They'll take you in.'

The children run off, some with hope; others, on wings of despair.

I take the blind girl's hand. 'You come with me.'

She starts trembling. 'Why?'

'You'll get lost. I'll hand you over to the Mediators. What's your name?'

'Sofi.'

'You'll be all right, Sofi. I promise you.'

I settle her in my jeep.

I drive towards the Mediators' lines.

The dawn spreads herself gloriously, but I am unmoved. How can there be beauty when there is no hope?

When daylight comes, we pause by a stream.

I share my ration with Sofi.

She wolfs it down.

We lie down to rest.

The sun warms us.

Then we hear shooting in the distance.

I leap up.

Sofi grabs my hand. 'Is it the children?'

I yank her up and drag her to the river.

I push her in. 'Stay there. Don't move. It's thick with bulrushes. No one will see you.'

The cold water makes her gasp. 'Where are you going ...?'

'I'll be back. If I don't, wait until nightfall. Then save yourself ...'

The shooting is still going on.

I jump into the jeep and drive towards it ...

I opened my eyes. I'd drunk too much. Memories were becoming unbearable.

I was sitting under the carob tree.

Night had fallen.

The full moon covered the earth in silver.

The mill looked like an enchanted abode.

If only there was another soul living in it ...

I still heard shooting.

That bothered me. Normally, I'd hear shooting whenever my thoughts went back to Sofi – usually several times a day. But once I had stopped remembering, I'd only hear a brief, melodious susurration which, I'd come to believe, was my mind trying to soothe me.

We all need respite from memories.

Definitely, I had drunk too much.

The shooting stopped. There had been only a few shots.

It hadn't been a memory. Those were real shots.

Hunters in the woods, I assumed. Full moon is a good time for nocturnal hunting; no need for lanterns to spot rabbits and woodpigeons.

I decided to sleep in the open. I laid out my pallet.

But the sound of the shooting had disconcerted me. I felt tense. And the gut-feeling that warned me something was wrong kept seething. I thought of going in and picking up my gun. Then I decided it was the drink affecting me. What could be wrong on this idyllic night?

I poured what I promised myself would be the last drink of the day, lit another cigarette and wandered towards the meadow.

I paused by the footpath which Bostan and the Kristof women used to take to go to the *lavanderi*.

I missed Bostan.

I gulped down my drink to stop thinking about him. Or, at the very least, to quieten down the apprehension that still gnawed at me.

Just then Castor hurtled out of the woods. Seeing me, he started barking furiously.

When he reached me, he jumped all over me and kept turning towards the woods.

I grabbed hold of him. His coat was sticky with blood. I ran my hands over his body. He wasn't wounded.

'Is it Bostan? Hurt?'

Now barking, now whining, he grabbed my trouser leg and tried to pull me towards the woods.

I sobered up instantly. 'I'm coming!'

I tore into the mill, grabbed my bag and backpack from my trunk and picked up my pistol and my torch.

I ran back to Castor. 'Go, boy, go!'

Castor sprinted towards the woods.

I followed him, running as fast as I could.

We reached one of the tracks.

Bostan was sprawled in a pool of blood.

I scurried over to him.

He was still alive, but his pulse was weak. He'd lost a lot of blood.

I heard a rustle behind me. I spun round, ready to fire.

A woman's voice screeched. 'Please, don't shoot!'

I shouted. 'Come forward then, whoever you are!'

Hesitantly, Iona, one of the Kristof women, edged out from behind the trees.

Relieved, I opened my bag and started examining Bostan.

Iona crept towards me. 'Is he dead?'

'Near enough.'

The other Kristof women emerged, weeping and wailing.

Bostan had been shot five times. One bullet had just missed the heart. 'Right. Who is the fastest among you?'

A young woman, Aisha, came forward. 'Me.'

'Run to Dev. Tell him to get here as fast as he can!'

Aisha bolted away.

I turned to the others. 'The rest of you! Get some water! Clean – from the stream. Bring me some sheets! Bostan should have some *rakiya* in his bag. Bring that, too!'

As I started tearing off Bostan's blood-soaked shirt, the women shrieked.

Iona grabbed my arm. 'You mustn't!'

'What?'

'You mustn't undress him!'

I had exposed two full breasts. I pushed Iona away. 'I'm a doctor!'

I tore off Bostan's trousers, this time exposing her vagina.

The women's clamour became hysterical.

Iona shut her eyes. 'He wouldn't want to be seen like this. Not naked. He'd rather die!'

I shouted at all of them. 'He'll die if you don't get what I need! Go on! Water! Sheets. And *rakiya*. Move! Quick as you can! Go! Go!'

The women, still crying, scudded away.

'Castor, keep your eyes open!'

Castor started prowling, fully alert.

I began a closer examination of Bostan's wounds. The bullet that had missed the heart had left the body cleanly at the back. One bullet, having smashed the right shoulder, was still lodged there. Another was embedded in one of her ribs. The other two, in the arm and thigh, had passed through without causing much damage.

Even covered in blood, Bostan was a striking woman. Her vagina, hidden by thick pubic hair, reminded me of a photograph of a painting I once saw of a robust woman's genitals. It said that everything in the world originated in the loins of the female.

The Kristof women came rushing back, bringing buckets of water and their sheets.

I started swabbing Bostan's wounds, for once thankful that I had not relinquished my medical bag and surgical backpack when I had thrown away the rest of my army stuff.

Dev and Kokona arrived within the hour in their van. Only Dev could have negotiated the tracks in so short a time.

By then I had administered some morphine, cleaned and dressed Bostan's wounds, and taken out the two bullets lodged in her body. When I'd run out of my phials of antiseptics, I had used *rakiya*. Fortunately, as the Kristofs' designated man, Bostan always carried several bottles.

I had also given her a blood transfusion. I had the necessary reagents to test her group in my surgical backpack. That proved to be AB, which made her a universal receiver, able to take blood from any other grouping. Picking two of the Kristof women, I had transfused about two and a half litres of blood from them.

I ruled out transporting Bostan in Dev's van. She was barely alive and a shaky drive over the rough terrain would kill her. She had to be carried by stretcher.

I told the Kristof women to cut down some hardy branches, tie them together with sheets and so make a crude litter. A couple of blankets served as a palliasse.

All this proved possible because of the full moon. In that we had been very lucky. Though I had had the use of a number of torches – mine and the Kristof women's – their batteries had soon begun to run low and I could switch them on only for the more intricate procedures.

The Kristof women volunteered to take turns to carry the stretcher. I thanked them, but refused. Dev and I would do that.

Keeping a litter steady so that the condition of the casualty does not deteriorate needs muscles able to cope with strain for a good length of time. The slightest jolt, particularly in cases where bone grates against bone, can be so traumatic for the severely wounded that they can die of shock. Dev and I, being workers of the land, had the necessary strength.

We carried Bostan to the mill.

I have no recollection of that trek. I was like an automaton, functioning on reflexes. Bostan could well have been one of the many injured soldiers I'd carried during the Peoples' Wars.

However, I do remember looking at the moon once and begging it to fend off rain. When it rains, you need four stretcher-bearers. If there are only two, one of them might slip or get sucked into the mud, killing not only his charge, but also endangering himself and his fellow-bearer.

At the mill, we settled Bostan on my bed.

The Kristof women, still weeping, but not as agitated as before, related what had happened.

Viktor and his two mercenaries had ambushed them. Though Castor had sniffed them out, they had contrived to fool him. One of the men, acting as a decoy, had sprinkled the area with a strong stench. When Castor had gone after him, Viktor and the other man had appeared and while the latter had distracted Bostan by challenging him, Viktor had shot Bostan. On Viktor's instructions, the Kristof women, who had run for cover behind the trees, hadn't been attacked. Hearing the shots, Castor had chased back. By then, Viktor and his men had left. Seeing Bostan prostrate, Castor had whined and licked her. Then suddenly he had bolted away. To find me.

As they talked, I planned ahead.

I told the Kristof women to go home. I drummed into their heads that they should say nothing more than that Bostan had been shot by Viktor and that they didn't know whether he was alive or dead because they'd run for their lives, abandoning their washing. That account would give us a couple of days' respite while the islanders searched for Bostan's corpse and, having failed to find it, start wondering what had happened to him.

Since Skender's isolation deprived it of an adequate range of pharmaceutical products, I would have to treat Bostan with whatever I could find. Fortunately, over the centuries, the islanders had developed some effective home remedies and these, I hoped, would complement whatever basic medication was available. So I gave Dev a list of drugs and medicinal herbs, including opium, and instructed him to get as many of them as possible, whatever the cost.

Dev left to pick up his van, promising to bring the stuff by morning.

Then I crouched by Bostan's bed to monitor her.

Castor stood guard on the stone traverse by the mill's entrance.

Kokona came and squatted next to me.

I had forgotten about her.

She took my hand.

But I couldn't respond. I was still outside my skin.

Three hours later I gave Bostan another transfusion, using Kokona's blood.

As she lay down to rest, Kokona looked at me in that marvellous way in which she conveys her love. 'Will he – she – live?'

By then, I had somehow come down to earth. 'Her body wants to live. That can make all the difference.'

'And you want her to live ...'

'Yes ...'

'Desperately?'

'Yes.'

'Then she will. Your wills fighting together – that's a powerful life-force.'

At dawn, Bostan needed another transfusion. This time I gave her my blood.

After that, Kokona and I sat down, her hand in mine.

I kissed her hand, then put it against my cheek. 'You know, Teacher, when I found Bostan and saw how badly she was hit, it was as if I had seen it all before. I even thought, for a moment, I was treating Sofi. Bostan, I'd like to believe, has the same faith in a future as Sofi did. As if death – and all its terrors – were unreal. I couldn't save Sofi. But I'll save Bostan. Even if I have to give her all my blood.'

Kokona smiled, but looked troubled. 'And then what?'

'Then? It will be up to Bostan ...'

'Up to you, too.'

'She may not want me.'

'You don't really believe that?'

'I don't dare believe she might.'

'That aside, you'll madden many people. The Kristofs, for a start ...'

'No choice, is there?'

'One choice: keep faith in life.'

23

BOSTAN

I hovered above my body.

Trees breathed like bellows.

The air spun.

My blood gushed.

I watched, spellbound.

Amazing to have so much blood.

When Toma taught me to drink and shoot like a man, he always spoke about blood. We're born with bad blood, he said. We can cleanse it only with honour. We spill our blood to make it pure. We feud to give life to our souls. We honour Honour.

He was wrong!

Look at my blood! It's good blood! Beautiful. Pure. Like a spring of fresh water in the middle of the sea.

That's how we're born! With beautiful blood!

But we let bad people, mad people, heartless, brainless people make it dirty.

I've never looked at blood properly before. Never up close. Always killed with one shot to the head. Never watched it spurt.

Never looked at my own blood either. During my monthlies I wash my rags the way I used to wash Zemun's nappies. Mindlessly.

Blood is beautiful.

Not strong as steel or stone, as Toma says.

It's soft, tender, aglow like dawn, precious like breath. It's life. Spilling it is akin to turning day into endless night.

Its mission is not to clean – neither the soul, nor the earth, nor honour. It just gives life.

In one of Kokona's books, I read that people drink their enemy's blood to possess their strength. But that doesn't make them strong. Only pushes them to their own deaths.

I read other things.

Men breaking vessels that contain God's breath. All to worship honour. That's how souls disappear.

And one day, there'll be no world. Only dust.

Castor was licking me all over. Frantic, whimpering. Trying to revive me. Faithful soul!

Do I want to be revived?

A voice answers. 'You can return to life. Or enter the after-life. It's up to you.'

I turn towards the voice.

Valmir, my dead husband, sparkles in the air.

A string of dead Kristofs follow him.

Most have been killed in feuds. Their wounds still visible. Like age-rings in felled trees.

They are smiling. They look at peace.

Some beckon me. 'Come. Stay. It's very pleasant here. No feuds. No killings. Only harmony. You'll be happy.'

Happy! A word from Kokona's books. I never really understood its meaning, but I loved its sound.

'Can't I be happy down there?'

Valmir shakes his head. 'Have you ever?'

'I didn't get the chance. All the feuding ...'

'Feuding has nothing to do with it. No happiness down there. Not at any time.'

'I'm too young to die.'

The dead Kristofs murmur their disappointment.

Valmir takes my hand. 'Age has nothing to do with it either. You'll like it here.'

I look at Castor. He is still trying to lick me into life. 'Let me think ...'

Valmir sighs and nods.

I swoop down to Castor, whisper in his ear. 'I need help. Get Xenos.'

Castor pricks up his ears. He barks and darts off.

Was I shocked that I had asked for Xenos? Yes. But I felt glad I had.

Kokona says the body or the mind or whatever's inside us always knows what's best.

I turned to Valmir to explain; he had vanished.

So had all the dead Kristofs.

When Xenos arrived, I was very weak. I could barely breathe. But the moment he started examining me, I felt hopeful.

I stayed outside my body and watched him.

Strange, looking at a man from high above. The shoulders tell you what he's like. Xenos' were big. Obviously. He had a big heart. Big hearts need big frames.

When he started treating my wounds, his girth turned into a light beam. He darted over my body like a sun-ray through leaves. And my pains became bearable.

And when he tore off my clothes, peace cradled me. Iona was right. I'd rather die than have men see me unclad. But Xenos was not any man. I wanted him to see me naked.

For a long time, I've wanted him to see me as I am. A woman with a good body. A woman in need of a good man. A woman made for him.

My body pleased him, I could see that. That made me feel good. Maybe he, too, wanted to see me nude. He had realized I was a woman. I had sensed that long ago. Maybe realized it when we first met. The way he had looked at my chest. Pretended my breasts were a bullet-proof vest.

A bullet-proof vest in Skender, what next?!

Something else made me feel happy as I lay there naked. I didn't have to live unnaturally any more. I didn't have to pretend to be a man.

When I feud again, I'll feud as I am. As a woman. Not as a designated man.

I'll reclaim the name I was born with: Bostana.

It may be good to be a man – privileges, power, and the rest – but I prefer being a woman. Because that's what I am.

Xenos said he was a doctor. Imagine a doctor giving up the mainland to return to Skender?

He certainly knows how to treat wounds. He soothed my body very quickly. By the time they put me on the stretcher, my limbs were sweetly numb. And I was no longer in pain.

They put me onto Xenos' bed. His smell was on the sheets.

I breathed it deeply and went back into my body.

Kokona and Xenos were by my side.

They talked in whispers.

I tried to listen but I was too drugged.

I heard Xenos mention someone called Sofi. I felt jealous. Then I fell asleep.

24

DEV

On the way back, I have a puncture. Takes a while to fix. Difficult to hold the jack stable on rough ground.

I reach the Citadel after daybreak.

News of Bostan's death is roaring. Almost everybody's in the Plaza.

Four groups.

One with the Kristofs. Friends and sympathizers. Grieving.

Another around Viktor Mikhail. He is triumphant. Receives congratulations as if he has discovered the secret of youth. His wife, Yilka, tries to look cheerful, but I can tell she's gloomy. She knows someone else will rise to feud with her husband. Viktor's mercenaries, Sorin and Gjon, grinning and grinning. Bloodsuckers.

Third group around Toma, Lila and the *Morituri*. Toma's very happy. He gyrates: honour blessed again with blood. His purple cloak balloons. He points at the Palladion: Bostan will have a special plaque there.

Fourth group is Marius and friends. They're not happy Bostan's dead. They protest: they never asked for revenge for Anton. Enough feuding, they shout. Enough killing. Abolish the Law!

I slither through looking for Basil, the apothecary.

No one notices me. Freaks blend with the background. Like shrubbery. People see but don't see.

The Kristof women have a crowd round them. They give the story of the ambush the way Osip told them. When Bostan was shot, they ran.

Now another group forms. Bostan's son, Zemun, moves away from the *Morituri*. Gathers the Kristof men to bring back Bostan's body.

The undertaker, Kostandin, is ready with his hearse.

Zemun's telling the Kristof men he's not a youth any more, he must be their next feudist. He's ready to start – according to the Law – immediately after Bostan's burial. And he wants the funeral without delay.

Many admire his impatience.

Toma hears him. He and Lila go over to him. Toma gives his support. He's very proud of the boy.

Lila repeats what Toma says. As a good wife must.

Zemun puffs up like a frog. Eyes always on Lila. Showing off. He declares he wants not only to avenge Bostan, but also to be the Kristofs' headman. He's clever. The Kristofs have four new men, husbands picked by four widows on the Day of Persephone. They're older than Zemun. They can be headman and feudists ahead of Zemun. And Zemun wants to prevent that.

I glide by Viktor and the mercenaries. They're telling about their part in the killing.

Sorin, an intelligence officer in the Peoples' Wars, boasts how he kept Bostan under surveillance round the clock. Last night he spotted him sending a Kristof woman to gather the others for the *lavanderi*. He followed. As the other women assembled, he dropped a tiny transmitter device – indispensable in the intelligence business– in their washing. Then he called Viktor and Gjon. They followed the transmitter's signal and set up the ambush.

Gjon boasts, too. He's also a veteran of the Peoples' Wars. He explains how he fooled Bostan's dog with a scent no four-legged animal can resist. A dirty trick of shock troops. He knows many other tricks. That's how they ethnically cleansed province after province.

I spot Basil. Standing by a street lamp, keeping clear of factions.

I sidle up to him. 'Basil, I need things.'

He shows immediate concern. 'Who's sick? You or Kokona?'

I like Basil very much. He's a freak like me. An albino. 'Half-baked', people call him. 'Let's get away from here.'

Basil points. 'Into the shop.'

We slip away. Basil walks like a ghost. I walk below the line of vision. Both unseen.

I love Basil's shop. An Aladdin's cave. Packed to the ceiling. Huge cupboards and cabinets. Jars and flasks of all sizes. Strange smells from lotions, herbs, spirits, solutions, unguents. It makes my head spin.

Little space to move, but Basil flits about like a bee in a lavender field.

He sits me down. Brings glasses and *rakiya*. 'What's up, Dev?'

Besides Kokona, Osip and Bostan, Basil is the only other person who calls me Dev.

I give him Osip's list. 'All these. As much as you can get.'

Basil puts on his glasses. Studies the items. Looks up. 'Some are for gunshot wounds ...'

I pretend surprise. 'Oh?'

He serves me *rakiya*. 'For Bostan, is it? Did he survive?'

'For Kokona.'

'She's looking after Bostan?'

'Nothing to do with him. She asked me to get these ...'

'Dev, we've known each other a long time ...'

I nod. I hate lying. 'Yes.'

'Way back to when you killed those two men, then got sick ... You can trust me.'

This shocks me. 'How do you know about the men?'

'When Kokona was looking after you, I helped out. Remember? You were delirious for days. Kept shouting how you had killed them ...'

'Kokona knows, too?'

'Of course. But I knew even before that. When I saw the men's wounds. Practically disembowelled. The sort you inflict with a yataghan. Who on this island has a yataghan?'

'You never told anybody?'

'Not my nature.'

I feel ashamed at not trusting him. 'What can I say?'

He waves his hand. 'Now these medicines ... For Bostan, right?'

'Yes.'

'So he's still alive. Thank God.'

'Only just. Lost a lot of blood.'

'I can make up most of these. The antibiotics are a problem. I have some, but they're not the best. I'll order stronger ones. Still, what I can give you might keep him going ...'

'You're an angel.'

Basil leaves his *rakiya* untouched. Rises. 'It'll take some time. Then I'll go with you and help.'

'No. Don't come for a few days. If you leave the Citadel, people will start to wonder ...'

'To administer some of these drugs you need someone who knows what he's doing. You and Kokona – all heart that you are – wouldn't know how ...'

'That's no problem. Osip's in charge.'

'Xenos? How come?'

'He found Bostan. Called us. He's a doctor.'

'A doctor? You're fibbing.'

'I don't fib. You know that.'

'Where's Bostan now?'

'At the water-mill.'

Basil shakes his head. 'Xenos a doctor? Imagine that.'

I smile proudly. 'A very good one.'

'All right, Dev. Drink to your heart's content. I'll be as quick as I can.'

I don't drink. I want to be sober.

I watch Basil prepare the medicines.

He works like me. Only better. Puts his soul into it. He's precise. Has steady hands. Never rushes measurements. Never grinds in a hurry. Yet he's brisk. I think of Stefan and Anton. Playing their lutes. Like water in the river, flowing gently. But faster than the eye can see.

I hope I work the soil as well. Kokona says I do. She says watching someone achieve something fine – anything – is witnessing beauty. A creation. We stand back and say: that's good.

Hours later, Basil hands me a bagful. 'That's all I can provide at the moment. It'll do for now. I'll radio an order for the antibiotics straight away – they should come on the next ferry. The potions will be ready tomorrow. I need some herbs. It'll take me a while to collect them.'

I hand him the gold coin Osip had given me for him. 'You're a good man, Basil.'

He gives the coin back. 'No need.'

I leave the coin on the table. 'Osip's money. He insists!'

Basil is not happy, but accepts. He leads me to the back door. 'Slip out from here. You won't be seen.'

I nod.

Before I go, he holds my arm. 'Xenos must know then.'

'What?'

'Bostan's a woman.'

'Yes.'

'What do you think will happen?'

'Don't know.'

'If she survives, they'll end up wanting each other.'

'Yes.'

'That'll cause mayhem. They'll need friends.'

'They have friends. Kokona and me.'

'Me, too – for what it's worth.'

I hug him. 'You make the world nice, Basil.'

I cross the Plaza.

The undertaker, Kostandin, is back from the woods.

He's telling the people that Zemun and the Kristofs can't find Bostan's body. They've found only patches of dry blood and crushed leaves. They're still searching. In case Bostan crawled away somewhere.

I jump into the van and speed back to the water-mill.

25

TOMA

I'm very proud of Bostan.

As a paladin, he lasted a long time – second only to the accursed Anibal. And, as spiteful Fate would have it, it took more than one man to kill him – just as it did with Anibal.

That fluke aside, Bostan has been the designated man of my prophethood – even more so than Eleanora the Falcon. Not just prodigious with guns, but also a person loyal to her community. She was not a great adherent of the Law, just wanted to live a quiet life, look after her smallholding and bring up her son. But, in order to help out the Kristofs, she reluctantly agreed to become their designated man. Once converted, and having diligently trained with me, he stuck to his task assiduously.

Eleanora wasn't very good with guns – that's why she didn't last long – but, unlike Bostan, she did not hesitate to become a designated man. She was zealous about the Law, held honour above everything else and took up arms eagerly.

As I promised the people, I'll put a plaque for Bostan here in the Palladion. I'll also make sure his picture hangs in the tavern alongside the great feudists of the past.

Lila asked me whether I was sorry he had died. Well, of course I was. Like all good leaders, I feel that, in a symbolic way, any paladin's death is my death.

But that's a passing sentiment – belongs to that alien concept, conscience. I drive it out as easily as I drive out the Doubter when he starts haranguing me. Now neither conscience nor the Doubter has features any more.

In the past, both had Anibal's face.

Their virtual dissolution proves how right I have been in embracing the Law. Our nobility resides in our readiness to honour Honour. And wherever we spill our blood, there we establish order in this orderless world.

Lila is delighted by Bostan's death.

Good riddance, she said. Bostan was a freak; leched after Xenos. That's why, she said, he used to take the Kristof women to the *lavanderi* near the water-mill instead of going to any one of the others strewn around the island.

All told, Lila pronounced, Bostan was a pervert who shamed Skender's moral rectitude.

Was I surprised by her reaction?

Well, it certainly brought back my concern that Lila might have aberrant tendencies. How could a girl, still a virgin, know about lechery, perversion and morals?

So I wondered. Was it her jealousy speaking? Did she attribute vices to Bostan because Anibal's son desired Bostan instead of her?

But would one expect a young girl to imagine the nature or depth of the mutual attraction between Bostan and Anibal's son?

No! Not unless she dreams up indecent visions about the ways of the flesh.

Which I think she does. Don't ask me how.

Women: dangerous enigmas – even when young.

So Anibal's son remains my hidebehind.

Still, my time will come and I'll deal with him.

But it looks as if another hidebehind might enter the arena.

My first thought when Lila expressed pleasure at Bostan's death was that she was pleased because Bostan's son, Zemun, had seized the privilege of being the next Kristof feudist.

When, before our marriage, she used to train with my paladins, Lila admired Zemun; found his fervour and marksmanship inspirational.

And, of course, at the time, Zemun, too, was very smitten with Lila. We all knew that.

Does she still see Zemun as her inspiration?

And does Zemun still hanker after Lila? Was his bravura in the Plaza aimed at impressing her?

Well, one day – soon, in all probability – Zemun will go the way of all paladins.

Even so, I'd better keep an eye on him. Lila and he are about the same age. Who can predict what might happen when lechery and perversion are in the air?

But now to a more pressing matter.

What I found unacceptable in Bostan's death was the fact that Viktor had hired outsiders. I look upon that as contaminating the Law.

There are numerous provisions in the Law for alliances. But they are meant for internal use, for Skender only. They provide sanctions for weakened families to adjust the odds against them. Hiring outsiders lies outside the Law.

An unwritten law, perhaps, but one that, until now, had never been transgressed.

I did command Viktor to send his mercenaries immediately back to the mainland.

But he challenged me.

Inviting me to go through the articles of the Law with him, he made me concede that there were no specific stipulations debarring outsiders.

So I was thwarted. Humiliated. By Viktor, of all people!

As if to bedevil me, he had discovered, as Anibal used to in his days, an eyelet in the Law.

Well, we all know about Viktor.

Another person of bad blood trying to pass himself off as good.

Full of bluster when surrounded with allies. But, beneath his pelt, a coward through and through.

Terrified of dying. Ever since Bostan killed his allies, Urs and Rustu, he has kept out of Bostan's way, often locking himself up in his home.

Everybody knows he'd much rather live a life without responsibilities, waste away his years eating, drinking and enjoying his young wife. Yes, he, too, has a young wife, Yilka. She's only a few years older than Lila and pretty enough, but with lots of flesh – very much to his taste.

I'm sure, were it not that as a rich patrician, he'd lose all respect if he challenged the Law, he'd worm himself out of it – like that imbecilic Marius.

More to the point, if he did that, he would reveal himself to the Gospodins as the lightweight he is.

Come to think of it, he has probably already roused their contempt. I know for a fact that he hired the two mercenaries on the

Gospodins' recommendation. Asking for thugs from your employers is hardly an attestation of strength.

I keep telling myself I'll never be delivered from the Law's convolutions until I've revised it in *my own* image!

So no hesitation now. It's time to update the Law.

Over the years – in fact, since my confrontations with Anibal – I've been annotating the Scroll I have at hand – yes, the very one Anibal furtively copied. That was wise work. Now I have to collate those commentaries properly – like the Ten Commandments, or, in *my* case, the Hundred Commandments.

When Lila becomes fully proficient we will restructure the Law, add amendments to any clause that might provoke a disputation.

That shouldn't take too long.

And when we finish it, we'll call it Toma's Law!

That would be apt.

And, when I pass away, many years hence, Lila will rule Skender with Toma's Law!

Is there a better way to achieve immortality?

You might think my mind is wandering again.

Not at all!

I haven't told You this before, but, for some time now, I've been forging a power base.

That's one reason why I didn't get down to rewriting the Law.

Are You asking me why I need a power base?

You know very well why.

Every prophet needs a power base. You, the Law, My Law, needs it most.

So I've been active behind the scenes.

I've harnessed the Gospodins; made them my devotees.

While they poured lucrative commissions into Viktor's coffers, I convinced them that the real power here is *Me*, not that avaricious non-entity!

How did I do it?

As You know, we don't have telephones any more. But a few of us – me, Viktor, the apothecary and some others – have radios.

So I duped Viktor, flattered him, inflated his drooping ego and got him to boast about how he communicates with the Gospodins.

Once I had their coordinates, I approached them.

The Gospodins may be faceless, unnamed and living who knows where, but they're abreast of much of what goes on on this island.

And, of course, they had heard of me and knew of my sublime status.

And they rushed to eat out of my hands.

They've even sent me a new ultra-modern radio to replace my old one. As they're always on the move I can now keep in touch with them wherever they happen to be.

And when they find a great power who wants this island for a base, it will be *Me* they'll appoint as Skender's plenipotentiary.

So what's ahead?

Suddenly, there's more than enough.

There's still Anibal's son.

There might be Zemun.

When they both become food for maggots, I should have no more concerns about Lila.

Of lesser importance, there is that moron, Marius, now hell-bent on abolishing the Law. Who does he think he is? Anibal reincarnated?

In fact, I'm not all that bothered about Marius. Once Anibal's son goes, Marius will wither away. He'll get no support, moral or otherwise, from the people. Skenderis have always needed a strong leader.

Anibal's son remains the priority.

I had a thought tonight as I watched Lila show herself to me. Since Anibal's son and Zemun are the two men she probably dreams of while undressing, why not pit them against each other?

Implausible at the moment, perhaps, but then situations change all the time ...

When I studied the Europeans, I came across someone called Machiavelli. Europe's people, brainwashed with notions of democracy, consider him obsolete. But I thought – still do – he was the only thinker who made any sense. Wouldn't he somersault joyfully in his grave if, by pitting Anibal's son and Zemun against each other, I rid myself of both vermin?

26

KOKONA

The search for Bostan's body lasted for four days. Countless islanders participated. Starting from different ends, they meticulously combed every handbreadth of the woods.

They found the washing the Kristof women had left behind – though not the sheets Osip had used to clean Bostan's wounds; we had taken those with us. But except at the spot where Bostan had fallen, they could not discover any trace of blood. Nor could they detect any crushed undergrowth that an injured person, scrambling away, would have left behind.

All this increased Viktor's misgivings: though he had taken Bostan's rifle as his booty at the time of the shooting, he had forgotten, in the excitement of his triumph, to pick up Bostan's poacher's bag in which, everybody knew, Bostan always kept a pistol. And much as the Rogosins searched for it, they could not find it – on Osip's instructions, we had taken that, too.

Viktor became convinced that Bostan, though mortally wounded, was lying in wait for him somewhere.

During those four days, Osip nursed Bostan vigilantly. Keeping her sedated, he tended to her wounds, gave her transfusions, administered medication, toileted her as if she were a baby and fed her with infusions of special broths. He did not allow himself a moment's rest.

Only when he could do little else but wait for Bostan to respond to his treatment did he leave her to my care. He barely spoke. Just the occasional word to Dev when he got him to help set up traps at the approaches to the water-mill.

On the fourth day Dev, who constantly fetched stuff from Basil, reported that some of the people in the Citadel, stirring up old myths, had started to proclaim that, like Prince Lazar at the battle of Kosovo, a band of angels had carried Bostan to the eden of heroes.

Also around that time, Osip gave us a grain of hope. Eyes crimson for lack of sleep, he muttered that Bostan, though still in a critical state, was showing signs of improvement. Given her strong constitution, she could recover. Even so it would take her a good while to regain her strength.

On the fifth day, Viktor's man, Sorin, the one-time intelligence officer, had a brainwave. Having noted Dev's frequent visits to the apothecary and then discovering that both Dev and I had not been home for some days, he reasoned that we had met up with Bostan and were hiding him somewhere.

So he, Viktor and the other mercenary, Gjon, hauled Basil out of his shop and started interrogating him.

Basil, who would never inform on anybody, babbled about his growing belief in the islanders' rumours: that angels or houris or nymphs or mermaids had carried Bostan away.

That enraged Sorin and Gjon. They began to beat him up – this, despite many onlookers' protestations that the poor man was not only neutral in feuding matters, but also, as Skender's sole apothecary, a most important person for the islanders' well-being.

Mercifully, before they could harm Basil seriously, Dev arrived to collect some fresh potions for Bostan.

Instantly realizing what was happening, he rushed over to Viktor. 'Let Basil go! You have questions? Ask me!'

Viktor grabbed Dev by the collar. 'Where's Bostan? Where's he hiding?'

Osip had predicted that, sooner or later, such a confrontation would occur; that Viktor and his men, eventually noticing Dev's regular calls to Basil, would suspect him and me of helping Bostan and would try to question us. When that happened, he instructed us, we were to hedge until they started turning nasty – which, in all probability, they would. At that point we were to reveal Bostan's whereabouts. Our cavils followed by our disclosure would convince them. Then they would charge to the water-mill and find that Osip had prepared a special reception for them.

'I'm asking you, Shrimp! Where's Bostan hiding?'

Dev looked at him innocently. 'He's not hiding.'

'Don't jest with me! Straight answers!'

'He's with Thetis.'

'Who?'

'Achilles' mother.'

'I'm warning you, Shrimp!'

'That's what people say.'

'People will say anything. What do you say?'

'I believe the people. They know.'

Viktor, exasperated, dragged Dev to his men. 'Deal with him!'

Sorin drew out his knife. 'I've never failed to make someone talk, louse! If he plays the fool, I start by gouging out one of his eyes. Then the other. Then I cut off his ears. Then his nose. Then his goolies. And if he still doesn't talk, I cut out his tongue. That way he never talks again.'

Gjon, grinning, whispered to Dev. 'Take my advice, dwarf. Sorin never once got round to cutting off ears. Once he started working on an eye, his captive sang like an opera star. Do you understand what I'm saying?'

Dev did not have to feign fear; realizing that this was the time to stop the pretence, he nodded miserably.

Viktor bellowed. 'One last chance, Shrimp. Where is Bostan?'

'At the water-mill – Osip Gora's place.'

'How did he get there? We left him for dead!'

'Gora found him.'

'He did, did he? What in hell's name has our feud got to do with him?'

'He's a doctor.'

'You think an idiot like you can deceive us, Shrimp?'

'It's true. I swear. On my honour.'

Viktor laughed. 'On *your* honour? What honour?'

Dev scowled. 'More than yours!'

Viktor hit him across the face.

Sorin placed his knife near Dev's eye.

Viktor stopped him. 'Wait, Sorin. This is so preposterous, it could be true.' He turned to Dev. 'Xenos is a doctor, you say?'

Dev nodded.

'How come?'

'I don't know. He is.'

'And he's treating Bostan?'

'Kokona and I are helping him.'

'That's why you're getting stuff from Basil?'

'Yes.'

Viktor sighed. 'Yes, we thought something like that was going on. But it never occurred to us Xenos was involved.'

'Without him Bostan would be dead.'

Viktor smiled. 'Bostan's as good as dead, Shrimp! You're wasting your time!'

Dev shrugged. 'Time, we have plenty of.'

'We'll see about that.' He turned to his men. 'Let him go.'

Sorin and Gjon released Dev.

Defiantly, Dev walked over to Basil. 'Potions ready?'

Basil, trying to stem the flow of blood from his nose, nodded. 'Yes. The other antibiotics will come on tomorrow's ferry.'

He went into his shop to fetch the potions.

Viktor taunted Dev. 'Shrimp, tell Xenos that even if he can turn water into wine, it won't help! Bostan's days have run out!'

'Osip can do the impossible. If he wants to he can catch a bird with his mouth.'

Viktor, furious, glared at him. 'One day, Shrimp, someone will shut your mouth for good!'

Dev smiled defiantly. 'Yes – God!'

Basil brought out the potions.

Dev took them and climbed into his van.

As Dev started the engine, Viktor yelled. 'Shrimp, tell Xenos he's got till noon to hand Bostan over. If he doesn't, we'll come and get him! The Law says I can't touch Xenos. Or you or Kokona. But my men aren't bound by that! In fact, they're not bound by any law! As you very nearly saw, they do things their own way.'

And so they came.

In the heat of mid-afternoon, they appeared at the meadow. Not just Viktor, Sorin and Gjon, but all the Rogosins and their supporters.

On Osip's instructions, for greater safety, we had moved Bostan to the top floor, in what was once the storage room. A precautionary measure, he had said, trying to allay our fears, in the unlikely event that he and Dev might have to retreat to the ground floor and set up the barricades they had prepared.

It had also proved a sensible rearrangement. The bedroom downstairs, cluttered with improvised medical appliances, had become rather cramped for the four of us. Whereas the room above, taking up the entire top floor, was spacious and airy. Also, given the thickness of the walls, it would be a more restful place for Bostan, sparing her the everyday hubbub of coming and going, cooking and washing.

We watched Viktor and his crowd from the window. The nearer they came, the more they exuded a celebratory air. They reminded me of those American films where mobs set off to lynch black people.

Behind them we spotted another crowd – this one led by Bostan's son, Zemun, comprising the Kristofs and their supporters.

And behind them, a third crowd, not very large, led by Marius and some youngsters.

As Osip had expected, Toma was also there, struggling along as a fourth party. He was accompanied – or rather, propped up – by Lila. As the authority on all matters of the Law, this was a confrontation he could not miss. Moreover, puffed up by the fact that Lila had become his wife, he now made a point of taking her everywhere. After all, he told everybody, since she would succeed him when he eventually died, she had to start learning how to implement the Law.

Osip signalled to Dev. 'Let's go!'

Dev grabbed the pistol Bostan had in her poacher's bag and dashed out.

Osip picked up his gun.

Castor, now always by Osip's side, darted forward.

Osip took another look at the sedated Bostan, then turned to me. 'Watch over her, Mother.'

I looked up, startled. 'Mother, you say?'

'I've wanted to say it for a long time.'

I hugged him.

He kissed my hands then left, followed by Castor.

I watched as Osip – with Castor by his side – took up position a few paces in front of the carob tree.

I tried to spot Dev but couldn't see him. He was an expert at hiding.

Fear gripped me; despite the heat I began to shiver.

When Viktor and his men were about twenty metres away, Osip raised his hand. 'No closer, Viktor. I've set up traps.'

Viktor stopped. 'Traps?'

The crowd behind him stopped, too.

'You can't see them. But they're all over.'

Viktor, unsettled, turned to his men, wondering how to deal with this threat.

The men, looking equally disconcerted, stared at Osip.

Viktor resorted to his unctuous smile. 'I've no quarrel with you, Xenos.'

'Nor I with you.'

'But I must have Bostan. It's a matter of honour.'

'Then what?'

'That will be it. We'll leave in peace.'

Osip pointed at the Kristof crowd who had stopped a short

distance away. 'What about the Kristofs there? Will they let you leave without putting up a fight?'

'They won't interfere. They'll abide by the Law. Once Bostan is buried, his son, Zemun, will take over as their feudist. After that, things will continue as they were.'

'Well, you'll have to wait a while. Bostan stays here. Until he recovers.'

'Don't be a fool, Xenos.'

'There's another law, Viktor. Much older than your law of honour. The Code of Sanctuary. It's the one I practise. Whoever comes to my place has the right of refuge. It's a code that even your Law respects. A place of refuge is like a person's home. He cannot be attacked there. I've got a copy of the Scroll. I can show you.'

'That's a matter of interpretation. I know the Law, too. We can take Bostan by force, then discuss the finer points.'

Osip raised his pistol. 'You can try. As you can see, I'm armed. Move – and I'll shoot you. At the same time, Castor will attack Gjon. As Gjon tries to fend off Castor, I'll shoot him, too. By that time, Dev will have shot Sorin.'

Viktor looked shaken. 'The Shrimp? Where is he?'

'His name is Dev, Viktor! Dev! You can't see him because he's like the air around you – there wherever you turn. And his gun is aimed at Sorin. And after the way Sorin threatened him this morning, he won't hesitate, believe me.'

'Shrimp – Dev – doesn't know how to use a gun.'

'Would you like to risk that and see?'

Viktor tried to keep his nerve. 'Look, let's settle this amicably. Let's put it to arbitration.'

'It's already settled – as far as I'm concerned.'

Viktor shouted. 'It's my right to seek arbitration!'

'Who did you have in mind?'

'Righteous Toma. He's the authority on the Law.'

Osip smiled. 'That should be interesting. All right, I won't deny you your right. But I won't let you deny mine – whatever Toma says.'

Viktor called Toma. 'Righteous One! We need your advice.'

Toma shuffled over, not in the best of moods. Lila helped him.

As they approached, Lila looked at Osip brazenly. 'Did you undress Bostan, Doctor?'

The question flustered Osip. 'Naturally – to treat the wounds.'

'So you know.'

'What?'

'That he is a she. A woman who has become a designated man.'

Osip hesitated before replying. 'Yes.'

'Is she nice to look at? Not too old? Glowing skin like mine?'

Toma was shocked. 'Lila! What sort of talk is that?'

Lila patted Toma's cheek. 'Just curious, husband. I wondered what sort of a man Xenos is!'

Toma sniggered. 'A man with bad blood!'

Lila turned to Osip. 'You didn't answer me, Doctor.'

Osip replied brusquely. 'I don't concern myself with my patients' looks. I just treat them.'

Lila chuckled. 'You may be a doctor, but you're still a man.'

Viktor intervened impatiently. 'Excuse me, Lila! We've urgent business here.' He turned to Toma. 'We're in dispute, Righteous One ...'

Toma nodded. He seemed, for once, uncomfortable in his authority. 'Yes, I've been listening ...'

'You must arbitrate. Who's right? Me or Xenos?'

Toma, looking dismayed, pondered a while, then spoke wearily. 'I can only say we're facing a question between right and right.'

'So?'

'It's impossible to decide ...'

'What's impossible about it?'

Toma muttered falteringly. 'You, Viktor, have the right to pursue your enemy wherever he goes.'

'That's correct. That's all there is to it.'

Toma, still faltering, fidgeted. 'But much as I detest this man with bad blood, he has the right to provide sanctuary to whomsoever he wishes.'

Viktor shouted. 'Surely my right is greater than his!'

Toma shook his head. 'No. The rights are equal.'

Viktor became furious. 'They can't be!'

Toma sighed miserably. 'Alas, they are. A place of refuge is inviolable.'

Osip turned to Toma. 'You're a misguided man, Toma. But you're fair in your savage world. You have my respect!'

Viktor stooped over Toma threateningly. 'Righteous One – think again!'

Gravely, Toma shook his head. 'You've asked for my judgement, I've given it!' He turned to Lila. 'I want to go now.'

Lila held him by the arm and led him away. Now and again she turned and looked back at Osip.

Viktor, enraged, turned to his men. 'I'm not accepting this!'

Osip addressed him. 'Go home, Viktor. Forget about Bostan. Until she – he – decides to resume the feud!'

'No! I'll have Bostan now! Come what may!'

'I've warned you, Viktor!'

'Even if you kill the three of us – our followers will trample you to death.'

'If they can evade my traps ...'

Sorin, who had been watching Osip the whole time, interjected sharply. 'These traps – the sort you use for animals, are they?'

'Same principle, Sorin. But more lethal. Modified – and improved – for humans.'

'How come you know our names?'

'Hearsay, how else? But we've also crossed paths before.'

'Then we should know you too.'

'It's been some time. Besides, I've changed.'

'How did we cross paths?'

'You used to hang around with an old acquaintance of mine – Dušan.'

'Dušan's dead.'

'So I heard.'

This time Gjon interjected. 'Killed horribly. By a trap.'

'Yes, I heard that, too.'

'One of your traps?'

'Maybe.'

Gjon turned to Sorin. 'It's him – Hekatonkiri!'

Viktor turned to them sharply. 'What are you gabbling about?'

Sorin looked dismayed. 'A doctor. In the Peoples' Wars. Devised traps whenever his unit retreated or was surrounded. Traps more lethal than a minefield. He could bring a whole forest down on a battalion. He was so clever they pulled him out of the field hospital and assigned him to the front. Hekatonkiri, they called him. The hundred-handed demon. That's him!'

Victor laughed in disbelief. 'What rubbish! Xenos is a drifter. Vomited by this island.'

Sorin and Gjon exchanged looks, then Gjon turned to Osip. 'Sir, we don't want to get involved in this any more. Will you let us go?'

Osip nodded. 'Dev mentioned there's a ferry tomorrow.'

Sorin, relieved, took a deep breath. 'We'll be on it!'

Viktor, who had been watching the exchange incredulously, yelled at them. 'You can't do that! You're contracted to me!'

Gjon gave him a terse look. 'Not for this! This is something else!'

'What something else? He's only a man!'

'Take my advice, my friend – go home. You don't stand a chance against his traps.'

He and Sorin walked away.

Viktor stood uncertainly, bewildered, then turned round. 'Righteous Toma! Why won't you help me?'

But Toma, held by Lila, was slowly crossing the meadow. He might have heard Viktor, but he didn't look back.

Lila, however, did look back, several times. Again only to eye Osip.

Osip turned to Viktor. 'Take Gjon's advice, Viktor. Go home.'

Viktor, finally deflated, pulled himself away.

His supporters followed him.

In their wake, the Kristofs left.

Marius and his group lingered.

Marius shouted at Osip. 'Thank you, Xenos! You've started a revolution! Know this: we are behind you! And we're gathering strength!'

Osip, looking drained, nodded. 'You go home, too, Marius ...'

Osip waited until everybody had disappeared from view, then, leaving Dev and Castor to stand guard, came inside.

He went straight to Bostan, checked her cannula, the drips, then started taking her temperature, pulse and blood pressure.

There are certain acts that transfigure a person. Every time he reverted to being a doctor, Osip radiated the feeling that the future will repair the past.

27

OSIP

I had checked the traps again. Nobody could get through. Kokona was attending to Bostan. So I lingered on the traverse over the millpond for a smoke.

As ever, Sofi's memory was tormenting me. Ferociously this night because here I was, a fugitive from conflicts, thrust into a new one. But this time I could not – would not – avoid it or drift through it – not for any haven in the world. This one was devouring me the way family, land, religion, ideology and – yes, honour – devour reason.

It was demanding, as Sofi once put it, that I find my true self. And demanding that I do so not in pretence or affectation, but as a man who finally understands that there is both goodness and evil in him, but that he has the courage to stand on the side of goodness; an act that would be the only achievement possible in an otherwise rudderless life. Even more vehemently, it was urging me to dispense with reason, to defy Skender's grim reality and attain the god in me so that Bostan would accept me as her man. Thus empowered, it further insisted, we could even create the beatific illusion that Sofi would return from the ether as our daughter.

Can there be reality in unreality?

I began to open my heart to Castor. A recent habit, this. It was easier to meet the solicitude in Castor's eyes than in Kokona's or Dev's.

Oblivious of the fact that a voice carries in the night, I was lamenting away, discharging that volcanic anger that had settled on my shoulders like Sinbad's Old Man of the Sea. And, I imagine, I wanted to be heard. By Kokona. By Dev. By Bostan. By everybody. Even by God. Particularly by God, if he existed.

It was Dev who came out. 'All right?'

'Yes.'

I offered him a cigarette. He took one.

'Bostan – all right?'

'Sleeping. Kokona's with her.'

As I lit Dev's cigarette, I saw how rigid my hands had become – as they had been during the Peoples' Wars. Ossified into triggers. Was I reverting to my old self? Was this how I'd engage the god in me? Were the few months of peace in Skender merely specks of illusion stolen from the real world?

Dev squatted by my side.

I stroked his head. My hands still stiff, still possessed by Death. Isn't this the true me? The true everybody? Aren't we born simply to kill? Isn't the yearning for a blameless soul just a perversion? What makes me think I can be different? So far, with a ruse here and a bluff there, I've avoided killing in Skender. But what about tomorrow?

Would I let Bostan die? As I let Sofi die? Not this time! Not this time!

Dev had brought out some *rakiya*. He served me a glass. 'You were telling Castor – the children's massacre ... I overheard ...'

I nodded in anguish.

'Sofi died. I know. Kokona told me. She died in the river?'

'No. Not then ...'

'I ask because I care ... Don't tell if ...'

'You know I've no secrets from you – or Kokona.'

'What happened? After you left Sofi in the river?'

I drive towards the shooting. I know it's too late. I'm always too late.

The shooting stops.

Jets of flame erupt in the distance.

I smell napalm.

And burning flesh.

I stop the jeep.

Instinct takes over. I jump out. I must abandon the jeep. Dušan will be waiting for me. I'll be ambushed.

I roll the jeep down a fosse by the road so that it turns over.

I lean against a tree. Trees give strength.

At least they shot the children before torching them.

The tree nudges me: when Dušan realizes you're not going after him, he'll come looking for you. You're unfinished business for him. And he'll rape Sofi.

I bolt back to the river.

Sofi is still huddled in the bulrushes. Shivering in the freezing water.

I pull her up. 'We've got to run.'

'The children?'

'Too late.'

Her mouth heaves.

I punch her unconscious before she can scream.

I haul her on my shoulders and run.

Dev emptied his glass. So did I. He filled them again.

Sofi regains consciousness. 'Leave me, Osip. Save yourself.'

Her mouth is bleeding from my punch. I clean it up. 'Just hold onto my hand. And don't let go.'

We run. And run.

Dušan is an able tracker. His men are veterans.

Sofi is not used to running.

For the blind it's all the more difficult. I guide her as best as I can.

And she's caught a chill in the river and is coughing.

But her spirit is indomitable. She runs with her heart.

Somehow we keep a step ahead.

After some days, Dušan's men get bored. Today's new breed: they expect killing to be fun, not hard work.

They drop out one by one.

But Dušan doesn't give up.

Luck comes to our aid.

At another river we find an abandoned boat.

I row at night. We get across. I sink the boat.

Dušan loses our scent.

Still he doesn't give up.

We hear he's put a price on our heads.

The countryside teems with informers. Denunciation has become a lucrative trade.

We can't risk going into villages.

And the cities are ruled by gangs of bashi-bazouks.

We have to live in the forest.

But Sofi's not well. Her cough is worse. And she has a fever.

I lit two fresh cigarettes, passed one to Dev. 'The forest would have been ideal. It's a place that's alive – as if just created. And at night luminous, like the sea reflecting the sky. Gypsies will tell you: grand place to live. Plenty of game. Mushrooms like fields of gems. All sorts of plants – some I'd never seen. But Sofi knew them all. She'd smell them and say yes or no.'

'Was she a Gypsy?'

'Could have been. Or a Jew. Or a Muslim. I never asked. To me she was someone from another earth – stranded on this one.'

Dev murmured. 'There are such people.'

'Yes. But they don't survive.'

She has developed pneumonia.

Unless I can get some medicine, she'll die.

I remember an abandoned shepherd's hut on a hill. I take her there.

I start preparing traps.

She asks. 'What are you doing?'

'Traps. To keep you safe. I'm going into town. To get some medicine.'

'I'll be safe. You've lit a fire. Animals keep away from fires.'

'These aren't for animals.'

'For people? But they'd get hurt. Killed even.'

'Let's hope they'll bear that in mind ...'

'You're not a killer, Osip!'

I laugh.

'You saved me. And tried to save the children.'

'An aberration.'

'Don't talk like that. Don't pretend to be what you're not. You're not a killer ... You were forced into being one. That's what they do to all the innocents. They lock up their love. Now, you can unlock it ...'

I don't like fanciful philosophy. She piques me. 'If that's true, where have they locked it? Where is the key?'

'In you.'

'Sofi ...'

'A god. That's what you have in you. That's what we all have in us.'

I laugh again, but I am really nettled. 'A god, of all things?'

'Actually a she-god.'

'A she-god, no less?'

'That's who god is – a woman!'

'The only she-god I know is called Sofi.'

'That's one of her names. She has many. They all mean love. My father called her Philia.'

That ends my animosity. The word 'father' always churns up memories. My voice sounds like a hyena's. 'Your father ... Do you know where he is? I can take you to him ...'

She smiles. 'He's dead.'

'Your mother? Brothers? Sisters?'

'All dead.'

'Killed?'

'Yes.'

'And you still believe in this shit about the god in us?'

'They'd have been alive – if the people who killed them had found the god in them.'

'Sofi, listen ...'

'No, you listen. Promise me, please: you'll never kill!'

'What if they come to kill us?'

'Talk them out of it.'

'These people don't talk, Sofi. They just fire away.'

'Disarm them. Then talk. You can do it.'

'Sofi, I admire – respect – your views. But open your eyes ...' I pause,

ashamed of my insensitivity. I apologize for my blunder. Then I beg her. 'Just bear in mind what's happened – what's still happening ...'

'All because people reject the god in themselves ...'

'And what if it's the god in us that makes us killers?'

'She doesn't. It's not in her nature. She's like a mother ...'

I feel like puking. 'A mother?!'

'A good mother.'

I stopped. I realized I had begun howling.

Dev poured me another *rakiya*.

I drank it in one gulp, but it didn't pacify my anguish.

In the end I don't lay any traps. She threatens she'll set them off herself if I do. And I give in.

I go off to get her medication.

The city is in chaos. Looted from one end to the other. Any produce coming in is seized at checkpoints by gangs. People terrified. Most of them starving. Searching for scraps. Hopelessness in their eyes. Only the black market flourishing.

I know the city well. I used to work in the municipal hospital.

That's where I go. I might come across someone who still remembers me.

Again luck lends a hand. One of the pharmacists is Yakov. I used to play chess with him.

I give him a couple of gold coins. For some time now, I've been converting everything to gold. Valid currency everywhere. Good Gypsy advice.

I get the antibiotics I want.

I return to the hut.

Sofi's burning with fever.

I give her the antibiotics.

I prepare a broth.

I paused, turned to Dev. 'I don't think I can go on …'

Dev nodded. 'Don't …'

'I should. I've come this far …'

Dev nodded again.

She manages to drink some of the broth.

Suddenly I sense danger.

Too late.

The door is kicked open.

Dušan bursts in! Pistol in one hand, flame-thrower in the other. He is grinning from ear to ear.

He points at Sofi. 'When you were running, I kept hearing her cough. I put two and two together: wisp of a girl; obviously getting sick; bet you, he'll try to get some medicine. So I had look-outs in hospitals and pharmacies. And what do you think? – I get a call …'

'Not from the pharmacist?'

'No. Two comrades. Sorin and Gjon. Not from our unit. But you might have seen them at the HQ. I used to drink with them.'

'Yes. I've seen them.'

'They work the black market. Do anything for money. I paid them well. They sniffed out the pharmacist. He refused to talk. Silly fool! So they made him talk. And here I am!'

Suddenly I feel too tired. I'm ready for the end. Let it come. 'So here you are. Get on with it!'

'That's my dilemma. Get on with what first? I'm tempted to kill you slowly. Then fuck her to death. But she can't see. So not much fun for me! On the other hand, making you watch what I do to her – that should thrill me.'

Incredibly, despite her condition, Sofi stands up and moves towards Dušan. 'I want to talk to you.'

Dušan leers. 'Wrong man, girl! I don't talk! My pecker says all I've got to say!'

I shout. 'Sofi, get back!'

Sofi throws herself at Dušan.

Dušan, not expecting an attack, loses his balance.

As they tumble, he falls on the flame-thrower's backpack and is winded.

Sofi shouts. 'Disarm him, Osip! Disarm him!'

I launch myself at Dušan, strip him of his flame-thrower.

Dušan rebounds. He still has his pistol.

We fight for it.

He fires once.

Twice.

I kick him in the groin. He doubles up.

As I wrench the gun from him, he fires again.

This time I'm hit.

But I have the gun. I shout. 'I've disarmed him, Sofi. You still want me to talk to him?'

Sofi's voice is weak. 'Let him go! Let him go!'

I aim the gun at Dušan's head. 'Never!'

Dušan begins to weep. 'Osip ... Please ... Don't ...'

I hear my voice thundering. But it's somewhere in the distance. I am drifting. Into myself? Or out to nowhere? 'Oh, I will! I will!'

Sofi clings to my arm. 'Osip ... Don't ... The god in you ...'

I turn to her briefly. 'Sofi, he's ...'

I stop drifting. My eyes scream. They don't want to see what they see.

Blood is gushing out of Sofi's shirt. She was hit while I was struggling with Dušan, when he fired those shots.

'Osip ... Let him go!'

I want to weep. But I can't. Since leaving Skender I've forgotten how to cry ...

Sofi turns to Dušan. 'Go now!'

Dušan runs off.

I can still shoot him. But I don't.

Sofi mumbles. 'Save yourself, Osip. Find the god in you. Live! Live! Live!'

Then she dies quietly in my arms.

And I manage to weep.

Dev refilled my glass. 'Your wound? How did you ...?'

'I'd had worse. The bullet had gone through cleanly. That made it easier. I still had my medical bag. I stopped the bleeding. And waited.'

'Why?'

Dušan will come back. He knows I'm wounded. He'll wait until I weaken.

He wants to kill me slowly. Dismember me. The way the Ustashi killed in the Jasenovač concentration camp.

First cut off my balls. And my tongue. Stuff them in my mouth. Then cut off my arms and legs. And look into my eyes until I die.

But I'll surprise him.

I set up a trap, using his flame-thrower. I make sure the backpack is where it was when he ran away.

Time passes.

Sofi's body begins to smell.

I can't bury her until I've dealt with Dušan.

Dev had blocked his ears with his hands. 'Don't tell me more. Please ...'

'I have to, Dev. I must. I must. I can't stop now. I can't keep this to myself any more.'

Dušan comes three days later.

Finds me leaning against the wall, opposite the door, seemingly unconscious, cradling Sofi.

Everything in the hut looks just like it was.

He walks in. He has a sharp knife and a cleaver. Ready for my slow death.

The spring of the trap is three steps inside the door, invisible.

He steps on it.

The floor gives in. A coil of rope winds itself around his legs.

Simultaneously another spring opens the flame-thrower's valve and lets out the pressurized liquid.

A loop of wire, battery-heated, serves as the trigger.

As Dušan tries to understand what's happening, the flame-thrower ignites.

Dušan burns to death, screaming.

I watch.

But revenge is not sweet.

I've broken my promise to Sofi.

Dev moved up to me. He stroked my cheek, wiped my tears.

I seized his hands, tried to push him away.

Later, I bury Sofi and leave.

It takes me an age to come to my senses.

But I never kill again.

Then one day I listen to Teacher's voice. It had been with me through all those years but I'd always ignored it.

And I make my way back to Skender.

I couldn't push Dev away. My fingers had unfurled and weakened.

He held my hands, then kissed them. 'I love you, Osip.'

I let my head rest on his copious hair.

28

BOSTAN

I don't know where I am.

The light is harsh.

As if I'm looking into the sun.

I'm in pain.

But I can't feel it.

And I can't sense my body.

Am I in a cocoon?

In a womb?

I'm strong, yet here I'm weightless.

There's someone near.

A woman.

I can tell by her breath.

My mother?

I try calling her.

But I can't find my tongue.

Strange – it doesn't worry me.

Far away, people are talking.

I recognize the voices.

Dev and Xenos.

I want to join them.
But I can't move.
If I'm weightless, why can't I float there?
Xenos is speaking. Shouting.
I can follow what he's saying.
Even see it.
As if he's talking in picture-words.
But I can't get the meaning of what he's saying.
In this bright light the picture-words stalk each other.
As in shadow plays.
A picture-word keeps popping up.
It's a name.
Sofi.
Not anyone I know.
Xenos' woman?
Men need women.
I want to find my body.
I want to be a woman.
As I used to be.
A woman to a man.
Women need men, too.
I want a man.
Xenos?
Someone says: I love you, Osip.
Is it the woman?
No. It's Dev.
I want to say that, too.
Only I can't find my tongue.
But I can make a picture-word.
I love you, Xenos.
Xenos ...

29

DEV

Zemun is impatient to start as the Kristofs' feudist. He's already the Kristofs' headman. But he doesn't come to see Bostan and sit by her side. Nor asks how she is. Heartless boy. Mirror of Toma.

Kokona won't forgive him. She says he's in a frenzy because Bostan's still alive.

Then unexpectedly he comes to see her. Five days after Toma arbitrated between Viktor and Osip.

I am by the carob tree. With Castor. It is now our caravanserai. We're keeping an eye on Viktor. He has camped on the meadow. Other men – Rogosins and their allies – surround the water-mill.

Viktor has come to accept Toma's verdict. He had no choice. But only as long as Bostan stays in Osip's care. The moment she steps outside the water-mill, the Code of Sanctuary will be dust. Viktor will have the right to restart the feud.

Zemun walks past Viktor. Brash, like a rooster in a farmyard. Salutes Viktor. As the Law demands from feudists.

He calls from a distance. 'How's Bostan, Shrimp?'

'Still critical.'

'I'm here to see him. Guide me past the traps.'

'Wait!' I whistle to the water-mill.

Osip looks out of the window.

I shout. 'Zemun to see his mother!'

Zemun snarls. 'Not my mother, Shrimp! Bostan! Bostan!'

Osip waves at us to come.

I point at Viktor and his men to Castor. 'Raise the Devil, if they move!'

I lead Zemun past the traps.

He tries to see where they are. But Osip has made them invisible.

I bring Zemun to Bostan's room.

Osip is replacing a saline drip.

Kokona is disinfecting instruments in boiling water. When she sees Zemun, she spits out her words. 'High time you visited her.'

Zemun barks. 'Him – not her!'

Kokona, in disgust, ignores him.

Zemun turns to Osip. 'You there, Xenos! How is he?'

Osip doesn't look at him. 'Fighting for her life.'

Zemun goes closer. 'Looks like he's dead.'

Now Osip turns to Zemun. 'You know how the dead look, do you?'

'Will he survive?'

'That's our hope.'

'If he recovers – how long will it take?'

'Depends how long his cock is.'

Zemun is shocked. He splutters. 'He hasn't got a cock!'

'I thought all men had one.'

Zemun growls. 'You're making fun of me!'

'Why would I do that?'

'You think I'm still a boy. I'm not! Not any more!'

'Then stop acting like one!'

Zemun boils. 'This is serious. We have a feud. How do you think I feel every time I see Viktor? Or walk past him as I did just now! And know that if Bostan weren't alive, I could kill him – easily.'

'Or Viktor could kill you.'

Zemun blusters. 'Never!'

Osip frowns. 'Invincible, are you?'

Zemun seethes. 'I need to know! How long before Bostan recovers – if he recovers?'

Osip sighs wearily. 'I don't know, boy. When I do, I'll tell you. In the meantime, keep visiting her. If she starts rallying, I imagine she'll be happy to see you.'

'He! He! I keep telling you! She's a man! Why won't you listen?'

Osip loses his patience. 'The way she is now, she's a woman. And that's good news. Women have stronger constitutions than men. I'm relying on that.'

Zemun looks long at Osip. Confused. Also full of hate.

Then stomps out.

30

TOMA

You, My Law, Toma's Law, You're forsaking me!

Can't you see, I'm being set against You?

They're usurping me – forcing me – to pollute Your very foundations. To undermine Your interests. Skender's interests. The world's, even!

Is this fair?

Am I being tested again – as in Anibal's time?

Didn't I defeat Anibal and forge the only right path?

Didn't I prove myself a veritable Hercules?

Are you commanding further labours from me?

And with Anibal's son, of all people, as my bane, as the Nemean Lion incarnate?

Is this a divine joke?

My Last Judgement?

So be it!

I won't fail! I'll come through!

Diligently! Honourably!

But I want You to know, the pain is unbearable.

Sometimes I think my wits are also forsaking me!

Would You have suffered the kind of humiliation *I* suffered?

Would You have stood on that meadow without an option, without recourse, and arbitrated between Viktor and Anibal's son?

Would You have stomached judging once again in favour of Anibal's son?

Would You have battled, without a weapon at hand, with the Doubter?

Wasn't it enough I'd already done that once when Anibal's son ensnared Viktor, Urs and Rustu?

I could have judged in favour of Viktor.

Don't think I didn't want to!

But to what end?

By laying deadly traps, Anibal's son had turned the water-mill into a fortress.

Besides, as You know, I don't tamper with the Law. That way perdition lies.

I stand where I've always stood. Strict adherence! Come what may.

In any case, even if I could have circumvented You in favour of Viktor, Anibal's son would have come up with all kinds of ploys.

Sorting those out would have been like sorting the gravel in a sack of rice.

You, the Law, My Law, must be immaculate, unassailable.

Ploys mean disorder.

You, My Law, means order!

It means everybody lives as *We* prescribe. Strong and contented through the consecration of Death.

Immune from humiliation.

Immutably prescribed!

That's why I'm going to update You! Make You Toma's Law!

Perhaps You can assign that as one of the labours you intend to impose on me.

Are You listening to me?

Is the voice in my head Yours or mine?

It's ours.

Must be.

You and I are One.

But the humiliation!

As hurtful as when I was a student in Europe, when all and sundry mocked me as 'retarded', 'crazy', 'megalomaniac'!

Worse: as 'alien', 'barbarian'!

Can You believe it? Me – alien, barbarian?

But look where Europe is now and where *I* am!

You didn't answer: would You have endured my humiliation?

In front of all those people?

People who worship You, the Law!

Who worship Me!

What must they be thinking now?

That I'm losing my authority?

That maybe You, My Law, is as inhumane as that delinquent, Marius, keeps shouting over the rooftops?

Yes, that's his new incantation!

And he's begun distributing pamphlets: 'The Revolution has started! God bless Xenos!'

Imagine Marius referring to Anibal's son as Xenos!

Xenos! The Stranger! The Alien! The Other!

Are strangers to be seen as our saviours now?

Can *We* tolerate that?

And what will the Gospodins think?

They back *Us* because they know that You, My Law, is what this planet needs!

They want order and believe that *Our* order is the only way!

What will they think when they hear that people with bad blood – strangers, others – are advocating the abomination of revolution?

And what will we do if the Gospodins look elsewhere to award their panacea of power?

I won't let that happen!

I'll come through the labours You've set me!

But does it ever occur to You how unbearable is the agony You inflict on me?

And how it's even more painful to keep asking which way is right for *Me*, for You, for *Us*, for Skender, for mankind!

I was saddened when I heard Bostan hadn't died.

That divests him of an honourable death.

But if he can take up feuding again, then honour will revert to him.

He will return to *Us*!

There is some light on the horizon.

My idea of pitching Zemun against Anibal's son looks as if it might flower earlier than I'd hoped.

Zemun is as enraged as the Erymanthian Boar.

He's desperate to start as Kristof's paladin, but cannot as long as Bostan is alive.

And as Bostan is being cared for by Anibal's son, Zemun feels profaned.

Imagine the anguish of a youngster who knows that a man with bad blood is revelling in his mother, touching her constantly, putting his fingers – maybe his cock, too – wherever he wants.

Whenever he wants.

Judging by the despicable way Lila baited and lusted after him, Anibal's son obviously has an appeal for women.

Why have You sent him, of all people, to scourge me?

Even the Furies could not have invented such a torment.

Pining for my manhood – that's another humiliation, another grief. But I've never forgotten the power of love, the joy of love.

I want to do to Lila – day and night – what Anibal's son must be doing to Bostan.

And the pain that I can't is worse than the pain of my castration.

Incidentally, I haven't forgiven Lila for her philandering before Anibal's son.

Even though she has been very loving since then and keeps trying to make amends not only by memorizing the Law, My Law, assiduously, but also by walking in our quarters in the Palladion naked all the time so that I can look at her as much as I want.

Another man would have killed her.

Zemun, for instance. On hearing Lila taunt Anibal's son, he looked as if a ram had dug its horns into him.

But, as you know, I'm not another man.

I don't live for the moment.

I can take blows.

That's the price I pay to secure my place in the future.

To immortalize Toma's Law.

Now, Zemun.

How shall I use him?

He told me he had visited Bostan.

He'll go to her again.

To make sure she doesn't fall for Anibal's son.

And also because he's impatient to start feuding.

I was just like him – before they shot off my balls.

I was even ready to wrest the feuding right from my own father, good man that he was, if, opportunely, he hadn't been killed.

So I'm sure Zemun is praying for Bostan to die.

I'm also sure that if she doesn't, or takes a long time to recover, he'll force her to renounce the paladin's mantle.

Failing that, he'll lock her up in her house for having besmirched the family honour.

Once he becomes the Kristofs' paladin, I'll persuade him to take on Anibal's son as his first engagement.

He can claim – it is within My Law – that Anibal's son defiled Bostan, if only because he saw her naked.

He could even allege they've fornicated.

Since we all know a man and a woman cannot live under the same roof for weeks on end without eventually throwing themselves at each other, he would be believed.

Of course, when Zemun attacks Anibal's son, he'll probably have to kill Bostan also.

That would dishonour Bostan.

Which is not right.

But that's how, sometimes, Fate arranges things.

Lesser rights are expendable for the benefit of the greater good: the right for order!

The means justify the end.

31

KOKONA

Bostan needed another transfusion.

Dev had given blood before going to stand guard.

Now I was about to take some from Osip.

You're a master of the loom, he had said, you'll be fine with a catheter. I was. I had learned quickly – without reducing veins to pin cushions.

Osip scrubbed his arm for a good while. He had been smoking all morning and did not want the smell of nicotine on any of the utensils. Cigarettes for him, I'd come to understand, were like the crochets of the clingers we find on seabeds. They enabled him to hang onto life whatever the turbulence. But when it came to ministering to Bostan, he made sure that Dev and I were, as he put it, completely aseptic.

I put the catheter into his vein.

He stared into the distance, thoughtful. 'Tell me about Bostan, Mother.'

'You know most things. Not much more to tell. Basically, a good person ...'

'But a proficient killer ...'

'Aren't we all – one way or another? That's what you said once ...'

'You're not.'

'Not literally, but ...'

'No. You refused.'

'I've also stood by when others got killed.'

'What could you have done?'

'Not put myself beyond people's reach. Not just live in bliss with Dev. I should have found the god in me – as your Sofi put it. And in others.'

'Saying is easy ... You struggled hard ...'

'Even so. Sofi was right, Osip. So were you. We're all killers because we don't do enough to stop the killings. We turn away. Or mumble in protest. But, in the main, we sit back and swallow the reasons the real killers give us for their blood lust. Insane justifications. The hunger for power masquerading as sanity – as in the Peoples' Wars. I've often protested, yes, but that's not enough. That still makes me a bystander. I should have challenged the Law every step of the way – as your father did.'

The plastic bag for the blood was half full. I got up to pull out the catheter.

'Take a bit more, Mother.'

'We don't want to drain you.'

'We won't.'

I sat down again.

'When – if – Bostan recovers ...'

'She will. I have great faith in you, Osip.'

'She'll go back to feuding, won't she?'

'She'll be expected to, yes.'

'She once told me she was very happy being a man.'

'Did you believe her?'

'The privileges men have ...'

'Privileges – for some men. For most others it's a somnolent existence. How can life have a meaning for men if women aren't their equals?'

'That's what I mean. The need for the same birthright ...'

'And with it comes the most fundamental right: the right to be who one is, to live the meaningful life one wants – that's the real need for everybody.'

'I can see that, but – in Skender? How?'

'You know, when a woman becomes a designated man, she destroys everything that denotes her gender. Everything, starting with her clothes ... She even dons a false moustache.'

Osip nodded. 'Yes. My mother did that. Burnt all her dresses. Glued on a moustache ...'

'Bostan didn't. She barely changed her name: from Bostana to Bostan. Refused to wear a moustache. And she kept her clothes.'

'She did?'

'She has a hideout – in the catacombs. Dev discovered it. She slips away there when she can.'

'I don't understand ...'

'That's where she keeps her clothes. Where she can go and be the woman she is.'

'If so ... maybe she can give up being a designated man?'

'There's that old abomination, honour, at stake. More importantly, there's her son. She'll protect Zemun come what may. That's why she became a designated man in the first place. To prevent Zemun – and the other Kristof boys – from becoming feudists.'

'She has no choice then.'

'Unless a reconciliation can be arranged ...'

'A reconciliation? Would that be possible?'

'Yes. Through marriage ...'

'You mean, if Bostan marries one of her enemies?'

'No. Once a designated man, you can't become a woman again. But if a member of the Kristofs marries into an enemy family ...'

'Who?'

'That's the bind. There's only Zemun. He's still young. But that can be overlooked. The problem is he's loathsome. And brainwashed by the Law. Who'd want him?'

'What if we put up some money? Buy a bride for him? I have enough funds ...'

'It's a thought. But if, with Zemun being who he is, the marriage breaks up we'd be back where we started with an even more bitter feud on our hands.'

'I see.'

'On the other hand, Bostan could find another reason – a good, personal reason ...'

'Like what?'

I went over and took the catheter out. 'I think you've given enough for today ...'

'What other reason?'

I showed him his blood, then sealed the plastic bag carefully. 'A reason to live ...'

'What are you suggesting?'

'Might give you a reason to live, too ...'

He looked at his blood. 'Toma would say that's bad blood ...'

'Sofi would disagree. She'd see life in it. Love, too. And a god. Who would you rather believe?'

'If Bostan and I ... That would mean dishonour for her. And her family. For ever.'

'Yes. She'd have to leave here.'

'Where could she go?'

'Wherever you take her.'

'Would she – would she do that for me? What about the family honour?'

'You and I don't believe in honour. When she recovers, she might come to agree with us.'

'That still leaves her son. Would she abandon him – given his craving to feud?'

'No. That's the crunch for you two.'

'No hope then.'

'Never say that. Hope loves the hopeful. So keep hoping.'

32

OSIP

Bostan regained consciousness on the thirteenth day, but only for brief spells. By then some of her wounds had started healing. It was on the seventeenth day that I finally saw some light in her pupils. She was still too weak to talk and only managed a garbled greeting. But the eyes held their gleam. And I, not having dared look at them directly before then, saw how beautiful they were. Almond eyes, as the Balkan poets describe their loved ones in ballads.

Earlier, at dawn, on that seventeenth day, coming back after my watch, I'd seen Dev and Kokona sleeping peacefully on the floor next to Bostan's bed. Dev had his head nestled on Kokona's lap and looked as if he was telling her that he would never stop drinking her. Then I thought he also looked as if Kokona was giving birth to him.

That vision possessed me. I envied Dev, kept wanting to have my head between Bostan's legs, to feel that I was being given life, too.

Though Bostan had lost some weight, her femininity was still striking. After nursing her for so many days, her contours were imprinted on me. And she looked like the woman I used to imagine whenever despair seized me. A woman in her true nakedness. A complete woman, mature and fully at ease with her womanliness. I knew in my bones that my flight of fancy held a truth that people perversely choose to discard. I've known a number of women, but, either because of my emotional paralysis or because they feared I might take something away from their existence, I never came across one that I could call my woman, the flesh of my flesh, feminine in her soul, the completion of my self, created for me and for whom I was also specifically created.

I felt certain Bostan could vivify me, reclaim the essence that had been snatched away from me by a loveless, motherless, death-draped world. Looking back at how I'd kept dreaming of such a woman, I understood that it had been my intuition that had seen Bostan as she was and as she could be; and that had made me feel I had at last come to the right place, that all that sophistry about seeking a refuge had been just an affectation. Skender was where I belonged because here, I had sensed, I would find the woman who would give meaning to my life. I had foreseen, even as I'd envied and cherished the way Kokona and Dev loved each other, that Bostan had the same gifts and only needed the chance to anoint me with them.

I had thought at first that Bostan might be an androgynous person who, though more female than male, had found greater comfort in masculinity. But, after a few meetings, I had realized, from certain comments made either in earnest or in bluster, that, despite her accomplished impersonation of a man, she hadn't dispossessed herself of that unique feminine softness that exemplified her womanhood. Now while tending to her wounds, keeping vigil by her side, wrestling Death for her life, feeding her with infusions, keeping her clean, I'd come to see that there wasn't any demarcation between her flesh and her soul. She was body and spirit seamlessly fused.

Sofi could look deep into my thoughts. And one day she told

me, swore in fact, that, at some point in my life, I would find the woman I yearned for and would have the resolve to surrender to her wholeness.

About Sofi: I never saw her naked. Not even when we undressed by a stream to wash ourselves. I always looked away. I think she did want me to lie with her – if only as an enfolding wing. But she had become like a daughter; her flowering femininity sacrosanct. She had to bestow it not on me but on the fine man I expected her to meet in better times.

I never stopped hoping she would meet him – or had already – wherever good souls meet in death. So many young people, just as exceptional as Sofi, perished in the Peoples' Wars.

Sofi's wisdom was prodigious. She wrought my destiny as if she were Athena. In the few weeks we were together, she revealed all that was meaningful in life. She tore off the calluses that had encrusted me. But for her, I would have remained a presence without substance, an empty man who could do little else besides drift into soldiery and who, having started as a field doctor with the impulse to save lives, had tamely abandoned himself to the brutalization – no doubt already part of him – that conflict engenders; and, thus, easily, had become a killer. I had never fathomed, in those days, the insatiable hungers I now feel for peace and for love; for an end to nothingness; for accepting myself as who I truthfully am; for a woman whom I can inhabit and who can inhabit me; to whom I can say you are my woman; and yes, to have children with her.

Later on that seventeenth day, I lay next to her.

Dev had gone on guard with Castor and Kokona was busy cooking and washing.

In order not to brush against her wounds, I left a wide gap between us. The bed was big enough, had to be, given my nightmares.

In truth, I wanted to lie between her legs.

Instead, I gently stroked her head.

She opened her eyes again after a while.

She smiled. Her eyes turned even more luminous.

I kept on caressing her. 'Rest, lovely one. Sleep.'

She strained and pushed closer to me. With her good hand, she managed to pull up my shirt.

I was so shocked I didn't know what to do. 'Bostan!'

She replied, faintly. 'Bostana. My name was – is – Bostana.'

'Bostana, you must rest.'

She strained again and placed her mouth on my breast. 'Bostana. Yes.'

She started sucking my nipple.

I should have pushed her back. But I couldn't. I was overjoyed.

Weak as she was, she could only suck a moment or two.

Then her mouth slipped from my nipple and she fell asleep.

I kept still. It was bliss holding her.

I heard a rustle; turned round.

Kokona was standing by the door.

She was smiling. One of her gracious, tender smiles. But her eyes were misty.

33

BOSTAN

It was the way he stroked my face. Not how our men do – if they ever do. So gentle, yet so male. As assured as someone who knows how to pick ripe figs.

Isn't that how we should touch?

A man is more of a man when he touches gently.

At first I didn't know where my body was. I thought I was watching him stroke someone else. But it was real. He was caressing me. Me, Bostana!

Except for my mother, no one had touched me so tenderly before.

My mother suckled me until I was five. Sometimes even when I was older. When I'd be afraid of something, she'd give me her nipple and make everything right. You like breast, Bostana, she'd say, you know how good it is. If you remember that, you'll be fine, vigorous and soft as women should be. You'll be the best, strongest, softest woman ever.

That's what I wanted to be.

I sucked all her wisdom. But I never imagined I'd end up a designated man.

I felt so good being a woman, so at ease in my skin, even when I was married to Valmir.

Valmir's mind was always on feuding. I tried to make him happy. I knew I wouldn't have him for long. Like all our men, he was born to a short life. So I gave him everything I could – cooked things he liked, kept his clothes clean, oiled his guns, lay down with him every day – including when I had my monthlies. And whenever his mind drifted away, I aroused him.

So easy to arouse a man.

I just washed in front of him. When he turned to look at me, I bent down, let his eyes feast on my behind, showed him how wide and ample I was, exposed my *amata*. 'There's a pearl inside this oyster, see if you can find it,' I said.

Or I wrestled with him.

Or straddled him.

Or sucked his nipples.

Or his cock.

We women could write bibles about the ruses we can think up to get a man going.

And I enjoyed doing all that. It didn't matter that Valmir never thought of pleasuring me. He was like a sudden squall, wild one minute, spent the next. I had to race like a dolphin to catch up with him. Half the time I couldn't.

Then he was killed. Just over a year after he started feuding. That's about the average survival time. Unless you're like me – a crack shot.

And a woman.

We women think differently. We're more aware of our surroundings. We can sense danger quicker than a deer. Also we're better at reading men's minds. Since almost all feudists are men, we can outfox them most of the time.

Valmir died before Zemun was born.

The tragedy was he didn't have to die so young. There were older men in the family. They should've taken up the feuding. But he couldn't wait. He believed honour provided the only admission to paradise. That's all he could think of. So he convinced the family and jumped the queue.

It hurt me deeply, his death.

But I was also relieved. I could stop worrying about when he'd be killed. I could have an ordinary life, be myself, a soft, strapping woman, a credit to my mother's milk – at least, until my son grew up.

I never married again. It would have been asking for more grief. Any man I'd marry would soon get killed.

But it was hard being alone. A woman without a man is like a moon without a planet. She needs him not only around her, but also inside her. Without a man, life is unsalted. I had to pleasure myself by myself. And that's a bleak activity.

I thought of taking lovers. But I didn't. I couldn't. Not in Skender. Here widow-watching is a popular pastime. Thousands of squinting eyes wondering how you'll smother your yearnings. Waiting for you to open your legs and dishonour your family. Waiting to stone you – not actually, not any more, thank God. But words and dagger-looks also hurt.

Of course men don't have that problem. They're free to fuck, free to kill, free to do whatever they want. So they prance like peacocks. And if they bed a woman out of wedlock – which is rare – their cronies pat their shoulders, tell them they've done what nature demands from true men.

Men can find reasons for everything.

That's why when eventually the Kristofs asked me to be their designated man, I agreed. I wanted to be free like a man.

But that was a whim. The real reason was that I was a mother.

Zemun, my son, is the rainbow that colours my eyes. He was growing fast, getting to be like his father. Imagine, getting to be like the father he never knew. Honour-obsessed. By becoming the designated man, I thought I'd save him from feuding.

Yet look at him now ... There's nothing of me in him. He's the Law's thrall, Toma's favourite pupil. Waiting for me to die so that he can take my place.

This is not what I intended. How did it happen? Where did I fail him?

Have I blinded him with my gunmanship? Made myself someone he wants to copy? Should I have refused to be a designated man and hoped for the best? Hoped that he'd turn out to be like Marius, a book person? He could have been. I taught him how to read and write. And he liked books until he fell under Toma's spell.

Ah, Zemun ...

If men could only give birth, they'd understand how precious life is, how good it is to live ...

When I gave birth, I felt I was Nature herself. I forgot the pain, forgot the fear of producing a monster ... or a stillborn infant ...

Giving birth is the completion of a woman. She has done what she was born to do. It's a joy only a woman can know. A joy that's entirely her own.

If you knew how good it is to give life, Zemun, you'd stop thinking about killing and dying.

Does it surprise you I talk like this – after all the men I've killed?

It surprises me.

But then, at the time, I was someone else. I was Bostan – not Bostana.

Now killing has become unholy ...

What changed me?

Xenos' touch.

Only that – nothing more.

Look how he's stretched out alongside me! Like a low cloud cradling the Earth.

Look at his chest. Manly breasts.

You like breast, Bostana, my mother said.

I do, I do.

Men in some tribes, Kokona once told me, take turns with their women to suckle their children. They don't produce milk, but whatever they produce is good for the child.

Xenos, I want your breast ...

34

DEV

Fighting for Bostan's life raises our souls. We forget the world.

So when I go to the Citadel for medicine and find nobody around, I think a djinn has come and is turning the island into paradise again.

But Basil reminds me it's Midsummer Day, when we pay homage to the Lords of the Brine. This festival, like the Day of Persephone, also imposes a truce. Everybody goes to the port.

Basil is eager to be off, too. He loves rituals. Also on Midsummer Day, the annual *Kriss* meets. He wants to see what will happen. By saving Bostan, Osip has created great confusion. Such a breach has never happened before. So this year's *Kriss* will be like no other.

I want to go too. I rush the medicines to the water-mill, then speed to the port.

The beach by the harbour is swarming. People are dancing in the water. They won't stop till they collapse. Then they'll stretch out, like shipwrecked Odysseus before Nausicaa, and give thanks because this year, too, they have escaped the sirens' fatal songs.

Zemun and the *Morituri* are climbing the cliffs. Without ropes. They act as if they have no fear of Eleanora's Falcons nesting there.

With this ancient rite, they'll prove they have the heart to embrace death.

At sea, the fishermen sprinkle libations of honey, perfume and incense. Then they slash palms, mix their blood with the swell and become blood-brothers with mermen.

On the cliff-tops, married folk stuff underpants with peaches, then throw them onto the waves – a covenant that binds those who will be born to them to the sea gods.

Also on the cliff-tops, the elders partake in a tug-of-war with a big rock. This is an ageless tradition, too. It re-enacts Poseidon's deliverance. By shifting the rock, they show how Zeus forced Cronos to vomit out Poseidon. Imagine, Cronos was Poseidon's father, yet he devoured his son.

After this, the *Kriss* will begin.

So I trundle up to the cliff-top.

On the way I throw my pants – and Kokona's – both bulging with peaches, into the sea. I had the wits to bring them. Of course it's impossible for us to have children at our age, but Kokona and I agree this is a ritual worthy of the Lover of Love.

The *Kriss* gathers on the plain by the cliffs. Here, Osip's father died. I pay reverence on behalf of Osip.

Usually people stand in a circle during the *Kriss*. Today they have formed three groups and are facing each other in a triangle.

In front of the largest group sits Toma. They've brought a chair especially for him. He's very frail now, a handful of bones lost in his big purple cloak. But, as always, he's stiff with self-importance. He waggles his mace like a caliph impatient to deliver *fatwas*.

His wife, Lila, stands on his right. She's beginning to look wild like Toma, the way dogs resemble their masters. Not surprising. Who can look human living with Toma?

The *Morituri*, wet with sweat after their rock-climbing, form a legion behind their prophet.

Further behind stand the families who have ongoing feuds. But Viktor is absent. He's still camped in the meadow, keeping watch over Bostan.

The second group is gathered around Marius Kaplan. They're youngsters who don't want to feud. And parents who abet them. Marius has written a leaflet and they are distributing copies.

Marius stands in front. His father and mother, Nexhat and Mimoza, next to him.

The third group consists of the neutrals. They are very curious. Some have taken Marius' leaflet.

Toma beats his mace against his chair and opens the *Kriss*.

Marius raises his hand, moves to the centre of the circle. 'I want the first word!'

Toma, angry, waves him away. 'I decide who speaks first!'

Marius stands firm. 'What I have to say is important!'

Toma rebukes him. 'We have a procedure! It's stipulated in the Law!'

'I'm following the procedure. I've raised my hand first.' He turns to the gathering. 'That gives me the right to start, doesn't it?'

A few of the neutrals shout.

'Let him have his say, Righteous Toma!'

'He has the right!'

'Let's hear him out!'

Toma is icy. 'Not unless I agree!'

Marius' father, Nexhat, moves forward. 'You must agree, Righteous Toma. The procedure is in accordance with the Law. You're a man of pure honour. You won't be biased.'

Toma sighs, fidgets. Coming all the way here must have tired him and it's beginning to show. But he likes flattery. He drinks it like an elixir. It revives him. 'Very well. You may proceed, Marius.'

Marius is imposing. 'I speak not only for my family, but also for all these good people standing with me. Most of all, I speak for my brother, Anton. Now dead. Dead long before his time!'

Toma nods sadly. 'Sweet Anton. Good boy. Wonderful musician. You should be proud of him. He died as he lived. Honourably.'

Marius ignores him, turns to the group behind Toma. 'You all loved Anton. He is a great loss to you, too. When he played, your eyes smiled as if they were seeing things for the first time. You relished your food and *rakiya* and felt you were at the gods' table. You thought the world was a land of hope. You wept and laughed and danced. You even bedded your spouses tenderly. Well, Anton is no longer with us. There's no one who can bestow on us his magic. Making his lute sing – that was his honour!'

Toma grunts. 'Get to the point, Marius. Or we'll think you're a mindless widow. Speak like a man!'

Marius, glowing with passion, continues to speak to Toma's followers. 'Now, you might think I've turned bitter because Anton was killed by Bostan – and Bostan's still alive. You might think I want revenge and to see Bostan dead!'

Gavril Rogosin, a *Morituri* and a nephew of Stefan, another of Bostan's victims, shouts. 'Now you're talking!'

Marius turns to him. 'But you'd be wrong! I don't want to see Bostan dead! Bostan didn't want to kill Anton. Like you, he loved Anton. Anton forced the issue. He even transgressed the Law! Went to kill Bostan at Bostan's home. Anton could take us to the clouds, but he was always the impulsive innocent. Bostan had to kill him – or be killed.'

Toma waves his mace impatiently. 'We know all that, Marius. No need to regurgitate it!'

Marius faces Toma. 'Another thing! And this time I'm speaking on behalf of my father and mother, on behalf of every parent who has lost a son to feuding! When Viktor shot Bostan, we didn't jump with joy! We didn't celebrate and get drunk! But we did when we heard Xenos had saved Bostan!'

Zemun and the *Morituri* protest. So do many in Toma's group.

'Shame on you!'

'You betray your brother!'

'You dishonour your men!'

'Anton died nobly!'

'He showed true blood! Good blood!'

'You're mad, Nexhat!'

The last scornful remark enrages Nexhat. He faces them. 'No! I was mad before! Mad, like you still are! But after Anton's death I came to my senses! If Xenos had been around when Anton was shot, Marius said, maybe Xenos could have saved him. Then I started thinking. This time without cobwebs in my brain. And I asked, as Marius asks you now: why was Anton killed? Why did he have to die?'

His outburst upsets him. He turns to his wife, weeps on her chest. She weeps also.

Toma seems confused, but pulls himself together. 'You know the answer, Nexhat! Anton died because he held the Law sacred!'

Marius moves closer to Toma. 'That's true! He honoured the Law! But what is this *Law*? Where did it come from? Who, of all the gods in heaven, gave it to us? And what sort of honour does it preach? What's honour anyway? The tool of despots! A chain to shackle people! What good is it if it kills? Answer that, Righteous Toma!'

Toma manages to find his old authority. 'Without honour, there's no life! The Law says: a dishonoured man ceases to be a human being!'

Zemun and the *Morituri* echo Toma. 'Without honour, life is unliveable!'

Marius faces the *Morituri*. 'Words! Meaningless words! We've been brainwashed with that drivel for generations! Life is liveable only when it's not poisoned by such nonsense! We get the chance to live only when we stop oppressors feeding us this nothingness as salvation! Life is to be lived! That's why it was created!'

Toma shrieks as if hurt in his soul. 'There's a way to live and a way to die!'

Marius turns to Toma. 'That's right. But making death noble – worshipping it – is not the way to live! Shall I tell you what killed Anton? The Law! Shall I tell you who really killed him? The soulless! Those crazy with power! The preachers of the Law! People who see life only through death! False prophets – like you!'

Exhaustion hits Toma. He pleads. 'Try to understand, Marius! Without honour, there's no life!'

Marius' passion explodes. 'No! The opposite is true! Without honour, there *is* life! Always!'

Toma strains to get up.

Marius addresses the crowd. 'Skenderis, listen to me! We must change our ways! We must abolish the Law!'

Toma hauls himself to his feet. 'Heresy!'

Marius is unstoppable. 'We must strive for peace, Skenderis! We must renounce feuding! Let's do it today! Now! Here, at this *Kriss*! Let's bury the Law!'

Toma, shaking his mace, staggers towards Marius. 'Never! Never! Nev ...!'

Suddenly he bends double, clutches his chest and collapses.

The *Morituri* rush to help him.

The assembly, in shock, fall silent.

Basil is the first to have the wits to act. He pushes the *Morituri* away, examines Toma. 'He's had a stroke.'

The *Morituri* protest in disbelief.

Lila starts screaming. Toma's supporters wail and beat their chests.

Basil shouts at the *Morituri*. 'Give me a hand! We've got to get him to my shop – quickly.'

Zemun and the *Morituri* lift Toma and carry him to Basil's van.

When they go, Lila stops screaming. She points her finger at Marius. 'If – if Toma dies ... You – and your supporters – will have killed him!'

Some of Toma's followers echo her. 'Yes! You! You! Murderers!'

Marius defies them. 'Have no fear. He's bound to live. Evil men always cheat death. Only the good die.'

Nexhat, still weeping, confronts Lila. 'You can't see it, but the truth is: if Toma dies, Anton will have been avenged!'

Lila laughs at him. 'You're a crazy old man. Go away!'

Nexhat, crushed, leans against Marius.

I go to them, take Nexhat's hand, stay with him.

Lila, now a wolf protecting her cubs, turns to the assembly. 'You heard what Righteous Toma said! Marius, Nexhat and those who agree with them are heretics! They have dishonoured us! May God forgive them! We, the true Skenderis, never will!'

Toma's followers applaud. 'Never! Never! Never!'

Their support bolsters Lila. Somehow mimicking Toma's

authority, she speaks as if she has memorized a lesson. 'Remember what Righteous Toma was saying! The Law lives! The Law is for ever! That's his judgement! The Law will remain our guide! That's what we will do! It will remain sacred!'

After this, Toma's and Marius' groups face each other, hurl accusations, ready to fight.

Lila seizes Toma's mace and outshouts them. 'I am Toma's successor. You know that's what he ordained. So listen to me!'

The groups fall silent.

Lila addresses the neutral group, who look at each other, confused.

The more she speaks, the more confident she becomes. 'We've been defiled by heresy here! Where does the blame lie? Toma has the answer. All the ills we Skenderis suffer, he taught me, come from bad blood! And whose blood is bad? The man who saved Bostan – Xenos! That's Toma's judgement! You all heard it! That bad blood now lives with Bostan: Stefan's killer! Anton's killer! Urs' killer! Rustu's killer! That bad blood, Xenos, stole Bostan's honourable death! Is it surprising then that the weak among us, like Marius, Nexhat and the rest, have had their minds poisoned? But bad blood goes as easily as it comes – that's something else Righteous Toma taught me! Xenos will go, too! One day he'll disappear! But the Law will live on! It will be honoured for eternity!'

Many shout approval.

Some, with Marius, Nexhat and me, protest.

Lila strikes the ground with Toma's mace. 'There's nothing more to be said! This *Kriss* is closed!'

35

TOMA

The albino, Basil, saved me. That half-baked man brought me back to life.

Whereas You, My Law, Toma's Law, You forsook me.

I could have died!

I could have died when I was ten ...

Diphtheria. My mother saved me. Bored a hole in my throat.

My mother loved me.

Then she caught my diphtheria. And died.

Again – this is the third time! – You let our enemies defy *Us*!

You disowned me. Left me humiliated!

They almost defeated *Us*.

They who live meaningless lives!

It wasn't Anibal's son who nearly defeated me. Bad blood, though he is, he's a formidable enemy – like his father. Defeating him would have been another laurel for me.

Instead, I faced that misguided lightweight, that bookworm, Marius! And the rest of the human dregs.

Books – what good are they?

When I went abroad to study I started reading everything.

Every book contradicted the other.

So I gave up, went after women.

Life is sweet when you are with a woman.

I was in love with one. Can't remember where. Can't remember her name either.

She left me. Said I was a relic from the Middle Ages …

Why? Because I told her the truth: that every god knows men are superior to women!

Did I deserve that disorderly *Kriss*?

If you're testing me, test me with someone close to my stature! Like Anibal's son.

So that I can defeat him. And I will. Soon!

When I recover!

When my mind comes back!

When my strength comes back!

I recovered from diphtheria! And from my mother's death! And from having my balls shot off!

Here is a heresy for You.

From me!

Are You brave enough to hear it?

Life is sweet! Even for a capon. More so for an old capon.

So …

So …

Is it right to condemn people to death?

Particularly youngsters?

When all they want is to live!

Ignore that! It's these wandering doubts. They catch me because I'm weak and fearful of Death!

Of course, it's right to send people to their deaths! How else would they accrue honour?

A man without honour is a dead man walking.

Without the Law there would be no order. Only anarchy.

And yet ...

Forgive my confusion ...

There are clouds in my mind!

Sometimes I can't tell whether I'm talking to You or to myself ...

It's not only You, My Law, Toma's Law, that confuses me ...

In the other room, there's Lila ...

She's with Zemun ...

They're talking ...

My mother and father used to talk like that, too ...

After my mother died, my father stopped talking.

Except when he instructed me on the Law. Which was most of the time.

Zemun visits me every day ...

Then stays on for hours with Lila ...

Does he come to visit me or her?

And do they just talk?

Or do they ...?

Am I being a typical old man with a young wife?

No such doubts about mothers ...

My mother loved me so much she wouldn't have another child ...

I melted when she cuddled me ... So soft and tender ...

But she also cuddled my father.

That made me jealous.

Why are mothers women – inferior like the rest? Why aren't they like men?

Then she died.

Father said she abandoned us ... Like You are abandoning me!

Father was right. Mothers do abandon their children!

They're spineless creatures – unless they are like Eleanora the Falcon.

Or like Lila will be.

Sometimes I think Death has an irresistible cock.

Father was lonely – bitter ... Wouldn't marry again.

So he married You, the Law ...

Zemun is a good boy ...

One day, he'll kill Anibal's son for me.

And he worships me ...

Also, Lila has changed ... She has bridled her sexuality ...

She now knows You, My Law, Toma's Law, perfectly.

She's a fast learner.

And she has taken an oath. She'll live and die a virgin.

The Virgin Lila!

She'll surpass Eleanora the Falcon! Surpass even my sweet, soft mother ...

She'll be the perfect successor when my time comes ...

Though that won't happen for years ...

We'll establish a dynasty ... Like old times – one family ruling for ever ...

Maybe that's why she's interested in Zemun ...

Admires his zeal ... His marksmanship ... Sees him as an intrepid defender ...

Of You, of *Toma's Law* ...

Of *Us* who are *One* and the *Same* ...

She's right, of course. Zemun's better – much better than Bostan.

And he has complete faith in *Me, Toma's Law*!

If necessary, he'll feud with all of Skender ...

To safeguard *You* and *Me* ...

My father trained me.

He was not an expert with guns. Not like he was about the Law.

That's why I wasn't the best shot in Skender.

Anibal was. But he was killed.

And I lived.

And made honour truly honourable.

Together, Zemun and Lila will smother *Us* in honour ...

Why did I say smother ...?

I meant they'll engulf *Us* with honour ...?

Engulf – that doesn't sound right either ...

I can't find the right words. But You know my meaning ...

Is this fear of mine, the fear of death?

One moment I'm able to think straight ...

The next ...

But I'll recover ... That half-baked man, Basil, will see to it ...

Do You know what he suggested? That I should let Anibal's son have a look at me ... He's a doctor, he said ... And he'd be happy to treat you ...

Happy – imagine?!

What humiliation!

I'd rather die ...

Lila said no – not Xenos! Never!

Lila knows my mind!

I won't die ... Basil will see to that ...

They're still in the next room – Zemun and Lila ...

I can't hear them talking. I think they're whispering ...

What are they doing?

I never heard my mother and father whisper ...

When they went to bed, they went to sleep ... Or so they said ...

But I kept picturing them naked ...

And I could hear their bed creak ...

If only I could get out of this bed ...

Soon ... Soon ...

That's what Basil said – soon ...

The stroke was minor.

Basil swears to that. Don't worry about the paralysed arm and the difficulty in speaking, he said ... They'll come back ... This is just a warning ...

Was it You who wanted to warn me?

Warn me about what?
That I must not think life is good.

I'll be out of this bed.
Soon ...
All I need is rest ...

You'll see, my strength, my mind, will return ...
I am Toma. *I* am indestructible!
Confusion. Doubts. What is truth?
Who is talking? Is it that young boy in Europe – the barbarian – before he became Toma? Before he embraced the Law, You, My Law, Toma's Law?
I am Truth!

One question before sleep ...
Do paladins fear death?

I did ...
So when they shot my balls off, I felt relief ...
Horrendous as it was being unmanned, it meant I was alive! I could go on living ... Enjoy the sweetness of life ... Carry honour without having to feud for it ...

Are we, *You* and *I* who are *One*, honourable enough to uphold honour?
Is honour good enough for man?

Disregard that!
My wits are wandering again ...
My Law, Toma's Law, will sustain *Us*. *We* are *One* and the *Same*.

36

KOKONA

The sky was dark as a nymph's eyes. A strong wind was sweeping the stars from one end of the horizon to the other. One of those nocturnal tempests which is a feature of our island and which we call 'the gods' rain dance'. The sort of night I love.

Dev and Castor were keeping watch.

Bostana was sleeping upstairs. Osip had moved into her bed.

Dev and I had stayed in the downstairs bedroom.

With Bostana's condition no longer critical, Osip was going through Anibal's papers once again. He felt certain that his father would have an answer to Bostana's dilemma; that somewhere in his writings on the Law lay a solution. Though the idea had struck me as implausible – no designated man had sought to revert to womanhood in Anibal's time – I had encouraged him to do so. At the very least, it would reinforce his determination to keep Bostana in his life.

I went to sit by the carob tree to let the wind garner my thoughts.

I should have been at the *Kriss*.

Bostan, Bostan
Wearing a man's boot
Come outside
And let's shoot

Viktor had started singing again. An old nursery rhyme rephrased to endorse the *Kriss'* judgement. He was still camped out in the meadow; he hadn't moved since the day Toma had arbitrated against him.

He was strutting around on a horse – Stefan Rogosin's horse. This pantomime, which he called psychological warfare, was his version of Achilles before the walls of Troy. He had let it be known pompously that the siege of the water-mill would be as relentless as that. He would stay encamped until Bostan recovered and left the water-mill. Then either he'd kill her or she'd kill him.

Bostan, Bostan
Wearing a man's boot
Come outside
And let's shoot

Now his entourage took up the refrain.

The water-mill was indeed surrounded. The many bonfires burning around the perimeter suggested that Viktor had formed new alliances. This tightening of the cordon, Dev had heard, had been requested by Lila as a get-well present for Toma. Thus Toma would be assured she was following in his footsteps.

The single mercy left to us – thanks to a clement article in the Law – was that we three were free to go to the Citadel to purchase whatever we needed, medicine and arms included. The Law exacted that feudists must be given every chance to be in good health; hence the blockade of provisions was prohibited.

The chanting stopped.

It would be resumed in an hour. And then again on the hour every hour. I had hated it at first, but now I found it silly.

As long as they bayed, Osip had assured us, we had nothing to fear.

I should have been at the *Kriss*.

This was the first one I'd missed since I'd earned the right to attend. For women that right is given only to those who have borne sons, but an exception had been made in my case for being a teacher; needless to say, a teacher for boys as, in the main, girls had not been encouraged to have an education.

Yes, this was one *Kriss* I should not have missed. Having grown feathers on my tongue, over the years, urging an end to feuding, I should have sensed that, during this particular *Kriss*, convening so soon after Osip had gravely undermined the Law by saving Bostana, my reasoning might have reached receptive hearts, might even have tipped the scales in favour of brave Marius, his parents and his followers.

But I'd chosen to stay with Osip and Bostana. They were my family now. And, like any good mother, I believed they would be safe only under my protection.

It's not only lovers who are befuddled by love; so are they who love the lovers.

One blessing, Dev thought, was Toma's stroke.

I disagreed. We have an old proverb that says successors always make us pine for their predecessors.

Toma, by virtue of Basil's intervention, had survived. However, given his age and the severity of the stroke – paralysed on one side and slurring his speech – it was unlikely he'd last long.

Osip had offered to have him installed at the water-mill and treat him, but Lila, parroting Toma, had declared that Osip was bad blood and that bad blood, always infectious, would hasten Toma's death.

Toma, we knew, had studied somewhere in Europe but, indoctrinated as he had been by his tradition-bound father, he had found the teaching too liberal, too seditious for Skender. There had been a time, between his return and his emasculation, when he had seemed wayward, purposeless and afflicted with doubts. But once blemished and disentitled to feud, he had, as he fervidly declares, surrendered himself to the Law. His doubts – we all know how pernicious they can be – must still exist. That, I always believed, explained why he hadn't succeeded in establishing himself as an all-out autocrat. His integrity within the scope of the Law, the way he judged fairly even when the decision was not to his liking, was indicative of that. Whereas a better-armoured Toma might even have captured the mainland, particularly during the Peoples' Wars.

I've come to believe that his odious beliefs provided him with some meaning after he had failed to find meaning in other human endeavours. I'm also convinced his vacuity has another source – probably unfathomable, but a source that must have been in his soul when he had gone abroad and could not absorb Europe's Enlightenment. Conceivably, had he been able to have children he might have found the meaning he had sought. Instead, he turned into a fanatic who, deep down, hates every male generation and marries them to Death.

But, at the very least, we could challenge him, even defy him.

Whereas now, with Lila posing as his apostle, I had qualms.

Lila, Skender's most desirable female, has always been popular with our men. When they see her they forget that women shouldn't be judged by their looks, but by their qualities. These days she is also the envy of our women. Moreover, since, under our fixed patriarchal order, women have almost no rights, Lila's empowering as the Law's prophetess, by Toma himself, has elevated her not only to the status of a man, but also to the rank of a Righteous One. In effect, she has reached, in one leap, a distinction far beyond that of a designated man. There has been no other woman in our history, with the possible exception of Eleanora the Falcon, to have attained such eminence.

Such power in one who is still very young frightens me.

What would she know about the evils of honour or the horrors of brutal death? She has yet to take a man inside her, let alone give birth. So what would she know about the blessings of love and life? And not least, after having been rejected publicly by Osip on the Day of Persephone and, irrespective of her marriage to Toma, she made it clear to everybody that she was a woman wronged. Should Toma die or fail to recover his speech, there's no telling what havoc her juvenile pride might wreak.

The arrogance of beauty is a Pandora's box. All the more dangerous for our people, who have been conditioned to seek leaders who'd discharge them from thinking for themselves and permit them to pursue their primitive obsession with violence.

I've been trying to hearten myself with the thought that Lila's youth, her lack of substance and experience are also deficiencies; that, conceivably, they might work against her.

But against that I bear in mind Zemun's interest in her. He has been seeing Lila regularly, ostensibly while visiting Toma.

Zemun's a firebrand. He has coveted Lila for a long time. How would we fare if we had a prophetess exploiting him when he's on heat?

I think what frightens me most is that there's a side to us women which we've always known about but rarely dared acknowledge. We can be as bad as our men. The designated men of the past – like Osip's mother – are proof of that. There have been shoals of women smitten with the desire to kill. Remember the generations of Skenderi mothers who, having given birth to boys, tore themselves from life and love and proudly offered their sons to the Law, affirming that by so doing they had done their duty as expected of them.

And it's not just Skenderi women who glorify conflict and death. Remember how the women of the mainland volunteered their voices and their wombs to their leaders, thus adding fuel to the Peoples' Wars? Remember also that, throughout history, all over the world, hordes of women have willingly sacrificed their children to countless despots, nationalists, religious bigots and every other harebrained ideologue who promised them an honourable death in this life and glory and paradise in the afterlife.

If that's how we women conduct ourselves, is there no hope then?

Yes, there is. There's still time to reclaim the natural tenderness and the innate love of life in us, to reclaim these virtues as the Lover of Love bestowed them on us. We women have been charged with creating the future. And we have been ordained to safeguard it.

We have to find a way to save Lila – and us – before she tastes blood and death.

Bostan, Bostan
Wearing a man's boot
Come outside
And let's shoot

An hour had passed.

Viktor was on his horse again, singing his banal refrain.

I stood up, ready to curse him.

But then I realized that his singing had lost its fervour. He looked uncomfortable on the horse. I felt certain he'd rather be at home, contentedly drinking *rakiya*, making love with his young wife, Yilka, and then going to sleep to count, in his dreams, the wealth he had accumulated from the Gospodins.

37

OSIP

Bostana was restless.

But she was recovering well and was in less pain; she could now move her limbs with some ease.

However, as she improved, her spirit darkened. I knew the nature of her anxiety. The same as mine: what to do when she was fully fit?

I tried to give her a sedative before she settled for sleep, but she refused it. That's not what I need, she said crossly. So I held her against my chest, wondering whether she had any idea how hungrily I, too, needed what she needed.

Then Viktor started up his taunt.

Bostan, Bostan
Wearing a man's boot
Come outside
And let's shoot

To conceal my own anguish, I asked her whether that stupid ditty was irritating her as much as me – but she shrugged her shoulders and repeated what I'd told her when Viktor had first started singing: jackals might bay all night long, but they can't stop the advent of a new day and so they must cease.

Then she pulled away, hugged the pillow and shut her eyes.

I waited for her to fall asleep, then moved to the office at the other end of the room where I'd been re-reading my father's papers.

My discovery of my lineage moved me in a way that I could not have imagined. It confirmed I had roots and a beginning. And it fortified my conviction that I had found my haven – of all places, at my own source – and that now, having attached my life, come what may, to Bostana's, I would stay here for ever. My odyssey had come to an end.

I had divided the papers into two lots.

The first comprised ancient invoices, receipts and promissory notes exchanged between the Goras, numerous Skenderi families and the foreign merchants and agents who had settled on the island when it was still under Ottoman rule.

They recorded prosperous and peaceable times. The water-mill, I learned, had been merely a sideline for the Goras. They had been involved in just about every enterprise, from chandlery of vessels to obtaining import licences from the Imperial Customs Office for merchants of various nationalities. And whenever a war broke out in the region – which it did regularly – they had provided warehouses and silos for ships unable to reach their home ports.

The Skenderis of those times, given autonomy by the Sultanate to conduct their affairs freely but equitably, had maintained that trade with everybody was the quintessence of civilization. This belief in coexistence had produced an ethos of goodwill: when, on occasion, the Mediterranean's fickle storms had sunk ships, wiped out fortunes, killed relatives, friends and associates, support and financial help had been immediately forthcoming. No wonder peoples of all races and religions had vied to settle here.

The second, and much the larger lot, contained the files, diaries and letters written over the years by my father, Anibal. Ochred from age, their ink all but fading, and composed in a fluent, classical style that nowadays is derided as old-fashioned, these texts, encompassing his reflections on a wide range of subjects, revealed that the good father I had so fervently idealized was a far more learned and loving person than my iconic memories of him.

Not surprisingly, there were a series of studies on Eleanora's Falcons – a number of which, judging by the appreciative responses to them, had been published in several ornithological journals.

What completely absorbed me were his personal diaries and the commentaries he had written on all manner of issues, particularly on the iniquities of the Law.

The most painful entries were those concerning my mother. There was an abundance of these and I had been able to read them only intermittently.

Their courtship had started joyously.

My father, captivated by my mother's beauty, had fallen in love with her at first sight. Firmly resisting his parents' exhortations to take his pick of the many maidens worthy to be a Gora bride – meaning daughters of wealthy families – he had convinced them to ask for her hand.

My mother's father, a widower who ran a tavern by the harbour when there was still some maritime activity, had readily accepted the proposal. A heavy drinker who regularly beat up his children – all of them girls – he had been only too pleased to get rid of one.

Nonetheless, refusing to give even a token dowry as was the custom, he had exacted a hefty prize – bride-money, he had called it – to keep him in *rakiya* for the rest of his life.

To my mother's delight, that had ended shortly. He had died a few months after her nuptials.

My parents' early months were harmonious. But in the wholesomeness of his love, my father had overlooked the fact that my mother had already embraced the Law and was deeply under Toma's influence. Indeed, that first time he had seen her had been when she had been listening to Toma's acclamation of the Law in the Palladion's *meydan*.

My father's initial disregard of my mother's religiosity had been an indication of his indulgence. He had considered it understandable that a young girl, forlorn after her mother's early death and seeking refuge from a vicious father, would be a natural candidate for the transcendental rites of the apostolic faith. But he had failed to see that the Skenderi Orthodoxy, to which my mother had submitted at a very early age, had been greatly influenced by the Law and, irrespective of its rapturous traditions, was just as uncompromising. The realization that my mother had veered towards fanaticism had dawned upon my father only when, almost overnight, she had converted from a devotee of Orthodoxy to a disciple of the Law. Needless to say, it had been Toma who had persuaded her to convert. Though by then my mother had grown into a young woman, she had not attained the maturity to resist Toma's fiery discourses.

Before the marriage was a year old, in fact on the day she had realized she was pregnant with me, my mother had barred my father from her bed. From then on, no matter how pitifully he had beseeched her, she had never allowed him any intimacy.

This had plunged my father into terrible despondency. At one point he had even contemplated suicide.

He had overcome that urge only because, by then, I was born: the son he had prayed for, to whom he could devote all his love. There are passages – so poignant that they always make me weep – depicting how, as I grew up, he would regularly sneak into my room when I was asleep, sit by my side and gaze at me for hours, murmuring that I was the miracle in his life.

It had been my mother, when still gravid, who had prompted my father to become the family feudist. He had accepted with deep reluctance. In fact, he had had little choice: the Goras were running out of men; those still alive were past their prime and some were approaching death; moreover, should he refuse, my mother had threatened, she would put herself forward as the family's designated man immediately after she had given birth to me.

However, I can't help thinking that, by agreeing to take up feuding, my father had hoped he would thus regain my mother's affection and, finally, be readmitted to her bed. In one entry, he had written: 'Hope lives, even in the hopeless.'

The notes on his views about Skender's feuding culture – some of which he had expanded into essays – revealed how brave, far-sighted and humane he had been.

These were the writings wherein I had hoped to find a solution to Bostana's predicament.

His reflections lamented the way Skender's erstwhile gracious life and the people's innate sense of fairness had disintegrated into a culture of violence within a few decades, with barely any resistance.

The decline had started after a band of soldiers of fortune, all seasoned warriors, had descended on the island. These reprobates – my father dubbed them *conquistadores* after the Spaniards who had devastated Latin America – had been roaming Europe in search of a rich, remote and vulnerable community that they could exploit unchallenged. Since, as my father had put it, Fate invariably favours evil men, the opportunity to fulfil their ambitions had fallen into their laps in the wake of the Ottomans' withdrawal from the archipelago, at the end of the eighteenth century.

Led by a monomaniac who called himself Timur and who claimed descent from Attila the Hun, these *conquistadores* had soon established a reign of terror on the island. Timur, who hated Christians, Jews, Muslims, converts and everybody else in equal measure, had proceeded, with cunning lies, to set families and businesses against each other by exploiting prejudices that had lain dormant for centuries. Soon the Skenderis, quaintly ingenuous after centuries of a peaceable life, had found themselves engaged in petty disputes.

Over time, deception and defamation had obliterated trust and honesty and petty disputes had grown bitter. Timur, offering himself as arbiter – and charging huge fees for the service – had formulated severe punishments for whatever he deemed to be an offence. By the time he died, a very rich landowner, those who could leave Skender had done so.

Under Timur's son, Chingiz – named after another Central Asian monarch – the descendants of the *conquistadores* had fully installed themselves as feudal lords. Chingiz, determined to maintain his rule and more skilful in governance than his father, had kept an eye on the political situation in Europe. At some point, he had come across the *Kanun*, a code of law entrenched in certain rural and remote Balkan communities which had as its principal commandment the safeguarding of honour – and, particularly, the absolution of dishonour by the spillage of blood.

Astute enough to realize that the strict observance of such a code, more restrictive and unforgiving than anywhere else in Europe, would not only ensure the continuation of his lineage, lands and possessions, but also create a society both submissive and apathetic, Chingiz had produced his version of the *Kanun* – now known as the Law – and had decreed it as Skender's constitution.

After that any act adjudged to contravene the Law had been interpreted as dishonour.

In the ensuing hundred years or so, as endless feuds had decimated Skender's population, the island's prosperity had evaporated.

By the beginning of the twentieth century, the descendants of the *conquistadores*, having despoiled the island's riches, had decamped. The Law and all its miseries had remained.

Actually, not all. Some changes did occur. Two major ones, in fact. Both initiated by my father, who had sought every opportunity to find saving clauses in the Law.

The first was his pronouncement that feuding should be limited to one feudist from each family. In Chingiz's *Kanun* all males from the age of ten, when outside the sanctuary of their homes, had been regarded as legitimate targets. Not surprisingly, this stipulation had vastly depleted the male pool, particularly through the deaths of young boys. It had also forced many of the surviving men to barricade themselves, in remote parts of the island, with meagre supplies of food, often for the rest of their lives, in fortified shacks where the only openings consisted of crenellations just large enough to push through a rifle. The immediate result was the desertion of ancestral homes. That, in turn, had caused the abandonment of agriculture and husbandry, reducing much of paradisal Skender to a wasteland.

My father, then still quite young, discovered that the Law's commandments on feuds had been based on Chingiz's *Kanun*. This itself had copied the praxis of classical times, when conflicts between factions were resolved by single combat between elected champions. Thus he had proposed that the Law should be amended to stipulate that each family should select, from its menfolk, a single feudist so that those two and nobody else would be targeted. Again, following earlier ordinances, he had further proposed that when a feudist was killed, his family should be granted a short respite to bury their man and to choose a new feudist.

Toma had strongly objected to the proposal, claiming that the Law, having been already amended by Chingiz, no longer had any links with the *Kanun*, and that my father had invented a gratuitous strategy.

The Skenderis, for the first time opposing Toma, had accepted my father's proposal and insisted on the revision of the Law accordingly.

But Toma had managed to repeal my father's most powerful adjunct: that in the case of a family that had all its men killed, the family should be judged to have atoned for the dishonour it had caused. Toma, never ready to relinquish his authority, had defined the adjunct as heresy with the argument that, since honour was canon and, therefore, incontrovertible, only the extinction of the family would see justice prevail. Thus the rule of designating a woman as the family's man had remained statutory.

The second important amendment my father had instigated, several years later, was a change to the rule of retribution. Once again referring to the *Kanun*, he had disclosed that, in certain cases, it had assented to a bloodless resolution – exercised by many kings and feudal lords of the past – namely, the payment of a ransom or the pronouncement of a public apology. Stressing that this rule, too, had been copied verbatim by the Law, he had proposed that, where possible, a *Kriss* should be convened during which the qualities of the offender would be weighed against his offence. Thus, should the offender be judged a good enough person, then redemption by blood should be remitted to redemption by reparation such as a public apology, or financial compensation, or a period of unpaid labour.

Though this proposal, too, had been accepted by the people – again, despite fierce opposition from Toma – it had been implemented only twice.

On both occasions it had been my father who had resorted to the amendment.

Though, in both those cases, the Goras had been the offended family, my father had chosen to take the blame upon himself and had demanded that he be tried at a *Kriss*.

In the first instance, aware that the opposing family had run out of men and had designated their newly married daughter as their feudist, my father, all the more reluctant to kill a woman, had asked the *Kriss* to acknowledge him as a humble penitent who, having inadvertently caused offence to the wronged family, was ready to offer a public apology. When the *Kriss* had accepted his plea, he had asked forgiveness from his adversaries, unmindful of some of the islanders' ridicule.

On the second occasion, when a young lad who could barely handle a gun had been elected as his opposing feudist, my father had again asked for a *Kriss* to be convened. This time, declaring that he had committed the offence inadvertently due to a severe fever – a lie endorsed by Basil's father, also an apothecary – he had obtained reconciliation by paying the family hefty compensation.

Distressingly, on both occasions, he had had to suffer not only Toma's censure, but also my mother's. The diaries don't reveal when my mother first showed her contempt for him. But they make it plain that her disparagement intensified day by day.

I also recognized something that made me feel, despite my love for Bostana, that I would never be able to emulate the depth of my father's love. Not only for my mother, or for the people of Skender, but also for myself.

Such had been my father's aversion to killing that he had planned, almost from the moment of my birth, how to spare me from the burden of becoming the family feudist when my time came. Unable to leave Skender because so many like-minded people depended on his guidance, he had desperately sought ways to liberate me from the shackles of the Law.

He had kept up a continuous correspondence with various contacts abroad – a few distinguished ornithologists among them – begging them to advise him where, in the world, could be found a place of peace where his son could be safe. When, to his great pride, I had proved myself an enthusiastic and intelligent student – to his mind, an indisputable indication that I would excel him in every way – the correspondence had become even more intense, with demands for information on the best schools and universities.

But none of the places suggested by his correspondents as safe had proved satisfactory.

Europe, he had concluded, was an assemblage of sharks at mob feeding time. On the evidence of the two World Wars and their aftermath, the nations of the old continent were ruled by kindred versions of the Law – but on a larger scale. Their feuds were just as relentless. And, like ours, their honour conflicts were dictated by their own historical pasts, though concealed in inflated verbiage such as 'imperial imperative', 'national interest', 'governmental sagacity', 'political necessity', 'military objectives', 'economic survival' and the myriad hybrids these spawn whenever expediency demands. All carrying the same meaninglessness as honour, all pursuing self-interest and aggrandisement.

The United States, he had perceived, had adopted comparable historical distortions to those of Europe.

He had dismissed the other continents for similar reasons and, not least, because most of Asia, Africa, the Americas and Oceania had lived – or were still living – under colonial rule. He could see no future for his son under such systems.

Finally, although he had acknowledged that the best places of learning were either in Europe or in the United States, he had rejected them all. Those were the very places, he had decided, where governments glorified conquests and military supremacy instead of taking pride in their many and important humanitarian achievements. 'Any country that has more men under arms and that either neglects or disregards its poets and philosophers', he had commented in one of his papers, 'must be as tyrannized by the same false myths of honour as Skender.'

Then the first of the Peoples' Wars had broken out. And that, finally, had broken his resolve. When news of the unrestrained barbarity on the mainland started reaching him, he had decided that there were no safe places in the world, nowhere where the enlightened would outnumber soldiers, nowhere where humankind's love for life could flourish, nowhere where the Law, in one guise or another, did not rule.

And so, according to one entry in his diary, since he loved me beyond anything in the world, he would not entrust my well-being to anyone but himself. He would keep me safe for years, until I, too, became as proficient as he in survival.

He had written that entry a few months before his death.

And that promise had been the only one, in all his life, he had not been able to keep.

I nearly jumped out of my skin. I suddenly realized that he *had* kept that promise.

There was a way to survive.

It had been there, trying to alert me, all these months, and I had not seen it. He had perceived how I could save Bostana – as I had known he would.

I rose from my chair. I needed time to think.

I came face to face with Bostana.

She had taken off her nightdress and, but for the few dressings on her body, was completely naked.

'Bostana ...'

She shut my mouth with her hand. 'Sssshhhh ...'

Then she pulled down my trousers.

'Bostana!'

'Sit on the bed ...'

'What?'

She pushed me towards the bed. 'On the bed. Lie down!'

Hesitantly, I lay down. 'But Bostana ...'

She lowered herself onto me. 'I want to be happy. If only for a day.'

I buried my face between her breasts.

38

BOSTAN

I mounted him. Willed my body to ignore its pains. Urged it to be strong, to remember what being a woman is.

He slid inside me. So tenderly. So easily. As if his birdie had been nesting in my *amata* all his life and knew her every twirl.

We stayed like that, moving gently. Timeless. I felt I was inside him as much as he was inside me.

We rested.

At one moment he said: 'I give you all I have, Bostana.'

And I said: 'That's all I want.'

Then he said: 'All the bad in me has evaporated. I flow into you with all the goodness in me.'

We rested.

Another time I heard Viktor singing:

Bostan, Bostan
Wearing a man's boot
Come outside
And let's shoot

I laughed. I wasn't wearing men's boots any more. I was a woman again. And naked. With a man inside me. My man. And I wasn't shooting bullets but overflowing with all the warmth and pleasure I had locked away in my belly.

We rested.

Osip kept whispering in my ear. 'I shall never have enough of you, Bostana.'

Each time, I whispered back. 'Me too! Me too!'

We rested.

Another time he murmured. 'Dev once said bodies don't lie. Now I understand what he means.'

I licked him, licked all the scars on his body, even though my strength was ebbing.

We rested.

Every time he drank my *amata*, he said: 'This is where your soul lives. This is where I've found my soul.'

We rested.

An age later, when all my limbs seemed to float around me, he laid me down on the bed, covered me and said: 'You're my miracle, my woman.'

39

DEV

Osip and Bostana are in love.

Kokona's very happy. Proves love always finds ways to sprout, she says. Even in rubble, it locates a chink and grows. Nothing stops it. Not laws. Not traditions. Not even Skender's death-ordained life.

But I worry. I shake with fear.

Almighty love, this one is. Endless Milky Way. They're so hungry for each other, like rain and soil. The way he touches her, dresses her wounds, washes her, helps her walk, rocks her to sleep. And she melts. It's like when Kokona looked after me. Always wanting to be one.

There'll be trouble. Big trouble. I say Osip can look after himself. Also Kokona and I are here. But trouble is like the thresher shark – you can never guess which way it will swerve and bite.

It's on its way, trouble. I feel the air is waiting for the graveyard wind.

Today Bostana comes down without help. Hair shining as if burnished by yellow berries. Caftan hugging her body. Radiant.

We celebrate, take *rakiya*, sit under the carob tree.

Bostana is so happy she decides to cook. Something special. She hasn't cooked for years.

We let her. Sea bass with quince. Delicious.

She gurgles like a child. Her mother's recipe, she says.

But Viktor spots her walking.

I see him send men to the Citadel, to spread the news.

Soon Zemun appears.

Zemun usually comes every three days.

But not as a dutiful son. Only to check on Bostana's progress. Will she recover? Start feuding again? That's all he thinks about – the feud. Time's passing. The Rogosins are gloating. The Kristofs' honour is in shreds, he says.

He is a bluebottle searching for shit. Impatient to take over from Bostana.

Today he's one day early. Comes in the afternoon. Afternoons he never leaves the Palladion's *meydan,* practises shooting.

Bostana's in bed, drinking mint tea.

I am sterilizing stuff.

Kokona's preparing dinner.

Osip's keeping watch with Castor. He must be surprised that Zemun's a day early.

But he guides him round the traps. Bostana's son has a son's rights, he always says.

Kokona offers Zemun tea. Wait until your mother comes down, she says.

Zemun refuses. Wants to see if Bostana is really resting. He heard from Viktor's men she walked this morning.

Kokona lets him come up.

Bostana's eyes light up when she sees him. 'Zemun! Son! What joy!'

The more I see Zemun, the more I detest him. Haughty turd! He's worse these days because now he can use guns as well as Bostana. He's still Toma's favourite.

We hear he goes to Toma's sickbed every day. I think that's because he's keen on Lila. Maybe he's waiting for Toma to die?

The wind that brings him has the smell of tombstones.

He grunts at Bostana, waves me away. 'Leave us alone, Shrimp!'

I'm sterilizing. I'm ready to argue.

But Bostana intervenes. 'His name is Dev, Zemun. And he stays. He's my friend.'

Zemun snarls. 'You and I have to talk – man to man.'

'Talk. Dev stays.'

'No!'

Bostana is firm, but gentle. 'Don't be a child, Zemun. I have nothing to hide from my friends.'

Zemun snaps. 'I'm not a child!'

Bostana gives a motherly smile. 'Good.'

Zemun huffs, points at Bostana's blonde curls. 'You should cut your hair! It's too long!'

Bostana remains sweet. 'It's nice long ...'

Zemun shakes his head. 'It won't do! And put a decent shirt on! Everything's bulging out! You look like a woman!'

Bostana stays patient. 'I am a woman.'

'No, you're not. You're our designated man. You should look like one.'

Bostana grows stern. 'This is how I am. How I want to look. It's not for you to tell me what to do!'

Zemun is furious. 'They'll be laughing at you – the islanders! Think of the family honour!'

Bostana loses patience. 'To hell with the family honour!'

Zemun is shocked, almost speechless. 'What ...? What ...? What has happened to you?'

Bostana weakens. 'Nothing. I'm just tired ...'

Zemun's voice softens. 'Just tired? Or still unwell ...?'

'Just tired. Otherwise fine. Osip says I should be bouncing in a month.'

'Osip says ...?'

'He's a doctor. He's been looking after me ...'

Zemun sneers. 'Yes, I know. Everybody knows. As long as that's all he's doing ...'

Bostana gets angry. And torn. She loves her son. She controls herself. 'You said you wanted to talk. So talk!'

'We have a feud. Our camp is getting edgy.'

'Well, tell them to simmer down. The Rogosins are still mourning Stefan. They've yet to name their feudist.'

'They don't have to. They're in no hurry. Viktor has taken over. Besides, you're still crippled. You can't fight just yet. When you're back in business, when – if – you kill Viktor, they'll name him.'

'So we have plenty of time!'

'Honour does not wait for time. We have to defend our honour.'

'Honour! Honour! Honour! Enough! I've lost half my life to honour!'

'You also owe the rest of your life to it! Honour is all we have.'

'I said – when the time comes ...'

'How long is that?'

'When I'm fully recovered.'

Zemun is scornful. 'A month? When you'll be bouncing?'

'I expect so.'

'Very well. In four weeks, you leave this place and do your duty as our designated man!'

'Are you giving me orders? Listen, my boy! I'm still your mother! Still head of the family! Be careful how you speak to me!'

'I'm not your boy! I'm a Kristof man! And I speak for the family! They believe in me! So does Toma ... And Lila ... They have faith in me!'

'But they haven't appointed you feudist yet! They can't. Not until I'm dead! Is that what you want? Me – dead?'

I see Zemun wants that. He tries to look sincere. 'No! I just want you to do your duty!'

'You know Viktor's out there waiting for me.'

'I know. If I'd been our feudist, I'd have killed him ten times over.'

'When he sees me leave, he'll have the advantage. He's got a perfect sniper's position.'

'That's a chance you'll have to take.'

'It's not much of a chance.'

'Whatever. You have to take it! Four weeks. Agreed?'

Bostana sighs. Nods. 'Four weeks.'

'I'll see you then.'

'Not before?'

'No. I'll let you get better. Besides, I must keep practising.'

'In case I get killed?'

'In case.'

'But I'd like to see you. I'm your mother. I love you. Doesn't that mean anything to you?'

'Honour comes before love.'

Bostana tries not to cry. 'Ah, yes. the Law according to Toma ...'

'He's a great man, Toma!'

'He is. He is. Of course, he is. He can even steal you from me ...'

Zemun turns and leaves. No tender gesture or loving word.

Bostana bursts into tears.

I go to comfort her, hold her.

Bostana weeps bitterly. 'Why did Osip save me? For this? For this?'

I don't know what to say. So I say what is obvious. 'He saved you because he now believes life is holy. And you are doubly holy because he loves you.'

Bostana groans. 'What's the use of love? What good comes of it?'

40

TOMA

I am not going to die!
  That's the verdict from Basil, the half-baked man!

I can now move my arm.
  And my speech is better; slurs only a little.
  So beware, world, beware!
  I, Toma, am still here!
  I, Toma, have immortality in my bones!
  I, Toma, have come back from Hades!

And Aníbal's son, beware, especially, for having dared challenge me!

A new world is dawning!
  Did You hear that?
  You, My Law, Toma's Law?
  I will honour *Us*!
  Our time is dawning!
  You who very nearly forsook me!
  Do You hear me?
  Our time is here!

No, You didn't forsake me!
You were testing me!
Again!
To my limits!
And see, *I* have no limits!
I have triumphed!
We stand victorious!

But here is something of interest.
Do You know why I'm recovering so quickly?
You won't believe it!
I will tell You nonetheless!

When I thanked Basil for saving me, for saving You, Toma's Law – for saving history, in effect – he said it was the medication prescribed by Anibal's son that had brought me back from death!
Grotesque!

That half-baked Basil deceived me.
That eerie albino went behind my back to consult Anibal's son.
I told him I would rather have died!
He said I was being unreasonable!
Me – unreasonable?!
He said: even bitter enemies should be chivalrous – that's in the Law.
Yes, it is. But it won't be in My Law!
He said: remember Avicenna: the human will can conjoin essence and existence, the inner and outer worlds.
Of course, I remember that!
I had schooling in Europe!
And unbeknown to anybody, I've kept reading whatever I could.

All imbecilic stuff!

But it gave me ammunition against free-thinkers!

I used it to promote the Law!

My Law!

Toma's Law!

Then I had a vision of Basil's father, also an apothecary, also an albino, healing some of the sick with leeches.

They sucked the bad blood and the person was cured!

So now I understand how Anibal's son made me better.

He's a leech, my personal leech.

He's been sucking the bad blood that wore me down with his medicines.

The bad blood he's poured into my soul since coming here!

You might think he contaminated me as he sucked my blood.

But he didn't.

He sucked his own bad blood – the blood that had contaminated me!

My blood is back to its original purity!

As untainted as it has always been!

A leech is a leech for ever. Whichever direction evolution takes, he can never become human!

And like all leeches Anibal's son will be crushed underfoot!

Zemun will do that for me!

Zemun tells me Bostan will be well enough in a month and will leave Anibal's son's place.

Viktor will kill Bostan the moment Bostan steps outside the watermill.

Then Zemun, my warrior, will serve my will!
He'll kill Anibal's son first.
Then Viktor.
Then whoever confronts him.

By that time I will be my old self, my blood purified by honour!

Zemun's here now.
In the next room.
Talking to Lila.
I can't hear their voices.
Their silence disturbs me!

Beware you, too, Zemun!
In *My* new world, you will be only a disciple.
No talks with Lila in dark rooms!
No talks with her anywhere!

Beware, everybody!
Toma is back.
Toma's Law will forge the future!
This time there'll be no casuistry!
This time *My Law* will replace all the laws as the monolithic pure *Law*!
It will conquer everybody!
Everything!
The world!

And *I* will live!
With Lila by my side!
Live and live and live!

41

KOKONA

Dev and I were sitting in the main room by the millpond, staring at our bottle of wine, too disheartened to drink.

Osip was outside, keeping watch with Castor.

Bostana had been pacing her room for some hours.

Zemun's visit had unnerved her.

And the ultimatum he had given her had shattered our complacency; time was ebbing away.

I had suggested to Bostana that we should consult Osip; that together we might come up with a solution. But she had preferred not to have any discussions yet; she wanted to clear her mind.

Then she had added dispiritedly that there were no solutions. No matter how well one winnows grain, there'd always be some chaff left.

She came down eventually.

She took out a bottle of *rakiya* and sat down at the table. She had been crying. Despite her strained face, she still looked luminous.

She drank several gulps in one go, like the Bostan of old. 'I've decided.'

Dev and I turned to her anxiously.

'A month's bliss. That's more than most people have. I'll be satisfied with that.'

'Meaning?'

She turned to me, her eyes shining. 'Osip and I are like husband and wife now.'

'I know.'

She looked at me in surprise. 'How? Did he tell you? Are we too noisy?'

I laughed. 'You glow.'

Dev chuckled. 'Osip, too.'

She beamed. 'We're so happy together.'

I filled up my glass of wine. 'You said you've decided.'

She became serious, drank some more *rakiya*. She nodded a few times. 'Yes ... You see ... Zemun – I have to think of him ... He's my son ... Not how I'd like him to be, but my son ... And I love him ... I keep hoping he might change – when he gets older. I'm praying he will ... Anyway, he must come first ... I'll have my month of heaven with Osip, then ...'

She paused, on the verge of tears.

'Then?'

She took another gulp of *rakiya*. 'Then I'll become Bostan again. And ...'

'Run into Viktor's bullets?'

'I can take Viktor ...'

'Not when he's got the vantage ground ...'

'Viktor's not a good shot. He fired all those bullets into me – and from close range – but still couldn't kill me. I'll take my chance.'

I tried to stay calm. 'All right. Let's look at your decision from another angle. You'll be Bostan again to stop Zemun from feuding?'

'Yes.'

'But if Viktor kills you Zemun will take over anyway.'

'I won't get killed!'

'That's not certain. Even if it were – sooner or later someone will kill you. Then Zemun will take over and eventually he'll end up dead, too.'

'No!'

'Bostana, listen ...'

She whimpered. 'What else can I do?!'

Suddenly, Osip's voice boomed. 'I'll tell you!'

We spun round. He was standing by the stone traverse, smiling. He came in. 'Your watch, Dev. Castor's on his own, wanting company.'

Dev sprang up. 'Sorry, I forgot ... I was listening ...'

He rushed out.

Osip came over, gently caressed Bostana's cheek, then sat down.

Bostana held onto his hand. 'Osip, listen. When Zemun came, he gave me a month ...'

Osip kissed her hair. 'Yes. Dev told me ... But I'd guessed as much. When he left his face looked like burnt wood.'

'Then you'll understand. Nothing I can do ... I have to think of him ...'

Osip poured himself a *rakiya*. 'There *is* something we can do, my woman ... I've found a way.'

'You don't understand ...'

'Reconciliation ...'

I perked up. 'I've already told you that happens through marriage between the feuding parties ...'

Bostana turned fierce. 'You're not thinking that I ...'

'No. Another way ...'

I became animated. 'There were two cases in the past – are you thinking of those?'

Osip nodded. 'Yes. Both instigated by my father. I should have noted them when I first read his papers. Now, having read them again, they shine like beacons. I was going to discuss them with you, Mother – a few nights back. But I wanted to keep going over the details and contrive a plausible way forward.'

'Those cases are forgotten now – buried away.'

'No matter. The amendment for reconciliation remains. It's still part of the Law.'

Bostana looked at us in bewilderment. 'What are you talking about?'

'Reconciliation by public apology. Or compensation as reparation. My father resorted to it twice – and succeeded.'

Bostana shook her head in despair. 'You forget, I've too many families against me.'

Osip stroked her cheek. 'I know, my woman. But let's look at how they stand. There are the Rogosins. It's been some time since you killed Stefan, but they haven't nominated a feudist yet ... They might see reason, accept the idea of a different future. Then there are the Kaplans. Both Marius and Nexhat, his father, declared at the *Kriss* that you had no choice but to kill Anton. They, too, haven't elected a feudist yet – and, given Marius' opposition to the Law, they won't want to if they can help it. They certainly didn't want Viktor to take it upon himself to avenge Anton ...'

Bostana lit two cigarettes, handed one to Osip and started smoking the other. 'Even so, two other families, the Eduards and the Nis, related to the Kaplans, also took it upon themselves to avenge Anton. I killed both their feudists, Urs and Rustu.'

Osip nodded. 'Nonetheless those families, too, haven't appointed new feudists yet. They might be tempted to accept a sizeable reparation.'

Bostana muttered despondently. 'Osip, my man – it's all might might might ...'

Osip took her hand. 'It's our only chance, my woman.'

She kissed his hand and nodded solemnly.

Osip turned to me. 'We have five families in dispute with Bostana – with, at the moment, only one feudist, Viktor, actively in the field.'

I nodded dubiously. 'We might win over two or three – but no more.'

Osip shook his head. 'I wouldn't suggest we approach all of them at once. They'll try to outdo each other and pretend their honour comes first. We should go to Viktor. He's influential on the island. He's also rich and getting on in years. And he has a young wife. The idea of a quiet life might prove appealing.'

Bostana laughed. 'But I can't go to Viktor. The moment he sees me, he'll start shooting.'

Osip smiled. 'You won't have to. In both the cases my father refers to, he used a third party. Much the better way.'

I clapped my hands. At last I could see a possible way out of the labyrinth. 'I can approach Victor!'

Osip kissed my hand. 'That would be best, Mother.'

My enthusiasm galloped. 'I'll do it tomorrow.'

Osip got up and took out some faded papers from a drawer. 'We'll plan well. I have some ideas. I brought these down – my father's notes on the two cases. They offer excellent guidelines. But you might think of some embellishments, Mother.'

'I'll read them tonight.'

'Thank you.'

Gleefully, I drank my wine. I was about to start pouring *rakiya* for them, but Osip stopped me.

'If you'll excuse us, Mother, we'll go to bed.'

I chortled. 'Go on then. Stop wasting time!'

Gently, Osip lifted Bostana off her chair. 'Come, my woman.'

Bostana, looking as if she believed in the possibility of a future, put her head on Osip's shoulder and let him take her up the stairs.

42

OSIP

We filled a hamper with food and wine. Then we went over to Viktor's bivouac in the meadow.

Having stationed himself there for over a month, he had a drained – almost torpid – appearance. His look-outs were still around – they were the ones who took turns to bring him provisions – but, except for the younger ones, they seemed pretty worn-out, too.

As we approached him, Viktor got up, stiffly. By then his look-outs were on the alert with their rifles pointed at me.

I opened my arms to show that I was not carrying a weapon. Then a few paces from Viktor, I let Kokona proceed.

I squatted, still a short distance away, to indicate that I would be privy to their conversation, but would not intervene.

Kokona greeted Victor like an old friend. 'Poor you, Viktor. You look like me when I get out of bed and have to lean on Dev for my bones to come to life again.'

Viktor offered a courteous smile. 'Old age looming, Kokona. Nothing I can do about it.'

'Make love as often as you can. Then you forget your age.'

'Ah, if only ...' His voice was hoarse and nasal. He was obviously suffering from a bad cold. 'A pleasure to see you, Kokona. To what do I owe this privilege?'

Kokona opened the hamper, spread a cloth on the grass and laid out the cheese, olives, *pastirma* and pitta she had painstakingly prepared. Then she brought out a couple of bottles of wine.

'I thought you might like a picnic.'

He looked amused. 'A picnic? Now – of all times?'

'And a talk.'

He became serious again. 'Thanks for the picnic. But what's there to talk about?'

'This and that.' Kokona offered him some wine. 'Here, drink some of this. It will help your chill.'

'I don't have a chill.' But he took the glass and drank avidly. Then he pointed at me. 'That Xenos – what's he doing here? Send him back. I hate him.'

'We've adopted each other – mother and son. He's also very gallant. He insists on looking after me.'

Viktor sneered. 'Gallant, too? What a world!'

'Full of surprises, I always say.'

'All the same, I'd rather he wasn't here.'

Kokona served herself some wine. 'He won't intrude. He might join in – after our talk. But only if you agree.'

Viktor sipped some more wine. 'The talk ... Is it about my singing?'

Kokona served him some *pastirma* in a pitta. 'No. Though I don't think that does you any justice.'

'Psychological warfare. Learned it from the mercenaries. Xenos should know all about it ...'

'Even so – not your class.'

'You won't talk me out of it.'

'I wouldn't bother.'

'So what's left to talk about?'

'Viktor – we've known each other a long time. And seen plenty ...'

'But our friendship lapsed. Ever since you refused to sell your farm to the Gospodins. One of my very few failures as their agent.'

'I wanted to die on my farm. That's all there was to it.'

'Looking back – and I shouldn't be saying this – you were wise.'

'I hope I still am.'

'On the other hand, I haven't forgotten how Xenos trussed me up. You just stood by ...'

'I never did. I urged him to treat you gently.'

Viktor nodded. 'Well, yes ... but ...'

Kokona filled his glass with more wine. 'Come on, Viktor. Admit it! You're a fair man. Always have been.'

Viktor made a face. 'Very well. I admit it. Grudgingly.'

'Bravo! That's the Viktor I know. And that's what I'm counting on – your fairness ...'

'Don't count on it too much!'

Kokona drank some of her wine. 'You've been stuck here heaven knows how many days. Your tongue must have dried up. You should be bursting to talk.'

He started eating ravenously. 'Good *pastirma*, Kokona.'

'May you always eat good things. I made it myself. Then there's your wife. She must be missing you ...'

'Now, that's a sore point, Kokona! You've no idea how much I miss her, too! Leaving Yilka at home is the worst part of this business!'

Kokona offered him another pitta with *pastirma*. 'I can imagine ...'

Viktor ate with relish. 'This is a great pleasure. Best *pastirma* I've eaten. Health to your hands.'

'Thank you. Let's talk about that – health. This chill you have. And feeling as if you're halfway to death. You're not a youngster, Viktor ...'

'I'm not old either.'

'Old enough. Look at yourself! Sitting stiffly as if a jetty has been shoved up your arse! Bet you, if it weren't for your pride, you'd be running home on three legs.'

'Let's not exaggerate!'

'What's the sense? Camping out here all these weeks. And more weeks ahead till God only knows when!'

'You know very well why! I'm waiting for Bostan. The moment he leaves the water-mill, I'll kill him!'

'And if she doesn't?'

He looked up, disconcerted. 'Doesn't what?'

'Leave.'

'Why shouldn't he? His family's honour's at stake!'

'What if she no longer cares about honour? What if, having been badly wounded, she thinks damnation to honour?'

'That would be heresy. And why do you keep calling him she?'

'Because she's a woman!'

'No. She – I mean he – is a designated man.'

'She now calls herself Bostana – did you know?'

'Bostana?'

'Her name before she became a designated man.'

'No! She – he – can't do that. Wouldn't do that!'

'She has.'

'I don't believe it!'

'Ask yourself, why has she decided to take up her real name?'

'I don't know. Maybe she's afraid of dying ...'

'Maybe. Or maybe she no longer wants to see herself as a man.'

'That's ridiculous! After all the people she killed?'

'Or maybe she's in love.'

'Now, that's a good joke, Kokona.'

'It happens.'

'Not to a designated man!'

'Designated men still have ovaries, Viktor. And we women never ignore them.'

Viktor stared at Kokona, aghast. 'You are serious.'

Kokona nodded.

'Who's she – he – she in love with?'

'Oh, Viktor – don't be so naive! Can't you guess?'

Viktor seemed unable to think. Then, suddenly, he grasped the obvious. Incredulously, he turned to look at me. 'Xenos?'

Kokona smiled. 'Who else?'

'That's impossible!'

'Would you still kill her?'

After a moment's hesitation Viktor barked. 'Yes. Whatever the reason. Makes no difference!'

Kokona served him some cheese and olives and offered him more wine. 'All right. Let's now talk about the *Kriss*.'

Looking at her quizzically, he drank a good mouthful. 'I wasn't there.'

'I know. Nor was I.'

'What about it?'

'Lila.'

'Ah, Lila ...'

'Are you happy to have her as Toma's successor?'

'Toma's still alive.'

'He might die any moment. And she's all but taken over. Do you like that?'

'Well, she's very young, but ...'

'But what?'

'But nothing. People have accepted her.'

'Not all the people! Dev told me half the Skenderis don't want anything to do with her or the Law!'

'So what? Too bad for them.'

'Too bad for you, too.'

'What do you mean?'

'I'm sure you know – can see – Marius' campaign is gaining ground. Lots of people are now against the Law. They're fed up with the killings. They want a future. A life that is sane.'

'They'll come round – they always do.'

Kokona offered him more wine. 'That would be, as they say, a Pyrrhic victory – for you. Because by then you'd be dead.'

'Come on, Kokona. That's Marius rubbish. Don't you believe it!'

'If – when – you kill Bostana, her son will take over. Zemun's young and everybody believes he's an even better shot than Bostana. Given your creaking bones, you'll be dead before you take a hundred breaths.'

'Assuming – if – that happens, at least I'll die honourably.'

'You can still die honourably and reach my age.'

He laughed. 'How?'

Kokona drank some wine, then filled Viktor's glass again. 'You're not drinking enough.'

'How would I reach your age?'

'Go on, drink!'

He drank. 'How?'

'You see the benefits of creeping age? Last year you wouldn't have listened to me, let alone asked that question. Now somewhere at the back of your mind you're thinking: with all the money I have, a peaceful old age in the bosom of Yilka would be so welcome ...'

'You're not about to give me one of your sermons, are you?'

'No. A proposal.'

He grinned. 'A proposal, no less. Well, go on.'

'Reconciliation.'

'Reconciliation?'

'Between the Kristofs, the Rogosins, your family and the rest ...'

'Just like that?'

'No. In accordance with the Law. There is an amendment, a procedure and precedents.'

'Since when?'

'Since Anibal Gora's time.'

'Another Gora! Another trouble-maker!'

'That's how it is with visionaries. But his amendment for reconciliation could keep you ensconced with your Yilka for years to come.'

That mollified Viktor. 'Would it satisfy my honour? And everybody else's?'

'If Bostana's given the chance never to revert to Bostan, your honour will have been satisfied anyway. You'd have killed Bostan, the designated man – which, to all intents and purposes, you already have done. So you won't need to go after Bostana, the woman. I think everybody would see the logic of it.'

'That's a wild assumption.'

'Wild assumptions can be special – like wild strawberries.'

'There are many families involved.'

'Yes. But if you, head of Skender's most important family, agree to reconciliation, the others might follow suit.'

'I doubt it.'

'Let's try and see.'

'Have you spoken to the other families?'

'No. I think it would be best if you approached them yourself. I'll talk to the Kristof camp.'

Viktor thought for quite a while, then shook his head. 'It's an unusual suggestion. And tempting. On the other hand, it doesn't feel right. It feels like heresy.'

'It will be conducted as a trial. At a specially convened *Kriss*. We'll ask Toma to preside. You can't get more legitimate than that.'

'Toma has had a stroke. He can barely talk.'

'He can use sign language. You know Toma: he won't miss an opportunity to judge – even in the state he's in.'

'It still doesn't feel right.'

Kokona started clearing up. She put the dishes in the hamper. 'Think on it.' She brought out the other bottle of wine. 'I'll leave this for you. It should help your thinking.'

He took the wine, but shook his head. 'Thank you. But no more thinking. Let's leave things as they are.'

Kokona sighed. 'As you wish. Take care of yourself.'

Viktor got to his feet – again stiffly – to see her off.

Kokona walked a few paces, then stopped and turned to him. 'Xenos has something else to say on this. Since he's here – can he speak to you – briefly?'

'I don't want to talk to him.'

'It won't take long.'

'No!'

'Come on, Viktor. As a favour to me.'

Viktor nodded resignedly. 'All right. As a favour to you.'

'Thank you.' Kokona summoned me. 'Osip!'

I went up to Viktor. 'Greetings!'

'Greetings, Xenos.'

I laid before him my pouch of gold coins. 'The principal requirements for reconciliation are reparations and the exoneration of the offended family's honour. The gold here should compensate all the families. Bostana's apology will serve as the exoneration of their names.'

Viktor, in two minds, stared at the pouch. Then, unable to resist the temptation, opened it. He spread out the coins and looked up, astounded. 'There's a fortune here.'

'Hold onto it. The families might want to see that the proposition is genuine. You can return it if they refuse reconciliation.'

Viktor gaped at me, bewildered that I would leave all that gold in his hands.

I walked away and offered Kokona my arm.

She didn't take it. 'I have one more thing to say to Viktor.'

She went up to him and held his head as if he were a child. 'Another heretical thought for you, Viktor ...'

'No, please. Enough is enough.'

'What if ...'

'Kokona, please!'

She overrode him sternly. 'Viktor, listen!'

He sighed submissively. 'All right! All right!'

'What if Osip – Xenos – is a gift from heaven? Think – here's a man, brutalized by feuds and wars, returning home. What does he bring with him? Not death – which he's seen a lot of and dished out a lot! No, he brings healing – an art that had been taken away from him by the Peoples' Wars. But more importantly, he brings love! Love, Viktor, given to him by the Lover of Love, the only god worth worshipping! To this island that has been immersed in hatred for centuries! Love, which you know all about because you're besotted with your Yilka! Can we spurn that? If we kill that, wouldn't we have killed everything?'

Viktor sighed sadly. 'What a romantic you are, Kokona.'

'We're all romantics, Viktor – deep down. That's what keeps me hopeful!'

43

BOSTAN

The *Kriss* for the reconciliation took place in the tavern.

The Citadel purred as if it was the Day of Persephone. A few old people remembered the reconciliations of the distant past. But dimly. No one else had participated in such an event. Or thought it possible.

A general truce had been arranged.

Everybody who could come came.

Shops closed. Stalls were set up. The wineries buzzed.

But no dancing yet. If we could achieve reconciliation there'd be a *paqe* meal.

Then there'd be dancing.

If only that would happen. I was much better and recovering quickly and wanted to dance till I dropped. Imagine the joy of dancing with Osip! The joy of a new life! Of a life without killings!

Osip thought the big turn-out was a good sign. The person who wished to apologize had the right to ask everybody to be present. And the right to ask them to attest to at least one of his good deeds. That was a provision imposed by Osip's father.

Osip considered this psychologically important. As Kokona

always stressed, no one was wholly bad. Even the vilest person had some goodness in him. For example, Stefan Rogosin. A real ruffian. But also an Orpheus. And he had loved Anton. Had taught him the lute so that there'd always be music on Skender. That's how people remembered him now.

So if people said good things about me, it would create a mood of forgiveness – not only towards me, but also towards all those seen as ill-natured.

I accepted Osip's word. How could I not? I loved him!

Yet I feared the hearing.

The previous night, I couldn't stay in my skin.

What if they all said bad things about me, I asked.

It might be close, he said. There's much bitter history in this island and many fools regurgitating it. On the other hand, half the islanders have had enough of feuds. That's hopeful. Moreover, you're apologizing when you don't have to, that's the best sign of goodness.

Then he held me in his arms all night.

I was also afraid of Toma.

Basil had told us that though Toma's paralysis and speech were improving, he was still very sick. And much of the time, he was delusional. On one occasion, Basil had heard him refer to the Law as Toma's Law.

Since, as the judge, Toma had the authority to veto everybody and impose his own verdict, this was of great concern to me.

At one point Osip had wondered whether we should get Lila to preside.

But Kokona had opposed the idea. Fanatic – and deranged – Toma might be, but he had integrity, she said. Over the years, he had impelled himself to abide, at all times, by the Law – we'd seen examples of that on the two occasions when he had ruled in Osip's favour. That conditioning would govern him, no matter how much he claimed that the Law was his law.

In the end, our discussion had proved irrelevant. Toma had decreed that since he was the sole authority on the Law, he – and no one else – would preside over the reconciliation trial. This was history repeating itself, he had added: he would face Anibal's son as he had faced Anibal.

I had a flimsy hope. I was one of Toma's former *Morituri*. He always had a soft spot for his students, especially for those who were good with guns.

And a far-fetched hope, too. I thought that, sick as he was, he'd be very possessive of Lila. Since, before choosing to marry him, Lila had proposed to Osip, Toma was likely to imagine that if I went back to feuding, I'd soon be killed, thus rekindling Lila's interest in Osip. An outlandish thought, yes, but it showed I was thinking like a woman again, considering every possibility.

Only the parties involved in the reconciliation were admitted to the hearing.

But Osip wanted the people outside to follow the proceedings too. His father's reconciliations had taken place by the cliffs, where we normally hold our *Krisses*, and where everybody can be present. The decision to convene in the tavern on this occasion had been taken because of Toma's condition; his health would have been at risk in the open air.

So, with Dev's help, Osip had set up a loudspeaker system in the Plaza.

Inside the tavern, the main parties sat at a round table.

A rusty microphone stood in the middle. It crackled and whistled but carried our voices.

Toma sat at the head of the table. His speech was slurred, but he could be understood.

That he had improved so quickly hadn't surprised Osip. Mind over matter, he had said. Though Toma, under Basil's supervision, had been taking the drugs Osip had prescribed, these normally wouldn't have worked so quickly. But Toma's drive to stay in power outweighed even his sickness. His constant references to Osip's father when his mind wandered – as Basil had informed us – were proof of that. He had kept going because he believed he had a final score to settle with Anibal.

Not an encouraging thought for me.

So my fears grew. Especially when they carried Toma in on a chair.

We heard him muttering that he was – and had always been – against the amendment for reconciliation; an amendment which he would soon excise from Toma's Law. He couldn't have done so on the previous cases, he grumbled, as, on both those instances, he had been fiendishly thwarted.

Viktor and a representative each from the Rogosins, the Eduards and the Nis sat to the right of Toma. Marius sat next to them. Nexhat, his father, had willingly ceded his place to his son.

Other members of their families sat behind them.

I sat on Toma's left. I wore, on Kokona's advice, a grey and sombre shift, the Skenderi women's everyday garb. This would declare that though I had returned to womanhood, I still abided by Skenderi traditions.

Osip, as my man, sat behind me.

Zemun, who should have sat behind me also, chose a seat at the back.

My son! He looked like a hurricane collecting winds. I felt certain that he wanted me dead, but kept praying that he would somehow remember me as the mother of his childhood and realize that my love for Osip in no way diminished my love for him. During the weeks in which Kokona and Viktor were negotiating the hearing, I had had terrible rows with Zemun. The moment Osip's name came up, lightning flashed in his head. Endless insults. Cunt-crazy man wallowing in dishonour. Filthy spunk from Priapus' cock. And so on. Had I been Osip I'd have thrashed him. But Osip had just ignored him.

Next to Zemun sat Lila.

Was that a surprise? But she sat as if she were in a trance. Her few expressions were like drops of water on snow. They barely marked her face.

Kokona was pleased. Lila's reign as the Law's prophetess had been brief. That was good for Skender. The reconciliation rules stipulated that only one judge would preside. So she couldn't even sit next to Toma.

Kokona sat at the other end of the table, opposite Toma. She had volunteered to serve as the *Kriss'* clerk. She had brought Osip's father's papers for consultation should there be any deviation from the established procedure. And she would record the proceedings for posterity. Osip hoped that this reconciliation would be the beginning of the end of Skender's troubles.

Dev stood by the tavern door. He'd usher in and out those who were willing to speak for or against me.

Castor, my dog – now also Osip's and Kokona's and Dev's – stood by his side in case some of the people in the Plaza became impatient and tried to force their way in.

Osip's gold coins were spread out on the table. When he'd offered them as reparation, I'd tried to refuse. It's best to be generous in reconciliation, he'd said. It's not right! What would you live on? I'd protested. He had laughed and taken me to bed, saying: don't you mean what would *we* live on, my woman? And then, as he made love to me and murmured in my ear, he'd said: we'll feed on one another, like this, like this, like this ...

Toma started the hearing by striking the floor with his mace.

I got up from my chair. That would show humility.

I was trembling.

I took the microphone. I made sure I met the eyes of each person at the table. Uprightness would go down well, Osip had advised.

Kokona had helped me write the apology and I'd memorized it.

'Righteous Toma. Honourable families.

'I am Bostana Kristof, known to you for some time as Bostan. I have reverted to my original name because I have renounced my position as a designated man.

'I stand before you today to offer my apologies – as well as reparations – for any offence my family, the Kristofs, might have caused your families.

'We have been in conflict for generations. We know how our disputes started. The warlords set us up against each other and invented stories which, they declared, grossly sullied our honour.

'It is said evil enters like a splinter and spreads like an oak tree. So the splinters became oak trees and we proceeded to kill each other to redeem this grand-sounding but meaningless concept, honour. Needless to say, once the killings started, we had real cause to carry on killing. An eye for an eye; a life for a life – that has been the oldest commandment for people who are afraid of life and so live by hate alone. People who discard their innate compassion as weakness.

'Today, I, who, until recently, had fed on our daily bread of hatred unthinkingly, whose hands are still as red as a field of poppies with the blood of those I've killed, want to put a stop to that cycle of slaughter. Today I appeal to your mercy. Today I stand here to ask you to grant me forgiveness for my wrongdoings. And I offer these gold coins on the table as my reparation. I do so in the fervent hope that your sons, my son, and, yes, Viktor and I also, will no longer die prematurely as feudists.

'You will remember that Anton, the lutanist, whom, to my great anguish, I had to kill, composed a song that started with the acclamation: "Living is such a beautiful thing!"

'I hereby beseech you: give back to life its rightful place. And its rightful place is within your individual existence. Because life is unimaginably more beautiful than your present occupant, death.

'Some of you might consider my apology a dishonourable act – one by which I forfeit my family's honour.

'Others might see it an endeavour that most upraises our honour.

'You, Righteous Toma, and you, the honourable families, will decide which. But before you do, let me remind you of an ancient myth that used to be part of our belief in the days before the warlords, when we, Skenderis, lived together peacefully.

'Every person, before going into a life beyond life, has to undergo judgement. They have to cross a bridge, called *ponte*, over a river of bubbling quicksand. For those who have the lightness of goodness in them, be it by only one accomplishment in their lives, the *ponte* is transformed into fragrant tilled earth and they cross easily. Those without a single good deed and thus heavy with wickedness are immediately sucked in by the quicksand and disappear for ever.

'I am prepared to stand the same trial before you. Instead of the river, *ponte*, I will traverse, despite my heels that are weighted with blood, the opinions my fellow islanders have of me. I will ask them to tell you, one by one, whether they consider Bostana Kristof, in essence, as a truthful and good person or as a false, bad person.

'If they find goodness in me, judge my passage across the *ponte* as worthy of redemption. If the opposite, then brand me as evil and let me perish.'

I sat down.

I was no longer trembling.

And I felt good. This had been the best deed in my life. The best, that is, after my love for Osip. But then, it had been Osip who had led me here.

I turned to look at him.

He smiled – my man – with all that gentleness in his eyes.

I turned to Toma.

His face was blank. Impossible to tell whether he'd heard me, and, if so, whether he'd understood what I'd said.

Then he banged his mace. 'Let the witnesses come!'

Dev opened the tavern door. The people were already queuing. Dev summoned the first in line.

***

The attestations lasted until late evening.

Those who testified that I was a good person ranged from mothers who praised the way I had wet-nursed their babies when their breasts had dried of milk to the poor folk who related my generosity with food, fish and game for distribution among them. One mother mentioned that I had sucked the poison out of her son's foot when he had been bitten by a snake. The old and the ill recounted how I would always cook for them and help out with this and that. To my surprise, some of the men acclaimed my beauty before I'd become a designated man; I embellished the island as orange blossom does, they said. Those who were children when I was still young and were now adults remembered the stories I had told them – stories I had read in Kokona's books. Basil, the apothecary, spoke about the countless times when, risking my life, I had collected medicinal herbs for him from inaccessible places. Many acknowledged my skill in shepherding goats and sheep. Others referred to my marksmanship and how I had taught their sons or husbands to use guns.

During many of the attestations, Zemun either protested loudly or mocked the speakers. Next to him, Lila, her face still expressionless, echoed him. The fact that only a few people paid attention to Zemun enraged him even more.

On the negative side, I was mainly accused of being arrogant as a designated man. When I pointed out that I had stopped being a man now and was starting life again as a woman, they were pacified – some even took back their accusations. The worst condemnation was that, at every engagement, I always aimed at my opponent's head, that this severely disfigured the victim's face, making it an even worse agony for the family when they had to wash him for burial. To this I replied that I would never fire a gun again, that this held true even if the hearing decided against reconciliation. I would face the feudists of the families I had wronged, unarmed.

Again, during these attestations Zemun constantly interjected, this time praising the speaker for portraying me as a born killer. And again Lila acted as his echo.

When the last of the people left, Kokona addressed the gathering and summed up. 'According to my count, Bostana has successfully crossed her *ponte*. There are several hundred testimonies to her goodness. Just over fifty against her.'

She turned to the families. 'Your say, now.'

As Osip and Kokona had expected, Marius Kaplan spoke first. 'I accept reconciliation on behalf of my family. And I commend Bostana for having had the courage to expose the inhumanity of our way of life.'

Viktor immediately followed suit. 'I accept the reconciliation also.'

Radu Rogosin was next. 'I, too. Though reluctantly.'

Then Sidi Nis. 'Same goes for me.'

And, finally, Dimitar Eduard who, after taking a long time to decide, gave his verdict. 'My allies have all agreed. I'll go along with them. I, too, accept.'

Yet again, as each one of them spoke, Zemun – with Lila parroting him – protested, shouting abuse.

'You dishonour your family!'

'Think of your paladins killed by Bostan!'

'You dishonour your relatives who died by his hand!'

Kokona, ignoring them, turned to Toma. 'Your judgement, Righteous Toma. You have the final say. We count on your integrity and wisdom. If you are against the reconciliation the positive votes of these five families will be nullified. Worse, their honour will be tainted for agreeing to the reconciliation. If you vote as they did, then reconciliation will rule them. They will share out the gold coins as reparation. And you will be remembered for ever as a just man.'

The moment Kokona stopped speaking, Zemun rushed towards Toma.

Lila followed him.

They shouted over each other, Lila, as before, repeating Zemun's protestations.

'No, Righteous Toma!'

'You must judge against reconciliation!'

'Skender's honour is at stake!'

'Bad blood is trying to buy us off!'

'Reconciliation defames the Law!'

'Don't destroy your life's work!'

'Remember that honour is more important than life!'

Toma, agitated by this onslaught, shuddered. He managed to mumble. 'Forsaken ... Again ... Damn Anibal ... Damn his son ... *My Law ... Toma's Law ... My Law ...*'

His mouth began to twist. His hand shook uncontrollably.

Osip moved swiftly over to him. 'He's having a heart attack!'

Kokona pushed past Zemun and Lila. 'Tap your mace, Toma! Once for reconciliation! Twice for against!'

Everyone stood up, silent and static.

Toma strained. He managed to tap his mace once.

Then, as he convulsed, he dropped his mace.

A moment later, he was dead.

Kokona was the first to gather her senses. 'He tapped once. You all saw it!'

Marius shouted. 'Yes! We saw it!' He turned to the other heads of the families. 'We saw it! Didn't we? We saw it!'

The heads of the families affirmed, one by one. 'Yes!'

Lila, suddenly animated either by shock or grief, screamed. 'No! He was going to tap again but dropped his mace!'

Zemun yelled. 'You're all deaf and blind! Throwing the mace was his second tap! That was his answer! He ruled against reconciliation!'

Kokona turned on them. 'Be quiet, you brats! Your eyes are so smeared with blood, you're mindless of everything else! Everybody here saw that Toma tapped once. That means reconciliation!'

Lila and Zemun were beside themselves. 'No! No! No! No!'

'Yes! Now get out of here or I'll ask these good people to throw you out!'

Zemun, his face contorted beyond recognition, looked at me. 'Bostan ... How can you ...? Our honour!'

I began to weep. 'What about life? My life? Why do you want me dead?'

Zemun hissed, pointed at Osip. 'Because life with him – and his filthy cock, his bad blood – is not life!'

I shook my head hopelessly. I managed to mutter. 'Go, Zemun, go, please ... This is for the good of everybody ... Go, now ... Go ...'

Zemun gave me a hateful – a desperate – look, then tore out of the tavern.

Lila ran after him.

44

DEV

Nobody wants to postpone the *paqe* meal.

So we bury Toma at first light in the morning.

Zemun accuses us of entombing his prophet with indecent haste, like Jesus, without giving the faithful time to mourn. For once, I think he's right.

Osip and I spend the rest of the day dismantling the traps around the water-mill. That's a condition of reconciliation before the *paqe* meal.

The meal lives up to its name.

Most people see it as a myth come true. They had heard of such a meal but never thought they'd see one. Everybody brings food, wine and *rakiya*. Maybe for the first time in their lives they eat and drink without their spirits aching. They toast: Death is no longer crouching by the door like Medusa.

And they dance non-stop.

Kokona and I dance, too. Sitting down. Pattering feet, entwining legs.

Osip and Bostana sit at the head table with the reconciled families. They don't dance. The proceedings have exhausted Bostana.

And Zemun's venom has turned her triumph into sadness. She just keeps her head on Osip's shoulder and tries to be cheerful. Even so, as Kokona always says, she glows. The full moon must be jealous.

Reconciliation is in everybody's mouth. It gushes as if there is a new spring in the Plaza. Even those who have difficulty with words curl their tongues to it.

Families that have been feuding for generations shake hands, arrange their own reconciliation.

This, despite Lila telling everybody that the reconciliation was a conspiracy by Osip and Bostana. I won't let deception happen again, she says. She struts as the Law's new protector, invested by Toma. And she has Zemun by her side. Her grey eminence, Kokona now calls him. It is Zemun's canker that she fosters.

Out of respect for the dead Toma, people let her talk.

She can fool herself, take any title she likes, it doesn't make her the Law's protector. That's not an official post. And not bestowed through inheritance. She must earn her rank over many years.

Also now that Toma is gone and reconciliation falls like manna, people might be ready to coffin the Law.

That's what we hope.

Not Zemun. He never stops cursing Bostana and Osip. Fortunately, few people listen. That angers him even more.

I keep my eye on Zemun. I now fear him. He's no longer an arrogant youth. The way he behaves towards Bostana – he has become rabid. He can't wait to foam at the mouth.

What troubles me most is his relationship with Lila. Always speaking to her. And Lila always agrees, and sometimes, she pats his hand. Together they can create mayhem.

I want to lurk around them, hear what they're talking about.

But I don't want to leave my Kokona. Nor Osip and Bostana. I want to be by their side in case there is trouble.

Then Bostana wants to go home. Kokona and I understand: she wants to lie with Osip, and forget Zemun if she can.

At the water-mill, I'm still worrying.
My guts say go back to the Citadel.
The *paqe* meal will still be going on.
Lila and Zemun will still be there, talking, talking, talking.
I must find out what they're scheming.
I jump into the van.

45

LILA

He kept telling me he'd be the new warlord, the new Timur. And I'd be his queen. Not just the prophetess of the Law, but a queen.

Lila, the great Queen!

And he made plans. All the time.

I, Zemun, will do this. I, Zemun, will do that. There are great days ahead, I have so many schemes.

He was planning even when Toma was still alive.

And my head spun.

As the Day of Reconciliation approached, his excitement grew. I know in my heart the decision will go against the whore, he said. He repeated this over and over.

He never called his mother Mother or Bostan. Always whore or cock-crazy cunt or spunk-drunk slut.

But never in front of Toma. I have integrity, he said, I don't want him to think I'm ploughing a field for myself.

And when the verdict goes against her, she'll be killed, he said. Within a day or so. Then we'll shroud her and I'll become the paladin. Then, in less than a year, I'll declare myself warlord, he said. The people will accept me. They'll salute my power. They'll realize there's no better man than Zemun in all Skender. No one else who can build a great future for them.

And he made bigger plans.

We'll have thrones. We'll tax the rich. Become wealthy ourselves – rich beyond imagination, he said.

And we'll build Palladions everywhere and spread the Law. The youngsters will worship us. They'll kiss our feet. They'll bow down to our sons because our sons will be our successors.

And the Gospodins, who have seen how strategic this island is and bought so much land here, will back us as rulers. They'll send gold and weapons. You won't have to draw water from the well to wash yourself. You'll have countless servants. A marble bath – filled daily with asses' milk, he said.

And my head spun.

Once I asked him, where do you get all these ideas?

From Righteous Toma, he replied. I've listened to him and absorbed his wisdom. He was the wisest man in the world. He knew everything there is to be known in this world.

Often, when he mentioned Toma, I felt guilty. I thought of the poor old man gaping at me as I showed him my body: eyes turned into one big eye; but meowing like a starved cat. How wise was that from a wise man?

Which then made me think what I really wanted was a real husband. And achingly. A man who would mount me like a lion, make a home for me, give me many children.

What I really wanted was Xenos.

The thought that he was having sex with Zemun's mother while I lay next to creaking bones drove me mad.

So I let my head spin.

And I listened to Zemun all the more.

At least Zemun was young. Strong. I could see him freeing me from my imprisonment.

True, my imprisonment had been my own doing. But what did I know about life when I proposed to Toma? What did I know about the spite that had made me do that? How could I have imagined that being married to such an ancient man – loving though he always tried to be – would have been like living in a mausoleum – the sort built by the warlords of the past?

Also, I hadn't expected Toma to live so long. Nobody had.

I think he lived on because he sucked out life from me.

Then he died. But too late.

And I was left alone.

A prophetess of the Law – but nothing else. What good was that to me? Where was I to go?

And my head spun.

To tell the truth, much of the time I didn't understand what Zemun was on about. And what I understood, I thought was unbelievable, no matter how exciting.

I'm not a thinker. Politics, the way Zemun went about it, is beyond me. For instance, though I'd heard about the Gospodins – Toma mentioned them a few times – I didn't know who they were, who they could be.

Yes, I could memorize the Law – memorizing is easy – but I had to pretend I understood all the things it said.

Pretending is easy, too.

On the other hand, I was delirious with the sense of power. I, a young girl, could make men and women stand with hands on their hearts just by putting on a serious face.

Power. That's another reason why my head spun.

It made me ambitious. The idea of being a queen. Of ordering what I pleased. Even ordering Xenos to leave Bostan's bed and come to mine!

But things went wrong.

The *Kriss* decided in favour of Zemun's mother.

All Zemun's and my protests came to nothing.

Zemun felt certain Toma wanted to condemn his mother. He had no doubt Toma was going to tap a second time if he hadn't collapsed.

I believed him.

But that witch, Kokona, and all the heads of families conspired. Dishonourable men bought off with Xenos' gold, Zemun said.

I believed that, too. But, I asked, what can we do?

Plenty, he said. I know the way forward, he said. If they can conspire, so can we. We'll go to the *paqe* meal as expected of us. Then when people are drunk and senseless, we'll move, he said.

I trusted him.

My head spun.

At the *paqe* meal Zemun and I sat together.

Zemun ignored his mother, kept cursing her and pretended to drink heavily. But all the time he was watching Viktor, who was seated near us. Viktor was the one person who was really drinking heavily. And happily because of the Reconciliation. He was teasing his wife, Yilka, lovingly, though she kept telling him he shouldn't drink so much.

I knew Yilka well. She was only a few years older than me. Always dressed like Snow White. But in pink. We called her Snow Pink.

She thought she was the most beautiful woman on the island. Not true. I am.

Then Xenos, Zemun's mother, the old witch and her Shrimp left. Too early, considering the Reconciliation had gone in their favour and they should have been celebrating.

Cock-crazy whore desperate for a fuck, Zemun said. And, for the first time since the verdict, he smiled. They have no idea what will hit them, he said.

Then he touched my hand.

I let him.

Why not? He had become my only hope.

Eventually, people started leaving. Most of the food and drink was finished. As if no one had ever eaten or drunk before.

Viktor and his wife were among the last to leave. Viktor was so drunk he had to lean on Yilka.

Zemun waited a few minutes, then said: let's go.

I went with him. My head spinning. This time not only because of his words, but also from the *rakiya*.

We followed Viktor and Yilka. Their farm was just outside the Citadel.

I asked Zemun: why are we following them? He said: you'll see. My head's spinning too much; I don't want to walk too far, I said. Just up to the Citadel's gates, he said, that's not far. I nodded. That was near the Palladion, Toma's temple and home. Now my temple and home.

Because the tables for the *paqe* meal had been set up in the Plaza, cars couldn't park there. So Viktor had left his outside the gates. That's the rich for you. They can't walk fifty metres. They have to drive everywhere.

By the time Viktor and Yilka reached their car, we, too, were outside the gates.

Viktor helped Yilka into the car, then staggered round to the driving seat.

At the same time, Zemun started running. He was holding a revolver.

I didn't know he had brought a gun with him.

Then I heard another motor. It was the Shrimp's van and it was speeding towards the gates.

Then – I can't remember what happened exactly because it all happened so quickly ...

Then ...

Viktor turned towards Zemun, looking surprised.

Zemun fired.

Viktor collapsed.

Yilka started screaming.

Zemun ran to her side and shot her as she tried to get out of the car.

The Shrimp's van screeched to a stop.

The Shrimp jumped out, holding a big sword.

Zemun swung round to face him.

As the Shrimp rushed forward, Zemun emptied his gun into him.

The Shrimp, gushing blood, but still holding his sword, kept crawling forward.

Zemun pulled out another revolver and started firing that one.

The Shrimp got very close to Zemun, then died.

I started screaming.

Zemun came up to me and slapped my face.

I wailed: I didn't want this! I didn't want this!

Zemun whispered in my ear: you wanted to be queen? This is how you become queen!

I clung to him, shaking.

He smiled, eyes grown into one huge eye – just like Toma's. And I am your king, he said.

He dragged me to Viktor's car, pushed me against the bonnet, lifted my skirt, tore off my pants, and entered me.

He hurt me!

My head spun.

I didn't want to be taken like this. It wasn't as I had thought it would be. Not how I'd imagined Xenos taking me.

When Zemun finished, I was still shaking.

I clung to him again.

He was my only hope.

I'd become his queen.

My head kept spinning.

Behind my eyes, I was screaming.

46

KOKONA

Yesterday was the first anniversary of the Day of Reconciliation – or the Day of Sham, as many of you call it now.

I started this account a year ago today. That explains the fury in my opening lines. But since then, as I went on writing and tried to convey the words and minds of the people whose destinies became entangled – three of whom have been a vital part of my soul – I've mellowed.

Why mellowed, given the horror of the tragedies? Well, that's human nature for you. In this part of the world, we believe catharsis helps. Maybe also I feel my end looms. It's been a struggle to get through the days and, particularly, the nights, without Dev in my bed.

Dev was found at the portals of the Citadel in the morning. He had been placed in a sitting position against one column. Against the other column, propped up in the same position, rested Viktor and Yilka. Both had been shot in the head, once the mark of Bostana when she had been the designated man. It had taken eight bullets to kill Dev – one of them, presumably the last, had shattered his beautiful face.

Before that, at daybreak, while we were wondering where Dev had gone – both Osip and I had heard him drive away in the night – Zemun and Lila arrived.

We discovered later that they had come in Viktor's car and, not wanting to be heard, had left it some distance away.

They looked feral; eyes fierce like those of wolves in a pack.

Castor, instantly on edge, stood up and growled at them.

Bostana rebuked him. 'Stop it, Castor! It's Zemun!'

Lila, afraid of Castor, withdrew to the stone traverse over the millpond.

Bostana, with hope in her voice, offered her hand to Zemun. 'Come to make peace, my son?'

Zemun, choosing not to touch Bostana, shook his fist at Castor. 'Watch it, dog, or I'll smash your head in!'

Osip pulled Castor to his side. 'It's all right, Castor. Zemun is family.'

Castor obeyed him, sat down by Osip's side, but kept his eyes on Zemun.

Zemun taunted Bostana. 'Never liked that hound! Never understood what you saw in him!'

Bostana, maintaining her maternal poise, answered him softly. 'He's beautiful. And faithful.'

Zemun sneered. 'Faithful!? That's strange – coming from you!'

Osip pulled up a couple of chairs. 'Welcome, you two. We're about to have breakfast. Join us. Let's make this our own *paqe* meal.'

Lila, still keeping her distance on the traverse, looked distraught. She shook her head. 'I'm staying here.'

Zemun leaned against the fireplace. 'We don't eat with dishonourable people! For us you are putrid corpses!'

Osip scoffed. 'Yet you can come to our home and speak with us – that's very commendable.'

Bostana sighed wearily. 'If it's not to make peace, why are you here? What do you want?'

Zemun faced her. 'Actually, peace sounds right. That's what I want. Peace for both of us.'

I tried to be friendly and calm. 'You don't have to sound so serious, Zemun.'

He faced me, his eyes looking even wilder. 'Oh, this *is* serious, ancient one.'

I shrugged. 'We're all ears, I'm sure.'

Zemun sniggered. 'Question is – where to start?'

Bostana snapped. 'Get on with it, son!'

Viciously, Zemun turned on her. 'All right, my whore Mother, let's start with you then.'

Osip, barely controlling his anger, rose from his seat. 'Listen, boy! You don't talk to my woman – to your mother – like that! Be warned!'

Zemun pulled out a revolver. 'I'll speak to her any way I like! Sit down! Before I shoot your balls off! And don't you ever call me boy again!'

I was so shocked, I froze in my seat.

But Bostana stood up, furious. 'What do you think you're playing at, Zemun?!'

Castor started barking.

Zemun waved his revolver wildly. 'Sit down both of you! And keep that dog under control!'

Then – and it happened so quickly that I barely saw it – Osip sprang forward, wrested the gun from Zemun and slapped him hard. He held him in a tight grip.

Zemun, his nose bleeding, whined. 'You hurt me! You hurt me!'

Osip retorted scornfully. 'I warned you, boy!' He turned to Bostana, uncertainly. 'What shall we do with him?'

Bostana went up to Osip. 'Let him go! Please, let him go.'

'He's not to be trusted!'

Bostana shook her head. 'No. No. He is only a boy. Playing at being a man. This will be a lesson to him. He'll come to his senses now.' She started cleaning Zemun's bloodied nose with her sleeve. 'If Osip lets you go, you *will* go, won't you, Zemun? Won't you?'

Zemun, now in tears, whimpered like a child. 'Yes, I will. Yes.'

Bostana stroked Osip's arm. 'See, my man, he'll go. Let him go, please.'

Osip nodded, but held onto Zemun. 'All right. But not with a gun. Pick it up. Throw it into the millpond.'

Bostana, relieved, did so.

Lila watched as Bostana went onto the traverse. Her mouth twitched as if she wanted to say something, but she could only stutter incomprehensibly.

Bostana hurried back to Osip. 'Done. You can let him go.'

Reluctantly, Osip released Zemun.

Zemun, less tearful now, straggled onto the traverse and disappeared from view.

Lila, whom he had completely ignored, sank to her knees.

Osip and Bostana sat down. I held onto their hands.

Some minutes later, Zemun reappeared, more composed, but chastened. He didn't come in, but stayed by the door. He spoke softly. 'I want to say something ... To my mother.'

Instantly Bostana became motherly. 'Yes, Zemun ...'

Osip remained seated, but kept his eyes on Zemun. He stroked Castor, who had started growling again.

As Zemun spoke his voice became harsher. 'What a strange fate, your fate, Mother! You who were the most honourable man in all Skender, the best designated man it ever had, are now the most dishonourable! And all because of that Xenos. There can be no greater dishonour to our family – or to any family! Going after a man of bad blood! Giving up your hard-earned manhood! If you tell me you've gone mad, I might – just might – forgive you! Tell me you've gone mad!'

Bostana, though weary, faced him defiantly. 'No. I was mad before – like most Skenderis. Mad to believe in the Law. With Osip I found sanity.'

'You took an oath never to be a woman again. You had all the privileges of a man. Giving all that up – surely that's madness!'

'No, killing is madness! Now that I won't ever kill again, I've found peacefulness, serenity. I found Osip. I found a man I can love. A man who loves me.'

'And to hell with everything else, is that it? To hell with your son, your family, our honour! We no longer count! You've traded our good blood for his bad blood!'

'No, you count – more than you can imagine. You are my flesh and blood. But you refuse to understand what I'm saying.'

'Love, love, love – that's what you're saying! If I don't understand it, it's because it's rubbish! At your age, you should be thinking about your grave!'

'I used to. And you're right. Now I only think about love. About being one body, one soul with Osip. About having you at home as our beloved son ...'

'I'm no longer your son. I won't be dishonoured by you!'

'That's what you refuse to understand, Zemun. I've stopped believing in honour. It has no meaning. It's just a word to justify killing. Or if honour exists, it exists in the way a man and a woman become one. That way they re-create the world.'

Zemun screeched. 'That cunt-crazy turd has emptied your mind! Every time you opened your legs, took his prick, drank his spunk, he broke you down!'

Osip was about to spring at Zemun, but Bostana stopped him. 'Sit, my man, sit. He's had his say. He'll go now.'

Zemun shouted. 'Admit it – he defiled you!'

'No, my son. He led me to the truth!'

'Is that your final say?'

'Yes.'

'Then it's my duty to purge Skender of you!'

And he pulled out a gun and shot Bostana.

He had snatched out this other gun so unexpectedly and had fired so quickly that none of us had had time to move. Who would expect a son to kill his mother?

And when we saw Bostana catapult back with the impact of the bullet, we remained frozen. Even Osip who had seen so many atrocities in his life sat like a stone statue.

Then time spun faster than the world.

Osip started bellowing. I can't imagine any creature howling with such pain. Then, slowly, like a leviathan rising out of the sea, he pulled himself out of his chair.

By that time Zemun was pointing his gun at him and shouting dementedly. 'You next, cunt-crazy fucker! First your balls, then your heart, then your head! Whatever remains of you will be a warning, for eternity, to all the bad blood in the world!'

Osip ignored him, lurched towards Bostana.

Castor, freed of Osip's steadying hand, launched himself at Zemun.

Zemun tried to fend off the attack. As he twisted round, he fired again.

He and Castor tumbled to the floor.

Zemun didn't move.

Castor, about to go for his throat, paused, sniffed him, then moved back.

Zemun lay still, blood oozing from his chest. Under Castor's assault, he had shot himself.

Osip had noticed none of that. He had been staring at Bostana, touching points of her body. Now, finally daring to look at her head where she had been shot, he cradled her in his arms and wailed.

Hesitantly, Castor approached Osip and Bostana. He sniffed Bostana, then crouched by them and whined.

Lila, who had stood transfixed on the traverse all that time, started screaming.

That's when I regained my senses. I rushed over to her and slapped her a few times with all the venom I could muster.

Lila collapsed. Then, crawling on the floor, she went up to Osip. 'I didn't want this to happen! I didn't want this to happen! I wanted to warn you he had another gun. But I – I couldn't speak ...'

Osip didn't seem to see her. He went on keening.

Lila turned to me. 'Zemun kept telling me: I've got plans! I'll put matters right. We'll go back to our old ways! We'll honour Honour! Stop all this reconciliation nonsense! You're Toma's successor! You're our prophetess! You'll be queen. I'll be the warlord. You must help me! That's what he kept saying – over and over ...'

I spat at her and went over to Osip and Bostana. I put my arms around Osip.

Lila crawled over to us. 'I didn't want this to happen. But Zemun was my only hope! To be somebody! So we went after Viktor. Then suddenly the Shrimp arrived in his van! He saw what had happened. Rushed at Zemun with a sword. So Zemun shot him!'

Another avalanche of ice covered Osip and me. We looked at each other. I managed to mutter. 'Dev dead?'

'And Viktor! And Yilka!'

I buckled into Osip's other arm.

Lila, out of control, started beating her head. 'I didn't want this to happen! I just wanted to have some worth. To be important – like Bostana! Like you, Kokona!'

Osip managed to mutter. 'Go away, Lila. Leave us alone ...'

Lila touched Osip's neck. 'I wanted to be important! But really I wanted to be a wife, a mother ... And I couldn't be ... You didn't want me ...'

Osip pressed Bostana harder to his chest. 'Lila! Go! Go!'

Lila hesitated a moment, then ran out, beating her head and screaming.

Osip and I sat on the floor holding Bostana, Castor and each other, oblivious of Zemun lying dead an arm's length away.

Later that day, after Osip had cleaned Bostana's head and laid her out on their bed, we collected Dev's remains.

Osip dug a grave for him in my farmstead, amidst the fig trees that Dev had planted many years back and which he had so loved.

Basil was the only other person to attend the burial.

After we had drunk to Dev and poured libations onto the orchards, the vegetable patches and the home that Dev and I had made a shrine to love, Osip took Dev's van and drove away, saying he'd be back shortly.

He was back within a couple of hours.

He'd brought his trunk and put it in a corner of my workroom. 'This is for your keeping, Mother.'

I didn't know what to say. 'What for?'

'I'm leaving you my things. And my father's papers.'

'Why give them to me?'

He put his finger to my lips to stop me talking. Then he hugged me and kissed me and whispered into my ear. 'Forgive me, Mother. I must go.'

'I'll come with you.'

'No. You're back in your home now. Stay here.'

'What will you do? Where will you go?'

'Whatever I do, I know you'll understand.'

I did understand.

And I didn't cry.

Not until I saw him stop momentarily at our crossroads.

I thought he might turn round for a last look. He didn't. He walked away.

That night the water-mill burnt down. The flames could be seen from most parts of the island.

By the time I and other islanders got there, nothing except the smouldering stone structures remained. The timber – so much of it – had been set ablaze with petrol, presumably siphoned off Dev's van.

Rummaging through the ashes, we found the charred bodies of Osip and Bostana entwined on the warped springs of their bed. At their feet lay Castor's remains.

Later, Basil told me he had given Osip, at Osip's request, an injection to put Castor down; after Bostana's death, Osip had told him, the dog had stopped eating. If he had known Osip had been planning to set fire to himself, Basil lamented, he'd have given him something to take, too. No one should burn to death – that's not why Prometheus gave us fire.

I should have guessed Osip would kill himself that way. Maybe I had, but refused to acknowledge it. It wouldn't have been difficult to read his mind. He had failed to save both Sofi and Bostana. The first had given him hope; the second had fulfilled that hope. He would have reasoned that torching himself would be an appropriate act of retribution – and a prophecy fulfilled.

We also found Zemun's charred remains, by the fireplace where he had fallen. No doubt he, too, had fulfilled his own prophecy: life and death touched only by the fervour to die meaninglessly.

A few days after Viktor's and Yilka's funeral – which I attended – the Law reclaimed Skender like undergrowth reclaims abandoned land.

Those families who had agreed, on the Day of Reconciliation, to make peace and declare amity disclaimed their pledges.

And the feuds resumed.

With added vengeance because people, believing they had been fooled by the dream of a life devoid of killing and unable to foresee a life without the intractable order of the Law, felt betrayed and fearful.

And they renamed the Day of Reconciliation as the Day of Sham.

So now ... To today ... The first anniversary of the Day of Reconciliation plus one day ...

There you all are, confused, unloved, untouchable, living in dread of being killed while worshipping death. You look upon the love between Osip and Bostana as a calamity that hit this island in bygone days. When you feel hunger in your loins you brush it aside as indecency. For all I know, you don't even undress in front of your spouses, fearing that desire might overwhelm you. You dare not live in case a grain of joy renders you dishonourable.

No. That's not quite true. You do have feelings: your devotion to Lila. You have come to accept her as the Law's prophetess because she lost her mind after witnessing the way Zemun killed Dev, Viktor, Yilka and Bostana. And you believe a deranged woman is wiser than a sane one. You even believed her when she told you that Zemun took his life heroically after killing his mother in order to restore the immaculate honour both she and he had enjoyed before Satan in the guise of Osip Gora had come to our island.

In all likelihood, in a generation or so, you will revere Zemun and crown him as the most honourable man in Skender's history. Deplorable as all that is, it shows your hunger for love. The same was true of the way you revered Toma. Indeed, your worship of honour, your obedience to the Law are indications of that hunger. Your hearts and minds want to give themselves to the very kernel of life. The tragedy is, you have yoked them to meaningless concepts instead of the flesh and blood that is around you, all of them as hungry to be loved as you are.

I've spent a long time reading and thinking over some of the writings Anibal, Osip's father, left behind.

As you will remember, he despaired of blood feuds and sought to eradicate them. Yet, in the end, he considered them a lesser evil than the endless wars that humankind endures – wars which he saw as blood feuds magnified into global dimensions. Invariably, in the meaningless pursuit of honour; invariably, fooled into that pursuit by the need to satisfy the hunger for love. He wrote in a diary entry that since prejudices propagated in the name of nationalism, religion, ethnicity, notions of power, superiority and possessions – all of them as vacuous as honour – ended up killing millions, even threatened the very survival of the Earth, it's better that a few should die, here and there, than whole peoples. Why worry about a few deaths when humankind, suppressing doubts, fears and its longing for justice, equality and happiness, is comprehensively killing itself?

And he kept asking over and over again: what is there in human nature that keeps denying the hunger for love, that very hunger that serves Creation? The eternal question – one to which neither religion nor philosophy nor science has found an answer.

And yet ...

Try and imagine the promise of life that those whose ordeals I've just recounted had in them from birth. Every person – even Zemun and Toma – was worth a people, a nation, a country. Every person deserved the kind of love Dev and I and Osip and Bostana found. Why deny that?

Think!

You won't believe this: there I was urging you to worship life when I had decided to go against my own advice. In a few moments, I was going to take a potion that I'd filched from Basil. And I was going to lay myself down to eternal sleep.

Now, I've changed my mind. I've convinced myself of what I told you: that hope is like love; you can't live without it.

So I'll follow my own advice and live. And I'll try and live till I'm as old as Methuselah.

And I'll continue urging you to forget hate and to embrace life and love.

Skender remains divided. Marius and his followers are still campaigning against the Law. Indeed, Marius has the potential to be another Anibal. He will be my ally.

Somehow we'll guide you back to Life.